ALAN FOX

ALAN FOX writes *love stories* about people looking for a sense of wonder in a brutal world, people pursuing beauty in the face of insanity. His previous novel, "The Seeker in Forever," is now available in a second revised edition.

For more information, please visit:
www.storyfocus.com

———

Praise for Alan Fox's Previous Novel "The Seeker in Forever"

" 'The Seeker in Forever' is an entertaining book that is a great read for anyone who enjoys a fast-paced, well-written political satire."
—Cherie Fisher, *Reader Views*

"Highly recommended . . . to be given high praise for an originality and cleverness that is as entertaining as it is thought-provoking."
—Small Press Bookwatch, *Midwest Book Review*

"A mind-bending world . . . This flight through the imagination requires a full and complete appreciation for the raw, elemental beauty of the human experience."
—Miranda Orso, *The Electric Review*

"This book will take you on a wild ride . . . A definite read for anyone looking for a rare adventure of violence, insanity, and power struggles."
—Adreann Stephens, *SLUG Magazine*

"An interesting read with a powerful message."
—Jasmine Greene, *Static Multimedia*

"The reader should be forewarned that this is not your mother's political satire, but instead a whole new animal altogether. . . . Prepare yourself for a bit of joyride the open-minded will undertake with gusto."
—Sylvia Cochran, *Roundtable Reviews*

Also by Alan Fox

The Seeker in Forever (Revised Second Edition)

The Girl Made of Cool

First Edition

Alan Fox

StoryFocus™ Communications
New York
www.storyfocus.com

The Girl Made of Cool (First Edition)
Copyright © 2010 by Alan Sean Fox

Published by:
StoryFocus™ Communications
New York City, NY
Tel (718) 775-5540
www.storyfocus.com

Printed in The United States of America

ISBN-13: 978-0-9762276-2-5 (trade paperback)
ISBN-10: 0-9762276-2-2 (trade paperback)

Txt: 2009_0714

Cvr: 2009_0714

Contents

The Girl Made of Cool

The Girl Made
of Cool

Act One

The Universe and
Boys and Girls

O UR UNIVERSE IS ONE OF THOSE THINGS that happens from time to
time—in the span of eternity.

Some say our universe has no edge. It is a form made of curved
space-time.

It's a strange place to live in—Just about anyone can tell you that.

It seems perfectly arrayed for physical "systems"—and for "us," little
systems within the greater systems.

It results in young men and women.

In spring-time.

In the longings of youth and desire.

For some reason and confluence of events—in some indeterminate
time in the past—there came to be a thing known to science and to great
generals of high military command as:

The Battle of the Sexes.

Some say, with bold speculation, that it may be that space and time
had an altogether different form before our now existent realm of creation
came to be. ... What we know is sparse.

Among the very few things we do know, is that we can say—with
some certainty—that at some indeterminate point, in the very distant past,
for reasons unknown, conditions unknown, circumstances unknown, there
came to exist the first moment of—time equals zero—of this thing now
known to these scientists and generals as the first moment of—

The Battle of the Sexes.

And within this cosmos of hot sex and cataclysmic battles, came the
stage called: *Dating: Or, getting to know someone.* ... Mind to mind; body
to body; tingling sense to tingling sense. There came physical encounters,
with the use of a bed and soft light—or with the use of darkness to en-
hance imagination.

And at some point, there came a moment where a young woman turned to a young man and said, "What is it you want from me?"

And his jaw went slack, and he started his answer with the statement, "Uh ... uhm, ..." And from there he did his level best to make sense.

And—ah—so it went ... and so it goes; you see many moments there were, there are, and continue to be in this battle of the sexes.

Now moving more closely into its cosmos, we find this thing called: *Body and Soul.*

Body is the physical of sex; soul is the "storytelling" of sex.

Body is when sex gets hot and penetrating—and thrilling. Soul is when sex gets stimulating, and gets to be a *sustainable* story—and sometimes leads to marriage contracts, which then brings it back to the physical realm, culminating in the honeymoon—which if all goes right is very physical indeed.

It's best when sex has body and soul. ... Oh, yes, this we do know—about this universe, that some say has no edge, and some say we cannot know in any absolute sense—that is, in any formal state of perfect sense.

And thus what we know is ultimately nonsense.

And to be enlightened is to understand nonsense.

And thus again to be enlightened—about sex, is to understand why sex doesn't make sense—just adventure leading to adventure.

And occasionally children. Did we forget to mention that? No matter for now. This is strictly about the beginning battles in this level of warfare, human strife, heartache and never-ending difficulty. This particular unfolding is about: *One girl, one guy, and one more guy. Three in all.*

Now, some say that that our universe began with a big bang. And it is all but certain that the battle of the sexes—of boy chasing girl, boy winning girl—began with an echo of the big bang.

And in the many years and in the many ways of the battling sexes since then there have been many "small big bangs," if you will. Some very hot; some with a great deal of bang.

And now—even as we speak so socially—at this very moment many hot-blooded young men are pursuing many curvy young women with offers of further big bangs—and new forms of curved space-time that new universes create.

The Big Bang that Wasn't

O NCE UPON A SPACE-TIME, there was ... an evening ... a nice, warm spring evening, ... and there was ...

A house. ...

And there was a black car pulling up to it. ... And a young couple dressed in black, set against rich, great colors. ...

Nighttime colors. ...

Orange, red, yellow, purple. ...

Blue, green, indigo, violet. ...

Set against a deep, dark blue night sky with many stars. ...

It was a quiet neighborhood. ...

There was a smallish sound ... of crunching gravel as the car tires came to a stop.

And then a longish pause ...

Then the metallic click of a car door opening. ...

Outside the House, Night

The young man and woman looked beautiful, as they stepped from the car.

When she emerged, she was a smile. This girl was a walking glowing beaming smile.

It was the kind of smile that owned the room, or owned the scene, wherever she was.

The girls that she met in her travels thought that it was a lovely smile.

The boys that she met ... wanted to be very close to that smile.

She was wearing a silky black evening dress. Sleeveless. Her arms and legs were gorgeous. She wore a silver bracelet on her right wrist. Her body moved with grace. Floating. She was wearing black heels.

Her eyes were shining with inner life. She glowed. Yes, this girl glowed.

He was wearing a tuxedo suit, with a black silk tie. A long, thin tie that cut a line down to his waist. There was a subtle pattern on the tie, a flow of waves. The suit was lean and gave him a tall line.

As he came out, he was struck by her. He was seeing her back in silhouette moving away from him, and he paused for a beat. *"Wow,"* he said softly to himself.

She walked as though she were coming off a fashion catwalk. There was something immensely sexy about this young woman. Her name was *Jayne Holly Wyatt*.

All the men fell for her. And quickly. Everything was 'right' about her.

She was a woman dangerously set. She had every man reeling or hanging or swaying or swooning, or moving softly through the air toward her. Every man wanted to lie down with her.

Ridley Richardson watched her walk toward his house. He was enthralled.

Ridley closed his eyes for a moment, before opening them and following her.

They were coming from a ballroom social.

They were both just past twenty years old. Just past twenty summers old. Both were recent graduates and they had recently met.

This had been a formal stepping out. And lovely, indeed, it had been. Filled with the thrill of the new. It had been an adult party. They were both so very young and it had been a new experience. It had been something beyond a nightclub, beyond a garden party, beyond a loft party. It had been a ballroom social. A boy-girl dance social.

It was the adult world, which—of course—was filled with crazy people. But they had all seemed quite nice at the ball.

Yes, he had closed his eyes in the moment of movement from one dream to the next.

Now he opened them and followed her as a gentleman properly would, should and does.

This was a very special evening for the young man, because he felt she was so truly special.

She was a seven-day-a-week woman. There was no higher beauty of woman.

What he felt as he entered the house with her was hope.

But there was a problem. A few important things he had said tonight about himself were ... well, what was the word ... oh, yes ... lies.

Well, that was harshly put. He had been: *untrue*.

Yes, that was much nicer. He needed to tell her the truth. He took in a breath. He was finding it hard to breath. He noticed his heart was now beating all too fast. His knees were wobbly and trembling. And his hands, were of course, also trembling.

Truth was best, he thought.

Inside the House

The young man and woman, Ridley and Jayne, stepped into the house, which Jayne was seeing for the first time. She looked around, observing a quite elegance.

Presently they were touring the house.

"It looks," she said, "like both bedrooms are being lived in."

"Oh, yes," he said, "I have a friend staying with me temporarily."

(This was: *Untrue.*)

The Living Room

They sat down.

"You said you're an executive at a public relations agency, right?" she asked. "Do you love it?"

"I enjoy it," he said. "It's a job, but it's commerce. And what can one find in commerce that leads to enlightenment?" He looked at her. "Actually I shouldn't say that. There's a lot you can learn from business people about leadership. ... Leadership is an important part of healthy spirituality—What fascinates me is behavior. Human nature. Relationships."

"I feel the same way," she said.

"Thanks for tonight," he said and looked into her eyes. "Thank you." He became quiet. And then said, "Do you feel like calling it a night?"

"No," she said.

They were sitting at opposite ends of the couch.

"What do you feel like doing?" he asked.

She reached across the couch and took his hand.

He gave it to her. "If I kissed you," he said, "would I be coming on too strong?"

"Is that what you're going to do?" she said.

He moved in for a kiss. Hesitated. Pulled away from her.

"I have to tell you something about myself," he said.

"Yes," she said.

"No, never mind ... Please forget it." He moved toward her for a kiss. He put his arm on her shoulder. Touched her skin with his fingers. ... And he brought his lips toward hers, until he was a whisper away. ... Here, he stopped.

The moment became very still.

"Would you like me to open the window?" he asked.

She looked at him.

"You're okay? ..." he said. "... Well, I want to tell you something about myself, ... mmm ... that is kind of important."

Jayne lay against the couch, and smiled. "Tell me what's going on in your head."

"I don't know how you'll take it?"

"You don't have to tell me," she said.

"Let me just say one or two small things." Ridley took a breath and stood up.

"Does it really matter," he said, "that I have this house? That I'm a business executive? That I dress elegantly? I think it's bull-mud."

"You should be proud of those things," she said. "What you do says a lot about what you are. How you dress says a lot about what you are. ... You're saying a lot of good things about yourself."

"What if those things really say nothing?" he said. "What if they're just a kind of front? ... How does a woman know the difference between a good dress and a bad dress?"

"I know what you mean," she said.

"Yes, right," he said, "when a woman wears a bad dress you notice the dress. When she wears a good dress, you notice the woman."

While talking, he was removing the tuxedo jacket. He took off his elegant silk tie and set it aside, carefully. "My point is that brilliant people don't need to dress to the hilt. They don't dress brilliant, they just are brilliant."

He opened the collar of his shirt, to reveal a white crew-neck undershirt. He tousled his hair, so that it would rest more naturally. His hair was wild and long. He pulled the sash from his waist, and he set it down gently.

"Do you really need to look like a million bucks? Do you need the *'million bucks front'*?"

"Well," she said, "most people would say you look better in the *'million bucks front.'* ... It's cool. It's *the art of cool.*"

He was trying to convince her. But first he was wondering if he had convinced himself yet.

"It's a high-bang-for-the-bucks move?" he asked.

"Yes," she said.

"Ah, I see." He looked at her. "Jayne ... I feel that you're a special person. ... I've done a few things that I don't feel quite right about. I wanted to put my best foot forward—See this tuxedo?"

"It's very nice," she said.

"It's not mine," he said.

"Oh ... That's okay ... Everybody, once in a while, borrows a tuxedo."

"You know the house?" he said. "And that person that's living with me temporarily ... He's the owner of the house. I'm just staying here—until I find a job."

She looked at him.

"I thought you said you're a public relations executive?"

"I could be," he said, "but I don't have the training. I'm telling you all this because I didn't want to get in so deep that you'd get a false impression of me."

She continued to look at him.

He sat back on the couch.

"So," he sighed, "I don't have a job—at this time. You can't tell that to a woman when you first meet her."

"I see," she said.

"There. That's it," he said. "Now those things shouldn't matter, I think."

"Of course not. It's so good that you've said these things to me. Most magazines tell you that *'You should see him for what he is, as opposed to what you want.'* I'm starting to see you for what you are. But listen ... I should get going. It's getting late."

She stood up.

"What time is it?" she asked.

"I don't know," he said. "I don't have a watch."

Walking Jayne Home

The Street, Night

Ridley and Jayne were walking from the house to Jayne's apartment, which was close by. They were neighbors.

"So what happened to your last job?"

"I got ... uhm, fired."

"Downsizing?"

"I influenced it in some ways when I told my, uhm, ... boss, uhm, to go ahead and uhm, ... fuck himself. ... He wasn't doing his job right. I was. I got caught up in an adrenaline rush. Do you know what that is? When your adrenaline starts shooting through you. Your heart beats faster. You start to lose control."

"Just like the way you were a few minutes ago, when we were about to kiss."

"Yes," he smiled, "you're right. You're very quick. That was an adrenaline rush. I wanted things to go right between us. I got nervous."

"So what happened with the boss?"

"Well, in business, honesty is not the best policy," he said. "... The whole thing happened, well, just a few days ago. It's got me a little startled. ... Oh, I don't want to get us into a total bringdown. ... I think it's all working out for the best. It's a positive."

"I see. ... But you had a rough patch there?"

"I said to him things like: You raging maniac, you psycho. ... I called him an insane bitch."

"But he's a man."

"Still it was true. ... You know ... now that I think back on it, I can see he wanted a reaction from me. He was pushing me to the edge. ... Well, he got a reaction. ... Like I said though—it's a positive."

"It sounds positive."

"Yes, it's nice when people can be open with each other. Honesty is so valuable."

She looked at him.

" ... Yes, I think it's working out for the best," he said.

"Were you an executive there?" she said.

"I was still gaining experience. Actually, I was still at the, uhm, junior level. But it really is for the best. I want to go into another field. ... I've always been interested in the study of behavior. Not just of people, but also animals."

"What kind of money can you make as a behavior person?"

"They're called zoologists. Or primatologists. Or behavioral scientists. It's not really a get-rich-quick scheme. Then again there's always an outside chance you could make a real killing in animal studies." He smiled.

"That must really be something—making your fortune in animals." She laughed.

"It's not like being a doctor or anything," he said. "The money is not there in that way. The deal does leave a little something to be desired. ... It's just something I feel a natural interest in. I'm hoping the money will come but that's not my first priority. I want to know about people. I want to know how the mind works."

"What happens if you meet a nice girl and you want to go out?"

"I'm hoping the young lady would be very understanding."

They continued walking.

"It really is beautiful out tonight," he said. He looked at her and then turned to take in the street.

She looked around. "I suppose. But it's just a street scene."

She saw houses, fences, sidewalks, lamps and cars with a little greenery here and there. Not exactly natural splendor.

"Can I show you a trick I got out of a book? It'll just take a moment." She smiled mysteriously.

He continued. "Stop here for a moment."

Opening your visual field

They stopped walking.

"Take a deep breath," Ridley said, "and let it out slowly."

She looked at him.

"Turn and look at that tree across the street." She turned. "Now look up there and would you, please, on one of its branches imagine there's a camera. Look into the lens. Do it with a feeling like you're the superstar of a great movie and they're filming you with that camera."

He paused for a beat to let her get started with the imaginary game.

"Look into the lens as if you're reaching for it with your eye. At the same time relax, and open up your peripheral vision."

He stopped a beat to let her take that in and then continued.

"Open your visual field. Keep looking into that lens with the center of your vision. The part that focuses and takes your attention. At the same time, open your peripheral vision so that you can see shapes and color on the outside."

She seemed to be following along and doing what he was suggesting, so Ridley continued.

"Imagine there's a feeler coming out from your eyes and going into that camera lens. Almost like there are lasers coming out of your eyes and shooting into that lens. At the same time, keep your peripheral vision so that your visual field is open. It should be almost like you have a two-way vision."

He paused. "How's it coming along?"

"I'm not sure, but I think I'm doing it."

"Now—take the things you've just done and scan your gaze along the street. Do a continuous, connected sweep. While you're relaxed, breathing easy, and keeping your visual field open. Move your attention along the street but the whole time keep your awareness of shapes and colors in your peripheral vision. ... Ready?"

"Yes," she said. Now she began looking around again.

He said, "Maybe try doing figure eights with your vision."

She did a slow figure eight with her gaze. And suddenly laughed. She did another figure eight.

Now he laughed.

"Do you notice a difference?" he asked.

She turned to him—then back to the view.

She saw lemon yellows. Spatterings of orange and red. Thick brushstrokes of emerald green. Blues—so many blues.

Dark blue streaked across the lower horizon and drew itself into black.

All around her she saw ...

Red. Orange. Yellow.

Green. Blue.

Indigo. Violet.

She turned back to him.

"Thanks Ridley," she said. "You're right. It is beautiful out here tonight. And I wouldn't have noticed."

"It's beautiful everywhere Jayne. ... Should we continue walking?" he asked. And extended his hand in the air, pointing toward her house.

She began walking. He followed at her side.

"Where did you learn that?"

"Oh, it was in a small little green book. I forget the title."

The Front Door to Jayne's Apartment, Night

As they approached her door, as they walked up the stairs to the patio outside her section of apartments there was a strange, thick awkward silence.

This was one of those strange things that happens in a relationship. In veering from moment to moment, sometimes the feelings between two people abruptly grew very strange indeed.

He had lied to her, presented a false front. ... There had been moments of fun; that last bit had been memorable and affecting. But there was something very disturbing. There was something she sensed that was bothering her greatly. She held it in. And held it down.

They said goodbye awkwardly.

There was a current of disturbance. Things were in an uproar beneath this quiet scene.

She opened her door, and stepped in.

"I had a wonderful time tonight," she said, feeling it necessary to be polite.

She had crossed her threshold, and now there was a distance between them.

He felt that to step forward would be to intrude into her personal space. He kept his distance and blew her a gentle kiss.

She smiled. And gently closed the door.

Oh, oh—that uneasy feeling

Once she had closed the door, Ridley felt something heavy and leaden hit him deep within his inner space. ... He suddenly felt that something had gone terribly wrong.

She felt rattled

Inside her apartment, Jayne paused. She took a breath. ... She was feeling some things that were quite un-right. ... She drew her breath and continued moving.

She walked into her apartment, turned off the main light, and made ready for bed.

The City Streets, Night

Ridley was walking the streets, thinking.

He was talking to himself.

Tonight, he was full of foolish song.

The words of one ballad moved in a persistent winding—round and round—inside his head.

"Lately, I find myself out gazing at stars," Ridley said the lyrics softly, while looking forward, and into the air before him. *"Hearing guitars, like someone in love. Sometimes the things I do astound me, ... mostly whenever you're around me."*

He stared outward wistfully as he took in the street scenery. He had come to a ridge. Spread out before him, he could see rolling lights and streets.

"Lately," he said, *"I seem to walk as though I had wings, ... bump into things, ... like someone in love."*

He stopped, took his gaze upward, and stared at the stars.

"Each time I look at her it happens," Ridley said to himself.

"Lately, I have trouble finding my way through things. It's almost like I'm in love. I'm feeling ... like someone in love. ... In love."

He looked upward and outward into the upper reaches of space—there were so many stars.

Chet Clifford
The Charmer

The Chet Session

The House, Later that Night

Ridley was talking to his housemate—*Chet Clifford*.

Chet was the actual owner of the house they lived in. He was good looking and a smooth operator.

Chet Clifford was stunning to women. He looked like a fashion model. ... Perfect body, perfect smile, ... perfect style.

The difficulty of launching into the world of adult romance ...

They were all young, Ridly, Jayne and Chet—and Chet was the eldest.

They were, all three, recent graduates. They were all fresh out of school and entering the adult world.

Now Chet was off to a running start. To a flying start. He had quickly gotten an executive job, bought a house, and rented out one of the rooms.

He had so recently been mired in that ugly stage of life called: *"college."* It was only a few years ago, but he had since emerged full bore, and displayed a natural talent for adult warfare and adult games.

Ridley was still emerging from his university days, and from the damage that a *good* college education can cause on the human psyche.

Chet was already over his college education. He had quickly realized that all of the important things you had to know in life—in order to succeed in sexual coupling, in business partnering, and in all of life's alliances—simply were not taught properly in school. Most teachers did not know and the others did not dare teach the things that Chet knew.

He was now helping Ridley to step into the world of *adult business*.

The Chet reaction

"You told her you got fired, you're unemployed, you're broke?" Chet asked.

"I laid it all out for her. I feel cleansed," said Ridley.

"Hmm ... I think you dug a hole for yourself," said Chet.

"Why?"

"Well, you made too much of a thing. Why would you want to confess all these things to a girl unless you were going to get married? You can't make the date that serious."

"You think I played it wrong?" said Ridley.

"She lost interest in you," said Chet. "You led her into the phony front you were putting up. Then you blew your cover. She got turned off by that."

"But you're the one who talked me into putting up a front."

"The front was fine."

"Maybe."

"You'll get over it. Girls like this are a dollar a dozen. Listen, in the scheme of things, it wasn't a presidential election. But you have to remember with the next girl—*You have to put up a little front.* Something. And then not blow your cover! You've got the thing going for you, she's liking you, and then all of the sudden on a first date you tell her well it's not my tuxedo. It's like you're deliberately into self-destruction. What are you a masochist?

"You completely sank this one. You're out of a job. She must have lit up when you told her that one. It's not your tuxedo. She had to know that, right? And why didn't you tell me you didn't have a fucking watch? I would've lent you one. Then you could have told her you borrowed the watch—You would have had more to talk about!"

Ridley was taking it in—He felt that Chet possessed a voice of odd wisdom.

"You were nice, polite, honest. That's all too sweet. Women can't get into that."

"What do you mean?" Ridley asked.

"Life is not rational. You study behavior, you know that. People don't behave logically. Do you want to know the secret of getting women?"

"Do you have that?" asked Ridley.

"You have to think outside the normal."

Chet let that hang in the air a while.

"I don't get it," said Ridley.

The Secret of Women
"Women's studies"—for men

"Life is not rational," Chet said. "People do not behave in a rational ordered way.

"You can't go about it rationally. It's not clinical. You can't go right down the middle. It's not straight—*It's curvy.*

"You have to be different than these other guys," said Chet. "They don't know what they're doing. They're disasters."

"Right, we're in favor of ... success," said Ridley.

"Let's look at what you do the next time ... when you go out dancing. ...

"Here's how to build a night sesssion. ...

Night-Time Chet Sessions
And how to seduce the sexiest of women

Setting up the room, the space-time of a dance floor
"Okay, here we go ... let's get a picture of the dance floor.

"It's crowded," said Chet. "There are lots of drunks on the floor."

"We were at a charity ballroom social," said Ridley.

"I hate you," said Chet. "Okay, the drunks were in tuxedos. Now some of the people—by that I mean all of the people—wanted to do what I'm going to explain now ..."

The curvature of space-time
"First, you've got the picture ... Correct?"

"It's crowded. It's a bar. ...

"There are lots of drunks on the dance floor. ...

"It's late at night. You're tipsy. ...

"It's a dark room. ...

"Slow, slinky, smooth. ... Lots of people here. ..."

"Now ... the girl ..."
"She has an inner dialog going," said Chet

"She wants to look fabulous. That's what you're helping her with. In your head, you're trying to get her into bed. That's where the night ends, if you do it right."

"I wouldn't say that."

"I would. Where's it supposed to end, in the kitchen? This is about getting into the bedroom."

Ridley said, "The way I think of it is this: You're polite. You make her look good. You show her a good time. You keep it simple. And then she'll want to dance with you again."

"Oh, you're saying you dance with her so you can dance with her next time? ... It's now or never. You go for it straight away."

"Go for what?" asked Ridley.

"What they want is a real man on the dance floor. A guy with confidence. Casual, cool, comfortable. He's not worried. He's in his world. He's in control. And he's treating her like the most important person in the world."

"What kind of dance do you want it to be?" asked Chet.

"It's couples dancing—but what do you want the dance to be?"

"You're caught up in ballroom. ... That's not it," said Chet. "... You want to be the guy women want to dance with late at night in a dark room, by a bar with the lights low and off in the distance.

"You want smooth dance.

"The destination is the bed. You want the dance that makes them want to go to bed. The dance with the guy they want in that bed. The smooth dance with the smooth operator.

"You want them to start thinking body-talk. ..."

Falling dance

"You want a *'falling dance,'*" said Chet. "You want a grounded dance. You want to be sinking into the ground with her."

The bare essentials of seduction on the dance floor

"Here are some quick basics.

"We're just going to cover her weight, her hips, and your hands. You'll get the idea.

"It's the bare essentials. We'll do this quick. ... And we'll go through some for-instances to make the picture clear for you. ..."

The Teaching Session
The Master Class with Chet Clifford

Weight Changes

Her weight

Chet put his arm around Ridley's shoulder.

"You meet a girl in a club. ... Offer to get her a drink.

"You want to get her tipsy.

"Tipsy is social. Drunk is out of control.

"Tipsy is you're falling forward. Drunk is you're falling down. You want tipsy. Tipsy is just tipping forward. You want a forward pitch. You want her on her toes falling toward you, not on her heels falling away from you. Got it? ... Falling forward you do in bed. Falling on the floor you don't do in bed. Are we clear?"

"All your concepts keep coming back to her bed," said Ridley.

"Yes, that's the beauty," said Chet.

Taking her into closed position

Chet moved in closer to Ridley.

"We seem to be one woman short for tonight's class, so you'll fill in," said Chet.

Chet brought Ridley into closed dance position—face to face—in a "slingshot" position, with Chet's hand on Ridley's back—where the woman's bra strap would be.

Ridley looked away from Chet, immediately uncomfortable.

"Look at me," Chet said.

Ridley glanced at Chet.

Chet said, "How do I seem? ... I'm confidant. Cool, casual, comfortable."

"Yes."

"And you—You look like a nervous wreck."

"I never danced with another man before."

"I never danced with a man either—Be cool brother. We'll both live through this."

Ridley looked Chet in the eye. He tried to do what he had taught Jayne about opening your visual field. About keeping your focus and your peripheral vision floating in your attention at the same time. It worked. He was able to look Chet straight in the eye.

"Better," said Chet. "Breathe and relax."

Ridley breathed.

"Incidentally, if she gets uncomfortable at this point, you tell her, *'This is the younger style. It suits you.'* "

"Thank you darling," said Ridley.

"You're welcome my angel," said Chet. "Let's get started. ... Feel me on you. Do you feel me?"

"Oh yes," said Ridley.

Spins and turns

"She gets tipsy. ... Then you take her dancing. I'll show you what I mean."

"But she's tipsy," said Ridley. "She won't be able to dance."

"Do you hear yourself talking? That's when you start spinning her."

Chet broke away.

He now pretended to be holding an imaginary girl in an open position and speaking to her:

"You tell her: *'Spinning is fun. Where are you from? From California? Oh, California girls love to spin.'*

"Make it fun. Then spin her."

He spun this lovely imaginary girl.

"She starts falling on you—Yummy! You brace her. You hold her. You stabilize her. You're a perfect gentleman—But look how close you are on her center.

"By the time Monday rolls around, you'll be waking up in her bed. Believe me."

Chet whirled the imaginary girl around and gave Ridley the sense that she was stumbling.

"You tell her: *'You're so beautiful doing this.'* ... You explain to her: *'What you want to experience is release. That anything is possible.*

" *'There's no ceiling. People think there's a ceiling ... of counting and steps. There's no ceiling.'*

"Then you find your way back into the set moves.

"You're continuing—until you're folded back into a connection.

"It's like the art of the hug—You do a goodbye—and then a hug again."

Chet looked at Ridley, "Now let's move to moment number two ..."

Hip Action

Her hips

Chet said, "Get her tipsy. Get her spinning and turning. Then you do *'The Mess-Around.'*"

He demonstrated by bringing Ridley into a very loving *'hug'*—a very close intimate, sensual embrace.

Now Chet wedged his leg between Ridley's legs—or *'her'* legs. He put his hip against *'her'* hips.

And what Chet did next was the sensational part:

He rotated their hips together in a circle.

This sexual move of joined hip motion was commonly called *'The Mess-Around.'* That's what dancers called it. But in the way that Chet did it, it was hard to tell the difference between this move and just plain *'fucking'* on the dance floor.

At the end of one nice sexy, smoldering circle of his-hip-rolling-on-her-hip, he stopped.

He separated from Ridley—or the *'her'* in this scene.

He rocked their weight away from each other.

And that was how the hip-on-hip move ended.

Chet smiled with great charm.

Ridley became very disturbed.

"Chet," he said, "isn't there such a thing as *personal space*? Aren't you invading a woman's—I mean a stranger's—personal space? ... You're putting your *'thing'* right in between her legs."

"You're fucking her," said Chet. "Yes, that's the beauty of the move. That's the nice idea behind it. ... Women love guys who know how to fuck them. ... Do you hear yourself when you ask these questions?" Chet continued. "Let's get back to work here. We're talking technique. It's a beautiful thing."

"How far in can you go?"

Chet smiled. And paused for effect.

"There's a lot to being a gentleman," said Chet. "What you tell her is: *'It's nice dancing with you today. Wow. You move very beautifully sweetheart.'* ... She'll forget where the property lines are—She'll be having such a good time."

Hand Connections

Your hands

"It's like a masseuse. Never take your hands off the client—I mean the woman," said Chet.

"Show her how a guy should put a hand on a girl's hip. ...

"Women love guys who know how to hold their hips while fucking them.

"Now, first, you play the game with her of *how to find the hips*. You say: *'Where is the hip?'"*

Chet touched his own ass. " *'This is not the hip.'* ..." He touched his own breasts. " *'This is not the hip.'* ..." Now Chet touched his own hip bone. " *'This is the hip.'"*

Now he touched Ridley's hip bone. He did it very tenderly, like a true gentleman—with just the tips of two fingers. It was a gentle touch. And then he pushed Ridley away gently but firmly. It had a very good feel to it.

Hand connections

"Here's what you do with your hands," Chet said.

"Show her the hand connections. Demonstrate what *not* to do with your hands. ...

"You tell her: *'What a gentleman does not do is this.'* And then you do it to her.

"You get naughty with your hands, but first you make it clear you're going to be naughty with her. Just with her. You don't do this with other women.

"Woman love guys who consider them a special fuck."

He moved his hand down her body, beginning on her shoulder blade, down the middle of her back, ... past her waist, ... her hips ...

Chet said, "Put your hand *almost* on her ass. Stop there. Because once your hand is actually on her ass, there's nowhere else you can go on the dance floor."

Chet finished dancing, and released Ridley. He patted Ridley's belly. And as his hand flew away, in the same sweep of his hand, he made a pistol motion and fired into the air.

He gracefully stepped from the dance floor like a lion king and moved to his throne—err, to his couch. He sat on the arm regally—instead of on the cushion.

"There, you have a start ..."
"Put things together," said Chet, "in unexpected ways—That's the joy. You want her to feel the joy.

"You know your way around the dance floor.

"Think of it as a pursuit you stay with. Don't let it be the end. It's so worth it.

"You've got a great start. Get it into your body. Music is awesome. Dancing is awesome. There are so many opportunities in this city."

The Master Class in Female Psychology
Chet Clifford and advanced studies

Domination

And the dominant male
"Try this out next week," said Chet. "Chalk up this girl tonight to experience. You'll get better."

"But I'm not looking past her," said Ridley. "I don't want to look past her. ... Chet, she's special."

"You want to know how to get her back? I'll tell you what it takes."

"What?"

"You have to get her respect. You have to be strong. The only way to do that is to be what women call a *caveman.*' I hate that word because it puts the wrong image in your head. But if a guy is too nice, too cooperative then they get turned off. Strength is a turn-on. You have to take charge. Listen, in every relationship there's always the dominant one and the one who submits. She wants to be the one who submits. You don't have two decision-makers. You have the one who decides and the one who follows. Life is about dominance. It's the same in everything. In politics, you rule your land. In marketing, you beat the competition. Look at the animal kingdom. Survival of the fittest. Show me a weak ape and then show me how many mates he has. Take the worst vicious ape, he has all of the other females around him. There we have dominance again. Equality is a myth. All men are created equal. That's a pitch, that's not truth. It's damaging— let's follow that and see where we end up."

Chet looked at Ridley.

"I'm real. Are you?" said Chet. "Life is nothing but a game of dominance."

"I don't like to think that way," said Ridley.

"Think how you like," said Chet. "I'm just telling you how life works. I could lead you down the garden path where nothing I say is true. If I wanted to live like that, I'd become a politician. You know her a little bit. You've known other women. Has it ever seemed to you that what they want is a guy who they can walk all over? You've got a little bit to learn about what makes a man sexy. I'm a feminist, but it doesn't work. Women want a real man. She wants a man who can lead. Now go in there and show some personality."

"I can't order her around."

"Don't order. Just give her a taste of confidence. It's what she wants. She'd never admit it. But trust me. If you want her to like you, you need to go over there and take care of business."

"You think that's what she wants?" said Ridley.

"Of course. But she'll never admit it. People don't say what's really on their minds. When was the last time you honestly told a woman what you were thinking?" said Chet.

"I don't know. An hour ago?" said Ridley.

"Do you want to listen," said Chet, "or do you want to talk? Most people tell you the opposite of what they really want."

"I think you might be right."

"You think or you know?"

"This is so mind-altering."

"You have something to say, do it now. It doesn't get any easier."

"Maybe you're right. Maybe I should fix this."

Now Chet Clifford went into the standard real man's advice:

"Go take a minute of her time for a straight talk. Lay it out for her. You'll feel better. Tell her *I've got you under my skin,*' or whatever love song works for you. Lay it out. Then you really will feel cleansed of sin. If you want her, go get her. If you're unhappy, it's because you're unhappy. Tell her how you feel. See what she says. You're a great guy. Why wouldn't she want you? Why not go over right now and tell her? You've got it bad, and that isn't good. It's no good. Now go over there and show her all your good intentions. I think it'll work."

"Thank you Chet. I wouldn't know what to do or how to do this without you," said Ridley.

"Hey, we're friends," said Chet.

"What time is it?" said Ridley.

"You're thinking too much. Forget the time."

"Okay, I'll forget the time, but what time is it?"

"It's like 9, or so, maybe 10. Ah, you've got plenty of time. The night is young—What the hell am I saying!—It's a Friday night for Christ' sake. Don't think up reasons to fail. You can make this happen. Go do this. ... You and me, Ridley, we're in this together. And we'll have you two together. It's going to happen. I can feel it."

Ridley walked out the front door.

Now Chet was alone.

Chet turned away from the door and moved into the living room.

What came next was a bit bizarre. It was a side of Chet and an experience that you could only call:

The Chet Show
Chet Clifford takes center stage and turns it all 'on'

Chet moves and Chet presentation

The light bounced off the walls filling the area with brilliance as though a spotlight had been directed onto Chet Clifford.

"I just gave him the best chance he could have," said Chet aloud to the room. "He's a good guy. We'll see what happens. Who knows? It's him, at this point.

"I'm a fatalist," said Chet, and his voice bore a rich resonance and a fluid tone that filled the whole room with a comfortable, friendly living room presence. "That's what I am. I'm a fatalist. Your fate is your character."

He was suddenly talking aloud—*to a large imaginary audience.*

This was a peculiarity—and a great virtue of Chet's. He had many magical qualities about him. And one of them was the way he was developing when it came to this thing—*to this imaginary audience that he always felt was before him.*

The "audience"

The principle Chet invoked here was: Use your imagination to start a fire— This was what Chet was doing now ... He turned and began to speak to a rich, colorful, streaming *imaginary "audience."*

The "audience" was always with him and there for him.

This was part of the game. *This was part of being "on."* This was the modern way. And Chet Clifford was the most highly modern young man. you would ever meet in your life.

Yes, the *audience* was always there. They were his friends. Always wondering to themselves, "*Oh, what was that Chet up to now?*"

In playing to his audience, he liked to reveal a series of inner thoughts that he would never share in daily life with actual people.

You see, with his audience, he felt free to deliver unusual advice as though it were perfectly normal. Almost as if the audience was filled with people who were just like him, who carried around the same kinds of thoughts.

The marketing show

Chet worked at a marketing agency. He was a public relations man. He was a campaign and warfare man. And he was always developing his act.

He was something like an adrenaline addict. He was addicted to marketing. In his field, he was Hannibal the Carthaginian general, he was Alexander the Great, he was Patton the field commander.

He couldn't kick it, he wouldn't kick it, he shouldn't kick it. It was him and it was heavy. It lent him the gravitas of great men, and he rehearsed his marketing constantly. His dream was to market to a sellout audience at the *Garden*—that great forum, the largest stadium within the largest city within the most powerful country on earth.

That would be the height of his soaring ambition. A great big spectacular marketing rock concert. It would just be him alone on a stage with a microphone and sharing his view of marketing greatness with his audience.

The art of the bastard

Chet was a master bastard, and he felt he was an example to other bastards.

He loved sharing moves—moves stewed to perfection. Oh, he did so very much love the high and right honorable art—the ancient art of the bastard. He loved presenting it to his audience.

Chet would sometimes think to himself, *Most people don't want to sound like the 'voice of god,' they don't want to sound like they're talking from on high. That's just ridiculous when that's exactly what you want to sound like—what you want is a really good 'voice of god.' The god voice works.*

And you have to practice, and develop a really strong god voice. You need it. If you don't have one, what happens when some guy comes along who does have the god voice? Why he's going to beat you cold.

Yes, Chet was a master bastard, and he was a shining example to all the other bastards out there. ... Now, in this moment, there was no rest for the wicked. Chet took to the stage and faced his audience of like-minded people.

"I'm a fatalist," Chet said again. "Your fate is your character."

This was how Chet stepped before his audience. This was how he opened the talk.

"This is Ridley's fate. I'll show you."

He paused for effect.

Once he had them in his grip, he walked them into the next room.

Ridley's Bathroom, Night

"This is Ridley's bathroom. Take a look at this."

He pointed to some towels that were hanging awkwardly. Then he pointed to the sink, which wasn't perfectly cleaned. It was rather disordered. The vanity held gels, soaps, brushes and razor blades.

"I don't have to use this bathroom but doesn't this tell you something about him? Come on, I'll show you something else."

Ridley's Bedroom, Night

The room was likewise disordered, filled with books and papers—which seemed to be spilling from every drawer and shelf. Apparently Ridley was a young man who studied a great many things.

"He lives in this. Go ahead take a look around."

Now Chet held perfectly still. He released his audience's attention to the environment of the room. He would let it sink into them.

When the audience at last turned back to Chet he was again in motion. He was opening the top drawer of Ridley's desk.

Chet lifted a set of green bills from the drawer, gracefully took one and replaced the rest.

Looking at the audience with a charming smile, he continued to educate them in his ways.

"I take $20 once in a while," said Chet, "... for expenses that Ridley doesn't otherwise cover. Once a week I have a cleaning lady come by. He doesn't chip in. This way I get the payments from him. I take 20 and I let him off the hook. I should actually take 25 but all right ... I'm a nice guy."

He held the moment. Then continued. ... It was a lighthearted aside, but significant for them to learn by. "You see simple acts like taking the bill come down to a question of confidence. You've got to make your confidence stronger and stronger every day. I don't like to take the poor guy's money, but your confidence is your most important asset. So when you come across a moment where you find yourself saying, 'I can't do that.' Then you have to do it."

Now he directed them to the body of the room. "Look at all the books he has here. He's got more in storage. As if the library at the college down the block didn't have enough ink on paper for you. He's got to be a know-it-all about everything. You talk about something that happened two hundred, one thousand, two thousand years ago—it doesn't matter when—he'd like to have a view. ... Is it important? Who knows, but it shows you something about him. He has an arrogant streak. Normally that's a very good thing, but not like this. He could learn all he wants about history, psychology, art. It doesn't mean he knows anything. Do you think ink on paper impresses me? He reads his books and goes to museums. Me—I'm real; I'm into the reality that's out there. I'm not an elitist.

"I deal only in facts—so I'm a cocky bastard," he said.

"I'm only interested in true success, and I'm ever watchful of failure."

He looked across his audience and made strong eye contact with them one at a time.

"I'll tell you some good things to learn. ...

" '*Get there firstest with the mostest.*'—That's an important principle.

" '*The pursuit is as critical as the initial attack.*' ...

" '*Reinforce strength, abandon failure.*' ...

" '*You don't fight alone—you have to bring in, and use allies.*' "

"These are the kinds of concepts you want. These are the things that matter. ... Listen, there's a lot to learn. Stick with me and you'll get it all."

He was performing what he termed a "*social job*"—teaching social jabs—teaching society punches.

And in his stance and manner he was teaching a subtle thing called "*The Ready Position*"—or what he liked to call the "gunslinger position."

... As he strode, he maintained a strong, light, elegant frame. His arms were floating slightly outward from his torso. He called this carriage of his frame the "ready position." It meant—'You can go this way, or you can go that way.'—Lots of great doings were possible, and each might happen at any moment.

He was always in the ready position. ...

He was a walking broadcast. And Chet's attitude held out a message to the world in which he said, *"I'm on my way. And my time has come."*

The Street, Night

Ridley was again filled with romantic ballads.

Ridley's talks and voicings were different than his friend Chet's. They were like songs. Like the jazz songs that people sang to themselves.

Ridley was talking to a himself-outside-himself. To a "him" standing beside himself. Whereas Chet talked to a developing, growing audience.

With Chet, the thoughts were growing major. He was talking to a stadium of imaginary people.

Ridley's style was different.

At long last love?

Is this forever? Ridley asked. The ballad repeated itself in his head. It was a famous ballad. Perhaps you might even have heard it yourself.

Is this for all time? Is this a fancy not worth thinking of? Or is it at long last love?

He was Hamlet—He had questions. He was racked by doubts. And the answers were elusive.

Is it an earthquake or simply a shock? Is it a cocktail, this feeling of joy—or is what I feel the real McCoy—Is it for all time?"

Is it for all time—or simply a lark? Is it a fancy not worth thinking of? Or is it at long last love?

They Disturb Each Other
The Viking Attack

Jayne's Apartment, Night

Jayne was on the phone.

"He seemed very genuine ... but you're right. How could he lie like that to me? When I imagine what he was thinking of me, it really hurts. ...

"... You know me. I have a healthy respect for money, business, ... and money. ...

"... But to pretend you have those things. I'll like you if you don't have those things."

Her doorbell rang.

Jayne opened the door and found Ridley standing there.

He saw that she had undressed and changed into her pajamas. She happened to look terribly sexy in pajamas.

"Sorry to disturb you," he said. "May I have a word?"

She looked at him.

He stepped in.

She picked up the phone.

"I've got to go dear," Jayne said. "I'll call you tomorrow, okay? ... Goodnight. ... Sweet dreams."

She hung up the line and turned toward Ridley.

"I was talking to her about some guy I went out with tonight and I expected him to be very sweet and very nice. He turned out to be a liar—and a dreamer. And we parted company. Little did I know that he would show up again around midnight. An interesting character, wouldn't you say? A winner. There's even more, the winner is about to say something. Okay winner, let's hear it. I'm all yours."

Abruptly, his insides went into overdrive. His heart started hammering. Adrenaline shot through him.

"Lately, I've been finding ... uhm, ... when you're around ... when I look at you, ... I, ... uhm, am, uhm, feeling as though ..."

He looked at her.

"I'm in love with you," he said.

She stood there.

"You just met me," she said.

"I know," he said. "Maybe I fell in love with you the moment I saw you."

"They all do," she said. "Do you have something serious to say?"

"Forgive me. It's my first time. I've never been in love with you before."

"Well, that's a good line. I like you when you're witty. But I don't kid around about being in love. It means something to me."

"I'm just getting the Zen of this. It's not what I expected."

"Surprise," Jayne said.

"I'm finding my way to the way you're supposed to do this."

Telling her he was in love was really, really hard. His adrenaline was coursing through him. He was disturbed. Pushing through extreme difficulty.

"It does happen sometimes. You can experience love at first sight."

"Yes, it happens all the time—in movies. But this is a place called reality."

"Why wouldn't I be in love with you?"

"Because we just met."

"That's how love at first sight works."

"Love is knowing someone."

"You're a girl."

"Yes."

"You're uhm, ... made of, ... uhm, ... cool."

"Yes, I'm cool. But there's more to me."

"So I'll fall in love with that later. I'm pacing myself."

"I have a different theory," she said.

"Yes."

"People go insane. That happens. Sometimes people just go crazy. That happens at first sight too. And around me that happens to an awful lot of men. It's my brooding, smoldering sexuality."

"There's always that possibility."

"No, there's always that reality. It's called being a scorching beauty. You get men coming up to you saying, 'Jayne, I think you're the girl made of cool.'"

"Well, I could have said it better. Lately I haven't been myself."

"How about we make this the night we called it a day! I'm not interested."

"Oh."

All the energy in him crashed, a thousand feet into the ground. He stood, defeated.

"This is the rest of me," she said. "How do you like it so far?"

At times, the sexes get cross with one another.
They fancy one another, get cross, and then fancy again.
Or they fancy one another, get cross, and never speak again.
What we know about how it all works is very slender.

Chet Session Two

Chet's House, Later that Night

"You told her you're in love with her?" Chet asked.

"Yes, I felt it was too early to talk marriage. It's better to keep it simple. Slow and steady wins the race."

"She's good," said Chet. "She's really good. She's at the top of her game. She turned it all around so she could take charge again."

"Are you saying she's maneuvering?" said Ridley.

"Women can do it. They know no man can deal with it. No man knows how to take charge of a woman—except me, but then I'm special. You know, I'm tomorrow but I'm here today, what can I say?"

"What do we do next?"

"We wait for her to call. The ball is in her court now."

"What if she doesn't call?"

"Then we taught her a lesson."

"If she never calls?"

"You stood your ground. You did the right thing. Now feel good."

Ridley was in agony.

"She'll come to you," Chet said. "Don't worry. Now you play hard to get. Take it down a peg."

"What if she doesn't come to me?"

"Don't worry. It's physics. It works like a charm. I've had a lot of experience in this area. You'll have to trust me. You know I have no problem with women. I'm trying to get you to that level. How many women have I been with since you've known me?"

"None of this is feeling natural to me."

"If it was easy, wouldn't everybody in the world sleep with as many women as I do?"

Ridley went to the door.

"Chet, I can't do it this way. It's not for me. I'm going to talk to her."

He opened the door and walked out. Chet immediately ran to the door.

"Don't go over there. You don't know what you're doing! Aah, all right! Ruin it for yourself! Go ahead, ruin it."

Ridley & Jane—Friends & Thunderbolts

Moments Later

Jayne's Apartment, Night

Ridley stood before Jayne.

Jayne's pajamas were hugging her hips, breast, buttocks.

Ridley noticed this.

As they talked he glanced at the bed. From where he stood he had an angle on her bed. The bed was part of his problem in this. Another problem was her scent, which he kept inhaling.

"I'm sorry for the way I acted tonight. Maybe we're not hitting it off as boyfriend and girlfriend but there are other things. Not every relationship between a man and a woman has to have sexual feelings involved."

He said this while looking at her breasts, her hips.

"There are other kinds of relationships between men and women. There's ... mother and son. And lots of others."

She smiled and then went deadpan.

"You're a night owl. What time do you go to sleep?

Ridley laughed. "Say you'll forgive me. You didn't catch me in a lie. I told you. No harm was done. I didn't trick you out of anything. I wanted to impress you. Now I feel bad because I have a high regard for you. I'm ashamed of myself. I'm taking enough punishment from myself. I don't think you want to chip in."

"Friends. We're going to be friends."

"Yes, friends."

Thunderbolts

Ridley and Jayne were sitting and talking.

"I've been through it before," she said. "Where you think it's right, but you're wrong. When it's right, you feel the rightness of it."

"Thunderbolts," he said.

"Yes!" she said. "You feel a thunderbolt."

"It's mysterious."

"Yes, it's mysterious. You know what I mean then."

"I've felt thunderbolts."

"C'mon, when was the last time someone made you feel thunderbolts?"

"Maybe, uhm, ... an hour ago."

"I do that for all the guys." She smiled. "You didn't really feel a thunderbolt an hour ago."

He answered with silence.

"I think," she said, "you thought you felt a thunderbolt because you wanted to feel one. You wanted someone who would make you feel a thunderbolt. And I happened to be the one standing there."

"Well, uhm, I think I know my thunderbolts." He looked up. "But I'll think about what you're saying."

Chet Maneuvers

Chet's House, Night

"Magic?" Chet said. "You two are talking magic. This is unreal. You ruined it. You went in and totally ruined it.

"Girls don't talk about feeling magic to guys they want to sleep with. They hide it from them. Let's play *'The Verdict'* with your host Chet Clifford: The verdict is you lost. ... You're killing me. You're killing me here."

The control fit

Chet threw himself against the wall.

Chet was now leaning against the wall with his head buried in his hands. He was pounding the wall with his fist.

"Are you out of your mind? You just went in there and undid everything. Don't you want this girl?"

"But I don't want to take a chance on losing her."

"That's what you did. You lost her."

"How's that if we just became friends?"

Chet arched his back in agony and now directed his fit in the direction of the ceiling:

"Oh goddammit. What am I going to do you—to get you to the light? How can I make you understand and see this thing?"

Now he talked to the wall. "How can I make you understand it's art? We're talking a pure true art. For real men." He was saying this to the wall. "How do you I make you understand? To see the beauty, the awesome splendor in a good seduction of a beautiful woman.

"And this girl Jayne is so sexy. She is just so damn beautiful and you could have been fucking her all night if you did this with some sensitivity and like a man taking a woman.

"You could have been pounding and banging her in her bed—instead you wanted to confess and talk things through.

"This isn't soul searching, this is the game of fucking women."

Ridley looked on—What the hell was this all about?

Chet turned to him. "Let's get to the heart of the matter. Do you want to fuck her?"

Ridley didn't answer.

"No," said Chet, "don't answer. You're you. I understand that. You have a different way to say things, a different way to experience these things, but I know what you want to do with her."

Chet concluded with:

"I've got to think," he said. "Give me a minute. This has a lot of moving pieces. Let me work through this. I don't believe in no-win scenarios. There's always a way to get past an ending with women.

"There are no dead ends—for men with true grit."

He walked out muttering, "Damn! This is troubling. What to do? What to do?"

Chet was on the strategic level of the great ones. He was on a tear— Chet was in the full throes of it now, as he exited the room.

Chet's Bedroom, Night

Chet entered the bedroom. He closed the door. And now had a talk with his private *"audience."*

These men and women in his audience were people like him. They could understand all of this. They could sympathize with his feelings here.

"So now they're friends," said Chet to the audience. "That's not the worst thing that could have happened. This may work out.

"Did you like the fit I threw? Very effective, huh? How did you like the part where I talked to the walls? It's a control technique. Very effective. I felt a strong impulse to punch one of the walls—I get these powerful sensations—but that would have been too much. You know what? Ridley isn't man enough for her. In a way it's for the best that now *I'm going to take her from him.*"

He looked at the audience. "Yes, we're talking a change of plan."

A worthy adversary

"It's good for him. He needs a worthy adversary. To get him on his game."

"I was thinking about it as I made the speech.

"She really is sexy.

"She is damn pretty.

"You've seen her.

"I had this image of her getting fucked, and then I got this picture of me fucking her. And then I got a better idea of what to do in all this."

Chet moved about now very expressively. There was a lot going on emotionally here. Things were really heating up.

"It's rough. The world is rough for people like Ridley.

"The lesson here is that: *You have to watch out for number one.* I have to do what's best for me. And now that I think about it—*Do I want to fuck her?* I ask myself. Yes, I'd really like to fuck her.

"Oh, of course, I would never use that word with her. ... *I would make love to her.*

"I'm very nice and gentle. I just think with what I'm seeing here that I could really be the kind of loving man she wants. She's looking for it. She's hoping to find a man who knows how to really make love to her.

"I'm realizing I'm it."

Chet let that sink in for a minute.

"I'm going to be her next lover."

Lesson time

"Do you want to hear the mistake he's making?" said Chet to the audience. "I'll tell it to you. A lot of people make the mistake. It's a real bear. Oh, it'll hang you up if you don't understand it.

"Are you ready for ultimate truth?"

He paused and let the audience consider the importance of it.

When the pause reached a peak, Chet broke the tension with a highly meaningful statement. Chet said:

"An entirely virtuous person is not interesting.

"You need color. Women love that."

"This is lesson time," Chet said. "Experience teaches you. And this is hard lesson time. I'll tell you, there's no substitute for experience in learning a thing. ... The man who grabs a bull by the tail is getting sixty to seventy times the information of the fellow who hasn't."

Destruction creativity

"This could totally break his heart, this could totally destroy him," said Chet. "But on the bright side he could learn something. He could be a new man once he sees where this is going now.

"There is an excitement, there is a creativity in destruction," Chet said.

"When you break something, you actully change the energy of it. For example, from glass to rubble. It's a different look.

"Smash 'em down. Tear it down. There's something in an explosion. You go, 'Wow.' "

He looked at his audience.

"Oh, good silence from you. Well done."

He continued.

"Mastering the flow—that's what we're talking about here. ... I like things that stop the flow, make it back away or ... make it go in a new direction.

"Think about it. You'll see what I mean. You have to master the flow with people. You have to be able to force feelings and thoughts to stop and find a new direction.

"Oh, yes, it's a great thing. ... I like things that stop the flow and make it go in a new direction.

"And this'll be a really good thing for Ridley. He'll learn a lot of things about the flow of life."

Chet stopped. He looked up at the ceiling.

He turned back to the audience.

"Yes, this could be beautiful."

He thought about it.

"... My God, ..." he said. "... It's going to be so beautiful."

Chet left it there and exited the room.

The Living Room, Night

"She knocked you off the scene," said Chet.

Chet walked over to Ridley.

"Technically, this area is called *'Death.'*

"You have to stop dying. It's not cool. Women don't sleep with dead men. True? Do you follow?"

Chet continued. "So how does a professional keep from getting good and dead?

"He uses allies. He has friends. ... I'm going to step in and help you."

"How?" said Ridley.

"I'll go ... and I'll have a talk with her ... and I'll state your business ... but very smoothly."

"Ah," said Ridley.

"Yes," said Chet.

"How would that work exactly?" said Ridley.

"Well," said Chet, "what I'll do is something very special for you my friend Ridley. We're pals. You two are meant to be together. I know that. I'm going to bring you two together. I want to see you two end up together. It'll do my heart some good."

"Hmm," said Ridley, "... on the bright side ... I made it through. I'll live another day. I guess."

"That's right," said Chet. "That's the attitude. You're going to live another day. You now are dead. You soon will live. It's all good. You'll see. It'll be up, up and away—in no time. Very soon. We'll rally. ... At ease soldier."

Ridley relaxed into his stance dutifully.

He held Chet's look with a level gaze.

"Thanks Chet. I'm glad for all your help. It means a lot to me. I really wouldn't know how to get through this without you. I would just be so confused. And I would blow it. It helps to get your wise, wise advice."

"Hey, we're friends. We're in this together—I mean I'm not going after her like you—I mean we're in this for you—For you two to be together."

Invitation
You and your smile hold a strange invitation

Chet's Bedroom, Day

Chet was dressing, before a full-length mirror.

He was a 'fashion model' getting into a suit. He knew his business.

The audience was, of course, watching in the background.

"Does everybody know why we're here?" said Chet.

"To hear a lecture on romantic literature," he said.

"No, no. You're going to watch Chet Clifford approach a young woman, a beautiful sexy young college graduate named *Jayne Holly Wyatt*, with lovely breasts, curvy hips and a cute personality. And you're going to learn.

"You're going to watch the Chet Clifford approach. You'll want to watch closely. Learn all you can. This is valuable. This is fantastic."

25 before 25

"She's going to be number 23. *Jayne Holly Wyatt*. Oh wow. You've seen her. She is really the most beautiful, the most gorgeous woman I've ever seen. I'll sleep with her—Then I have to start thinking about woman number 24.

"That's the important thing. I'm a businessman.

"She's going to be number 23. ... You aim high in your objective, and then you go for it. ... I'm only 24 years old. Hey, I happen to be wise beyond my years. But I've only slept with 22 women. She'll be number 23. I ought to have that done by the end of the week.

"Then I have to think about girl number 24. My goal is 25 women before I turn 25. See that's the important thing. You always want a clear goal and you want a way to measure against that goal. If you can't track your progress you don't know how you're doing.

"I set myself 25 before 25. It's a good, solid goal. Once you turn 25, it's time to settle down. You have to start thinking about your future."

He was finished dressing.

"Now it's show time," he said and he kissed himself in the mirror. "You're welcome to watch," he said to his audience.

Chet's House, Day

Chet and Jayne entered the house.

Chet said, "Yes, well, he is a little weird but he's a nice guy. His head is some place else. He lied about the job and all that?"

"Well he exaggerated," said Jayne.

"I haven't known him to do that," said Chet, "but it could be. A guy acts differently with a woman. I'm really surprised by what you're telling me."

"I think he's okay though," she said.

"He's a little naïve," said Chet. "That's what it is. He's a very good person but he's not totally in touch. You're a very attractive person and that threw him. Listen, I have some fresh-squeezed juice chilling. Would you join me?"

She looked at him.

Now they were each holding a glass of bright fresh-squeezed juice.

"What should we toast to?" he said.

"Success, success and, oh, how about ... success," she said.

They connected glasses.

Chet took a sip. "He said that you're looking for a new job. I think I might be able to help. Give me an idea of what you want."

"Something I could stick with, where I could work my way up—I'm looking to build things up. I want a job with no ceiling. I'm ready to move up. And I want a place where I see nothing but sky above."

"Such as ..." he said.

"Marketing," she said.

"And I work at a marketing agency," he said.

"Say, you catch on quick," she said.

"—Good! Excellent! ..."

He took another sip.

"What do you do?" he said.

"Well, at the moment I'm looking for a job. ..."

"... Ah hmm ..."

"I used to manage an international conglomerate with offices in 57 countries but it went broke," she said.

"Ah, what a shame! I have some friends in that game. Perhaps they can be of some help?" he said.

"I'm thinking of opening up a gun shop," she said.

"I see—There's a lot of money in gun sales."

"No. Actually I don't sell guns, I just shoot them, ... at men. ... Actually, I'm looking for a job in the traditional sense. ... Right now, as we speak, I'm in the reception game."

"Ah, the front desk game?" he asked.

"Yes receptionhood," she said.

"In the lobby of a company?" he asked.

"Oh, you're fast. Yes lobbyhood." She looked at him. "I also make some side money as a waitress."

"Do you know something?" he said. "I tell every young person that when you first get out of school you should spend some time in a service industry. It builds character. It's so important to develop a sense of dealing with people."

"You said 'young people.' How old are you?"

"I'm twenty-four," said Chet.

"Hmm." She took it in. She was an amateur detective (always on the alert for true crime).

"How about you?" he asked. "You look younger than me."

"Yes, a few years younger, I just graduated," she said (under the cross-examination).

"Oh, you're probably the same age as Ridley. He just graduated too."

"Yes, I know. But I don't hold it against him."

"Listen, I'm a big believer in networking. I do lunches, dinners, coffees with people. That's how I build business. How do you feel about networking?

"I'm all for it," she said.

"Excellent. Then let me toss an idea at you and tell me how you like it. ... Let me suggest something—perfectly reasonable—that may sound off-the-wall but it's something you might want to consider. I work at a public relations agency—"

"—I know—"

"—Good. I'm supposed to have dinner with a major client. And I don't want it to be a business dinner. I want it to be social. So I arranged for it to be at a nice restaurant."

"And you want me to be your date."

"No. I would never ask you to pretend we're dating. We'll be completely straight. We'll let him know we're just friends."

"Why do you need me?" she asked.

"He'll be coming alone and so if I come alone, it'll just be business but I want him to let his guard down. If you come it'll be social. And we'll be doing us both a favor.

"Are you hitting on me? Is this a date?"

"No, I wouldn't tell him it's a date if it isn't a date. It's networking among friends. C'mon go with me. I'll give you some killer tips about how to network. And you'll be doing a great thing for me. If you're not there dinner is business; if you're there dinner becomes social. It'd be a favor. You toss one into the favor bank for me, and next time I'll toss a favor into the favor bank for you.

"Believe me, you're going to learn a lot about networking. I'm the best at it. And every day and in every way, I try to bring my friends along.

"You know what the secret of networking is? It's not about 'what you can do for me,' it's about 'what I can do for you.' That's how you have to think. You help others make connections and then they make connections for you.

"That's why it's great. That's why I'm so passionate about it. Doesn't that make sense to you?" he said.

"Yes," she said.

"Total sense, or perfect sense?" he said.

"Absolute sense," she said.

He waved his finger at her and smiled, "You're a naughty one. I can tell. I like that about you."

"And you look expensive. I like that about you," she said.

He laughed.

He said, "I tell everyone: You have to get out there—the view from behind your desk is a narrow one."

He was talking at a fast pace. He didn't want to give her time to think it through too deeply. All he needed was a "yes." There was everything good in it. He smiled a lot.

She was fascinated. He made an impression.

"What's the down side?" he said. "You have a nice dinner; I make a good impression; he has a good time. What's the up side? Possibly you get hired over there or maybe as we're talking we think of somewhere else you could get hired, which would be great—You'll see how good my company is and I'll have a friend in an inside position. Companies are always wondering, 'Should we keep our agency?' ... 'Should we fire our agency?' ... 'What kind of job are they doing for us?' ... Having someone who could put in a good word is important. It's a crazy idea but what the hell."

She looked off into the distance, considering the idea. Then she looked up at him.

"Is that a yes?" he asked.

She smiled.

"Maybe. I want to hear a little more about this first."

She sipped at her juice and looked at him with a level gaze that did not blink.

Chet said, "I want to say something, and I'm not looking for remarks back or to put you on the spot in any way. ... I just want to say you're a very attractive, beautiful lady. ... I'm a man. I have to notice these things. And with you there's no way not to notice."

She held his look.

"And this wouldn't be a date?"

"Oh, of course not." He made a big show of a reaction to express his sincerity. "But if you want a date, just ask me out. I'm free next week. ... I'm single and I'd be happy to be seduced by you, but I don't even know if you're single. Are you?"

She looked at him and held silent.

Role Play

An Office, Day

Chet was now visiting the office of his childhood friend, *Nathan*.

Nathan was a very straight-laced, straight-minded, orderly personality. He was a top accountant who thrived in an environment of stability.

"I need your help," said Chet. "I met this girl—"

"Since when," said Nathan, "do you need my help to make a girl?"

"This is a very special girl. I need a tailored approach with her."

"Why don't you ever try honesty?"

"I'm not here to kid around," Chet said. "You can't just conform in this life Nathan. You have to think outside the normal. I want to create an impression of strength. How do I do that? By talking strong? No."

He stood up.

"Come here. Shake my hand. But when you do it, I want you to pretend you're *the strongest man in the world.*"

Nathan shook Chet's hand as though he had some real muscle, the kind of heft that could break an arm off.

"You're doing it," said Chet, "the way a thousand other people would do it.—Now shake my hand with *no effort.*"

Nathan shook Chet's hand again. This time with a light, easy confident motion. And as he did *Chet sank to his knees* in agony as if his hand were being crushed by a steel vice.

They paused the lesson there.

"Wow," said Nathan.

"See that," Chet said. "My reaction makes you the strongest man in the world. You can't do it yourself. That's why I need you. I want her to feel she's with a guy that really has it going on right there." He pointed to his biceps, instead of his mind.

"I want her to see some depth.

"We'll go to dinner with this girl. I'll pay you to do this for me and you'll pretend to be a big client.

"Throughout dinner you will treat me with enormous respect and keep asking me for advice.

"Make me an authority.

"What you'll get out of it is: You'll be paid for your time. You'll get a fantastic dinner. And you'll learn how to seduce a girl, correctly. It'll be worth your while."

Act Two

The Charming Dinner and
The Lovely Evening
Chet Clifford in the social element

A Restaurant, Night

Chet and Jayne were standing together at the main door of a posh uptown restaurant, as Nathan arrived with a dramatic flair. *He was with a very attractive woman.*

Presently, the group was walking toward their table.

Chet took advantage of a fleeting instant of movement to whisper to Nathan. "Who is that girl you brought? Why is she even here?"

"If you invoke the strongest man in the world principle for tonight," whispered Nathan in return to Chet, "then I think she's necessary because how big of a client am I supposed to be if can't get a date? So I brought her."

"When did you start seeing her?"

"I'm not going out with her."

"No? How do you know her?"

"She only cost us an extra 50. And 50 is a great price considering how much more she normally makes for a performance."

"She's an actress?"

"No."

The Restaurant, Night

The group was being seated at a booth by the waiter.

"Business is great," said Nathan and spread his arms wide. "Sales are going through the roof," continued Nathan and spread his arms upward. Then he brought them down with a passionate inward sweep. "Oh, I wish I had brought this month's sales report with me. Wait till you see it Chet. Phenomenal. Profits are going through the roof. It's an act of God."

"And public relations is part of the reason for that?" asked Jayne.

"A very big part. Chet is very good. His results are very good. Astonishing. We kill the competition."

"I don't know too much," said Jayne, "about public relations. Maybe you could tell me what Chet does."

"He hasn't told you?"

"No."

"He should stop being so humble."

Chet tried to take over—

"We try to spread the word about what his company is doing," Chet said. "We try to get stories placed in the newspapers, television stations, radio stations around the country."

"He is great," Nathan said. "He can sell. They don't want to write about us—it doesn't matter. He sells them on it. He gets stories running on us everywhere: New York, Washington, Denver, the Mojave Desert. It doesn't matter. He sells. He's a supernova. He burns through the atmosphere."

"I'm impressed," said Jayne.

"Oh, sure," said Nathan. "He's great. His agency is the best too. Number one in the country."

"Really? Are you putting me on?" said Jayne.

"Well some might say that," said Chet.

"We're so lucky to have him," said Nathan, "especially now when we're expanding our marketing campaigns. Oh yeah, he's putting together a real monster for us. We're launching a new product in four months."

"Just in one city," said Chet.

"That's one plan," said Nathan. "The other plan is really big. We go nationwide right away. I want to win in the top 50 markets or nowhere. I say if you're going to take a risk go all the way. I never do anything unless it's going to be major. This new product is going to be in every store within four months."

"That's impressive," said Jayne. "But as a practical matter Nathan, my goodness, what kind of budget does it take to go national?"

"You're going to see," said Nathan, "stories for it everywhere: The network news, the the magazines, the newspapers—"

Suddenly Chet stood up.

"Uhm, sorry to interrupt but—" said Chet.

"—You'll see it on talk shows," said Nathan, "you'll hear it on radio, you'll see it online—"

"Could I just show you something out front?" said Chet.

The Restaurant's Entrance, Night

Chet turned to Nathan.

"What if," Chet said, "I'm going out with her in four months and your roll-out doesn't happen?"

"Oh boy," Nathan said. "I got carried away, didn't I? I'm sorry. You know what makes me do it?"

"Stupidity?"

"No, insecurity."

"How do you figure that?" Chet asked.

"I didn't think she'd believe it otherwise."

"Just say we're launching in one city, as a test."

"But then the competition has time to analyze the product and create a counter-offensive. I think you have to go with a national roll-out—"

"You're going to get caught you idiot."

He grabbed his head, trying his darndest to resist smashing it into the wall.

"Keep it small," Chet said. And to himself thought, *Don't kill him.*

The Restaurant Booth, Night

Everyone was now back at the dinner table.

"So you're looking for a job?" Nathan said.

"Yes," Jayne said.

"What are you interested in?"

"I'm looking for something with room for growth."

"Why don't you send a resume to my office. I'll see if we have anything for you—"

Chet stood up.

"—Excuse me—"

The conversation stopped instantly.

"—Could I just show you one more thing out front?"

The Restaurant Entrance, Night

Chet and Nathan were talking.

"How can you consider hiring her?" said Chet.

"She's a nice person," said Nathan, "a hard worker."

"Right."

"She needs a job."

"So?"

"What kind of person would I be to not hire her? She'd hate me."

"You don't have a company."

"She doesn't know that, at this point."

"What do you mean at this point? I'm not going to argue this one—"

"All right. All right. I'll just give her a business reference. How about that?"

"No reference. Nothing."

"Okay."

Chet walked away.

Nathan, to himself, "Not even a reference?"

The Booth, Night

Everyone was back at the table.

"Public relations is a great profession. A dream," Nathan said.

"Isn't the competition rough?" Jayne said. "And what about all the politics you have to deal with?"

"Overemphasized," Nathan said. "The happiest, most interesting people I know work in public relations. There's a little word association going on in my mind. You say 'public relations' to me, I think of lots of happy people."

"If you'll excuse me ..." Chet got up. "I'm going to the restroom."

"Do I need to come with you?" Nathan said.

"No. I don't think you need to see the bathroom."

"Right, that's what I was thinking too," Nathan said.

"I'll be right back," Chet said, shaking his head the moment he turned the corner.

The Restaurant's Bathroom, Night

Chet was there. The bathroom was there.

A moment later, Nathan was there too and a drink had been thrown in his face. He was wiping away the red wine, which was dripping down his face and shirt. His expression was anguished, on the verge of tears.

"What are you doing here?" said Chet.

"She threw a drink at me?" said Nathan.

"Who? Your escort?"

"No, the other girl."

"Why?"

"I'm so embarrassed. It was all my fault."

"What'd you do?"

"After you left I suggested very subtly, discretely, like a perfect gentle-man I said, *'Why don't you unload Chet, I'll unload my girl and we'll get into something comfortable—like my place?'* It was just a question. Then out of nowhere she threw a drink in my face. I'm so embarrassed I can't go back there."

"You asked her," Chet said, "to sleep with you?"

"I didn't mean to."

"Then why'd it happen?"

"Insecurity," Nathan said. "I told you I'm very insecure."

"So you overcame it," Chet said, "by asking people to sleep with you?"

"If she had said yes that would have put me in a very secure place."

"You're going to apologize."

"I can't talk to her. I'm so ashamed."

"You're not going to say anything to her the rest of the night?"

"No. I'm not seeing her. I'm going home."

"You can't go home."

"I'm so embarrassed. Good night."

He started to leave.

"What about your showgirl?"

"Tell her she's got the rest of the night off."

"If you walk out that door you'll regret it. If not today, tomorrow. If not tomorrow, then soon and for the rest of your life."

"Goodbye Chet."

They wrestled but Nathan broke free.

The Restaurant Booth, Night

Chet was returning to the booth. With his head bowed, apparently making some heartfelt apologies on Nathan's behalf.

"He's flirtatious," said Chet. "In a way, it's a good quality. ... "He, uhm, ... he just likes people."

"Oh, he's a people lover," Jayne said. "Why didn't you say so earlier?" Jayne looked at Chet. "Well, there you have it. I bring that out in a lot of people lovers."

"Yes, my career depends on that kind of people love," said the show-girl.

The Living Room of Chet's House, Night

Chet and Jayne stepped into the house.

"Try out that couch," Chet said. "Tell me what you think of it. I just bought that a few weeks ago."

She sat down. He took out a bottle of wine.

"Feel the contour of it. What do you think? It's the kind of couch that really tilts back."

She found that it was practically a bed.

(He wanted to get her on her back.)

She caressed the couch and slowly wiggled her bottom in the cushions, almost as though she were making love to it.

"Mmmm—oooo, yes. I love getting on top of something so soft but firm."

Chet had to stop a moment when she hit him with that line.

"Now," Chet said, "I want to hear what you think of this wine."

He poured them each a glass. "They say you should take a sip, work the wine around your mouth for a few seconds, then suck in a little air through the wine before swallowing. Or they have all sorts of other fancy ways to drink wine."

"Yes, I've heard about some of them," she said.

"I say drink it however you like. Don't let the proper be the enemy of the good."

Jayne drank a little wine. She sensually licked her lips when she was finished.

Chet looked at her tongue cross her lips.

And she said, "Like that?"

She smiled at him. And Chet got an erection—so stiff and hard that it startled him.

She just smiled at him. And looked pretty. And waited for his desire to grow and grow. Then she had a thought. ...

"Oh, is Ridley home?" she asked. "Maybe he'll join us."

That didn't strike Chet as the greatest way to add to this moment.

But now all at once, she rose and began to cross toward the hallway and Ridley's room.

Chet popped up and stopped her.

"Uhm, that's okay. Sit and relax. Enjoy your drink. Let me go see," he said. "That'd be a blast if the three of us got to talk a little."

Ridley's Room, Night

Chet entered.

Ridley was studying.

"Would you mind," said Chet, "doing me a favor? Would you stay in here? I've got a girl and we're trying to get, uh, ... comfortable. She's shy so I gave her the impression we're alone."

"How long do I have to stay in here?"

"Maybe an hour. What are you reading? Greek history? Oh, yeah, you'll overwhelm girls with that. Didn't I give you a list of things to read? Stick with the list. I love you but God your head is in the clouds. All right, I don't want you to feel worse about yourself than you already do. You have low self-esteem. Ah, it doesn't matter. You can cover that up. You know a book I might suggest to you. You might feel it's far afield but 'Secrets of the Central Intelligence Agency.' You'll get so many good ideas on how to operate."

The Living Room, Night

Chet returned from Ridley's room.

"He's sleeping," said Chet. "I said come on, get up, it'll be fun but he's drained. The poor guy. He is just pooped. He studies until he collapses. He's set in his ways."

Chet refilled her wineglass.

"This wine," he said, "is not for the faint of heart, am I right? Although to the nose it's tame, more polite than forceful, it's a trick. In the mouth it shows plenty of fruit, fruit swaddled in tannins. It's a big, muscular wine that's going to take a few years to settle down."

He brought the wineglass to her mouth. She sipped it. Very romanticly.

"Mmmm ..." Jayne said. "I love the mouthfeel—I love tasting it—and I love the feeling of having a warm liquid bursting through my lips and lunging deep into my throat."

Chet looked at her. He felt something warm shoot through his groin. And a direct thought came to him of what he would like to do with her later that evening.

But for now, abruptly, Chet said as innocently as can be: "How do you like dancing?"

Chet and Jayne were dancing.

He took her into a turn. Then into a closed dance position, into a social dance position.

"Jayne," he said in a gentle lover's voice, "today's dance style is a lot different than it used to be. It's a lot closer."

He pulled her in gently, sweetly, lovingly.

"And it's not because it's more sexual but it's because spaces are so much more limited. You don't have room on the dance floor to make big moves. Still it should be driving and sensual. You keep it gentle, tender. Indulgent yet with a forceful, decisive rhythm. In and out, and around."

He took her through some very sensual turns.

"Soothing, smooth. But determined."

He took her into some sweetheart cuddles and some fun ladies' turns.

"It's one of the last places where the man and woman still have the old sex roles. The man dominates and the woman submits—or follows, if you will—but with a silky give and take. That's where the art of it is."

"My, you're a good leader," said Jayne.

"Why thank you," said Chet.

"Would you mind if I lead for a while?" asked Jayne.

"You can lead?"

"Yes," she said.

"Are you a lesbian—I mean do you know how to lead the guy's steps?"

"No silly," said Jayne, "I'm going to be the guy. You're going to be the lady—And use your hips! I want us to look good."

"What?" asked Chet.

She took over.

She threw him into a dynamic move—in which she brought him into her, whirled him around, and then threw him out again.

Chet was stunned.

"That move was good," said Chet.

Before he had a chance to recover, she took him into another move.— Again she brought him in, and took total control, as she threw him around the room.

"This one," said Jayne, "is called the *'Madman's Swingout.'* Don't you love it? I came up with the name."

She completed the move with total grace and sureness.

Now she shot him a look.

"Hey, do you want to try some aerials?" asked Jayne. "That's where I toss you into the air."

"Ow!—You just pinched my ass!" said Chet.

"Heh, heh," she said. "I did.—And just remember, Chet, if you ever try something like that on me—I'll slap you so hard you'll be lucky to stay conscious. No offense—But if you get fresh with me, I'll rip your throat off."

And she laughed, a girlish charming giggle.

"Oh," said Chet.

"You don't need a lot of fancy moves," she said, "just a few good ones, done to perfection. It's always about perfection, baby. Perfection is a turn-on."

"Who taught you these moves?" asked Chet.

"Those last two, I got from Ridley."

"Ridley!"

"Yes, the night we went out. He's a good dancer. He's a little shy so he does them differently than I do, but yes the moves were his."

"I'll be damned," said Chet.

"Why?" asked Jayne.

"I was teaching him about dancing, a few nights ago."

"You? He's good."

"Oh, just about approach."

"Ah, that makes sense. You have an unusual approach."

She took him into spins, pivots—and then dipped him. It was a big finish.

"Ooh, I'm tipsy from the drink," she said.

She gave the lead over to him for the next song.

They danced a little while longer and then—

—she started sighing. Taking long hot breaths.

It was a slow song. She laid her head on his shoulder.

She continued taking long, hot breaths.

He could feel her on him, and he was getting intensely aroused.

"I'm really enjoying talking with you," Jayne said. "Maybe we could take a rest and talk some more."

"Good idea," Chet said. "Let's lie down on my bed and we'll talk. Until we feel like doing something else."

Relax Max

Chet's Bedroom, Night

Jayne was seeing Chet's bedroom for the first time. She entered doing a dance and exploring the room with her body.

Chet watched mesmerized.

My God, I ... can't ... think ... with her around ... he thought. He really did not have enought blood to fill both ends of his body.

She voluptuously entered the bed. *Oh my God! she's on the bed.*

And she continued moving the curves of her body in her dance.

"Are you aroused?" she asked

He was delighted. My goodness, that she would be so blunt. What kind of wonderful was this? He joined her on the bed. He thought, *Yes, we're going to hit the same town at the same time. Glory, glory, hallelujah.*

"Do you have a raging stiffness yet?" said Jayne.

She put her hand on his engorgement—that was flowing in upward extension from his pelvic floor. She put her hand directly on it. No ifs, ands, or buts. No coulda, woulda, shoulda. There was nothing moderate about it. She was direct. She was firm. She looked him straight in the eye and measured his reaction.

"Oh good," said Jayne. "Now, do you know what game we're playing? Think really hard about what it is you see here."

"I think," Chet whispered, "I've played this one before. I'm very good at it."

"No you're not," Jayne whispered in his ear. "You're actually quite bad at this one."

She fell away from him and onto the plush mattress.

Now she stared, with a rocksteady gaze into his eyes. Her head was beneath his. She was looking up at a dynamic angle. And she looked terrifically sexy doing it. Everything about the light and the position flattered her curves.

She rose onto her elbows and raised her head toward him. "I'm just a country girl," she said through her sexy eyelashes, "and you've been trying to take big-city advantage of me."

Chet froze and contemplated all the problems of the world in her steadfast gaze.

She replaced her hand on his pelvis. More particularly, the area just below his pubic symphisis.—She held the head and the shaft of his being.

"Now," she said, "you're not going to do anything with this tonight. You deserve a little frustration after all the moves you put on me in the living room."

She smiled, very pleased with herself.

He dropped down and kissed her.

"We will not be having sex together tonight," she said.

"I respect that. Of course. I respect everything about you Jayne. But why is that though, I might wonder?"

"It has to do with how men think. If I slept with you before getting to know you, that would mean I would sleep with other men before getting to know them. Would that make me more or less attractive?"

He looked at her. She had stopped him cold, with no effort, he thought. *Good God, she's not a pawn in the game. She's the queen of the chess board. ... Well, how do you like that?*

Jayne was changing before his eyes.

"We're going to have a proper love affair," she said. "As the divine Dinah Washington used to say, *'Relax Max.'* ... Yes, my pet, control yourself."

She looked at him.

"My pet Chet." And she smiled. ...

"Relax Max," she said.

"Your nerves are kinda bad there boy.," she continued.

"Your heart is thumping with a crazy sound.

"Stay cool fool. Just take it easy, that's the rule.

"A kiss is no kiss without love.

"C'mon and relax Max," she said, completing the arc of it.

She was a take-charge girl. And she enjoyed taking charge of Chet's condition.

"Chet," she said now, "do you know how sometimes half the battle can be getting *'there'*?

He nodded.

"Well," she said, "this time your whole battle is going to be getting there."

He looked at her.

"And the plot thickened," she said to him. And smiled.

"Slow down boy," she said. "I like to take things slow. Real slow."

"Slow?" asked Chet. "Hmm, slow sounds lovely Jayne."

He looked at her.

She had made their first love scene ... into a scene about slowing down. ... She had made it perfectly clear. This might very well be her pattern. He would learn, in time. He would learn. But at any rate—She was in control of the tempo. And she was a hell of an orchestra conductor.

In swift commanding strokes, she had slowed him down to a crawl. ...

With the immediate effect being that—

It drove him crazy! He wanted her all the more. ... Oh God did he want her now!

She knew that slowing things down could be very good for a boy, very exciting for the male of the species.

It allowed time for imagination to do its work. When you slowed a relationship down, the man's mind started to go to work. You see, story and imagination worked with great power in romance. ... And ... she held the power. She was *'The Girl Made of Cool'*—as her friend Ridley Richardson might say.

Chet Clifford was formally meeting ...

Jayne Holly Wyatt. *The girl made of thunderbolt cool.*

... Chet looked at her. ...

Sex and the single career girl

They settled into the bed and lay beside each other.

"Now that we're finished with the activities for the evening," she said, "let's hear more from you. I want to hear about what you do with your days."

Chet said, "Do we really want to talk about work right now?"

"We don't, I do."

"Why is that?"

"We have to find out if there's a job for me at your office."

"Jayne, you're, uhm, ... you're, uh, ..."

"Unscrupulous. Ruthless," Jayne said. "A woman who wraps men around her finger and uses them."

"You wear manipulation well," said Chet. "But there's no way on Earth we're going to start talking about work right now."

There was a ... longish pause. ...

He brought her closer, gently. ...

Surrender wrestling

He kissed her softly and delicately. She surrendered to it. It was terrific. It felt so good.

She closed her eyes and enjoyed it.

After a moment of dreamy intensity she opened her eyes and looked at him.

"You're a good kisser," she said. "How did you know the way I like to be kissed?"

"That was simple. The way you kiss me, is the way you want me to kiss you."

"Clever boy," she said.

"Why thank you Jayne. Any man can think it through."

"You think about these things?" she asked.

"All the time."

"Why is that?"

"You have to treat a lady right. You deserve a gentleman, Jayne."

He kissed her again.

He was fascinating.

Now he kissed her cheek. So softly, so tenderly, so lovingly.

He kissed her neck.

She was in ecstacy and hugged him. She ran her arms along his back. He was gorgeous. And he was wonderful in bed.

He brought his lips to hers and kissed her again.

He ran his hand along her belly toward her skirt. He was going to slip his hand into *her panties.*

She grabbed his hand by the fingers to stop him. Now she slowly but very purposefully twisted his fingers in a direction that fingers do not go. She twisted them back until he winced in pain.

Meanwhile, they just kept kissing as if nothing else was happening between them.

And she just kept bending his fingers back.

With his other hand—without breaking out of the kiss—he tried to stop her from bending his fingers any further.

He couldn't.

Her hold became more extreme.

He started moving his body back to adjust and lessen the agony. Too far back. He slipped from the bed onto the carpet.

She grabbed his arm and twisted it up his back until she was on the verge of causing him real damage.

Now she kissed him by bending over the bed and wrapping around his shoulder.

She did *all of this* as though nothing unusual was happening.

"Control—," she said, "this is about control Chet. Can you appreciate that—a woman with a high level of control over you?"

He liked the thought of it. And couldn't say why. This was strange to him. Why was this turning him on so much?

There was a strong sexual fascination between them.

And now they were done. They stopped kissing.

And just lay in the bed.

She curled up in his arms like a babe.

She was very happy and serene in his arms. She lay there. With him, at midnight, cradling her gently in his loving arms.

Things became quiet in that way.

She fell asleep.

Chet looked at her. His breathing became long, slow and deep. And he just continued looking at her.

Chet's Bedroom, Later in the Night

The sexy sleepover girl

Jayne was still sleeping soundly.

But now Chet was sitting in an armchair.

He turned to his audience and spoke, ever so softly, to them. They understood his predicament. They were good people. ...

"Did you see how she teased me?" he asked in a whisper. "How she led me on? Now look at me. I'm sitting here and thinking about nothing but her body. And look at her."

He looked at her voluptuous figure.

"Isn't she marvelous? She knows how to play the game. You have to give her that. She's something else. What an act she has. And she does it all deadpan. She's hot. And she knows it. So she's playing it cool.

"I may have been wrong thinking I would go through her in one week. She's the kind of girl I could see myself being with for a spell.

"I'll be honest with you she's so on the ball, that if I don't act sharp, she might dump me. I better watch my ass."

He stopped, sighed, and stared at her. So pretty. She was so damned pretty, he thought.

Chet's Bedroom, The Next Morning

Chet was sound asleep. Jayne was awake. She was peering out of the bedroom door. She closed it softly.

She woke Chet.

"Did you sleep well?" said Jayne.

"Yes."

"Could you check if Ridley is around?"

"Why?"

"I'm going to head home and I don't want him to see me."

"What's wrong if he does?"

"It might hurt him. I think he still may have leftover feelings for me. They're fading feelings, those kinds of feelings always fade, I know that, I know how men are, but ... I'll tell him at a better time."

"Oh, is that what you're worried about? He likes you as a friend but he's over the rest. He's already past that. You don't have to worry about that Jayne. You don't have to worry about that at all. I'll talk to him later today. I'll feel him out. I'll let you know."

She looked at Chet lying there. He was gorgeous.

About last night

"I want to say something about last night," she said.

"You shouldn't try seduction games ..." she continued.

"I see through you Chet. ...

"Why do you play seduction games? Chet you're better than that. You're extremely attractive. I have to say, I, uhm ... think you're very handsome."

"Thank you Jayne."

She smiled. "Yes, you're hot. There's so much about you that's terrific and turns women on but you shouldn't play games with this young lady—the lady said pointedly. You don't need it. You can get her just with—*you being you,*" she said.

"This is a sincere moment, isn't it?" he said.

"Yes, it is."

"I could get to like these Jayne."

"Me too Chet, my dear."

She looked at him.

"You've got looks. You've got charm. You've got personality. Why do you pull moves?"

"Jayne, you bring out the devil in me. ... I love that you see through me."

"Does your act really work on women?"

"You'd be surprised."

"No acting with me, got it?"

"Or what?"

"Don't make me get mean on you. Don't make me hit you with my fist."

"You are the sexiest woman in town. ... No acting. I want to be sincere with you Jayne. ... I make mistakes. Not because I'm really a devil but because I'm mistaken. I want things to be right when I'm with you. Help me when I go wrong, please, Jayne. Will you?

"Sometimes I do things I shouldn't. Not because I'm bad. Or that I mean to. ... It's because I haven't thought them through. ... Jayne please help me to think things through. ... I want to do what's right by you. And when I stumble, please be patient with me."

"You're sexy," she said, "but the important thing is a foundation of ..."

"Of what?" he asked.

"Of ... friendship," she said.

He looked at her.

"Friendship?" He kept looking her. "Yes, you're right. Friendship is so important."

He stopped there.

She smiled.

"Now about Ridley ..." she said.

Openings

Chet's Kitchen, Later in the Morning

Chet stepped into the kitchen. Ridley was preparing breakfast.

As he entered from the living room, Chet said, "What a beautiful morning!"

"Yes," said Ridley, "good morning. ... Would you like some eggs?"

"That would be fantastic. I'll be right back." Chet turned around and went away.

An instant later, Chet was discreetly showing Jayne out the front door.

She dashed out, blowing him a goodbye kiss as she went.

And then Chet returned to Ridley, walking into the dining area, past a set of large day windows streaming with morning light.

"How's your morning?" said Chet. "It's a fantastic morning." Chet looked out the windows and continued talking to Ridley over his shoulder, "Oh, what a morning! My oh my, how I love this morning."

And now Chet turned around to face Ridley.

Ridley was cooking a full breakfast. And he looked up at the big day windows to glimpse that beautiful morning out there. Then he glanced at Chet.

Chet looked at Ridley. "And you're in a good mood too," said Chet.

"I feel good about my problem," said Ridley. "I see a way."

"With the girl?"

"Yes."

Chet sat down, joining Ridley at the breakfast table.

Ridley continued, "I was just doing some thinking about her."

"Ridley ..."

"Yes ..."

"I have an important confession to make."

"A confession? ..."

"Ridley you're my friend so this is very difficult for me."

Chet paused and then said:

"She's the woman I had here last night."

"Oh ... Did she leave after an hour?"

"No."

"I see. ..."

"Did you sleep together?"

"Yes."

"Did you have sex with her?"

"We made love. Over and over." Chet said. He took a breath. He looked at Ridley. "And the truth is I really didn't feel good about what we were doing."

"Oh, I see. ..."

And yes now Ridley did see.

This was the moment.

And it was the moment where it hit him, where it just absolutely floored him. He felt like somebody had come along and hit him with something very heavy. Just punched the life out of him.

He was dead again.

... And he knew ... that he would be a long time dead this time.

After a quiet while Ridley said, *"Well, I really misunderstood things. ... I've been a fool."*

"It's not you," said Chet. "It's me and her. ... I blame myself. What I did is—I had mad, passionate sex with her. And I shouldn't have done that."

"Well," said Ridley, "maybe I was mistaken. Maybe I didn't have a hope.

... And I don't have a hope now."

"No, don't say that."

"I want to face the truth. ... I must have been out of my mind. What chance was there for me?"

"You're good looking. You're a wonderful guy. "

"You don't have to, ... I understand."

"You do?"

"If you care and you're going to make her happy—"

"But it can't be anything near the way you feel about her—"

"I have to think about what's going to make her happy. ... If she's just not that into me. And she is into you. ... If she cares more about being with you—then maybe she should be with you."

"Oh no, no! She's yours," Chet said.

"If you would make her happy, if you're what she wants ... Well, I want her to be happy."

"No, fight for her. Don't let me get away with it."

"Do you fancy her?"

"Yes."

"Do you have honest and true romantic feelings for her?"

"Ridley don't let that get in your way—Yes, I have very strong, very sincere romantic feelings for her."

"You might be falling in love with her."

"That's possible," he said. And Chet suddenly became cheery.

"Then I have to step out of the picture," said Ridley.

"You're her friend. And you should stay her friend," said Chet.

"Oh god," said Ridley. That caught him and then he caught himself and recovered. "Yes, I'm her friend. I ... should ... be ... her friend."

Chet remained locked face to face with Ridley.

He draped his arm over Ridley's shoulder. And in a slingshot hold curled his arm around to softly touch the back of Ridley's head. Chet continued to stay face to face, to look him in the eye, like a father would a son.

"I'm sorry," said Chet. "I let you down. God, I'm so sorry."

"I love her so much," said Ridley, "that the only thing in my mind is her happiness. There should be nothing that comes before her happiness."

"You are such a *good guy*," said Chet. "... Do you notice that?"

Ridley's New State of Being
Walking alone along the boulevard of broken dreams

Several Days Later

Chet and Ridley's Living Room, a Bright Afternoon

Ridley stepped into the living room.

He stopped abruptly. In front of him, Chet and Jayne were hugging.

Ridley watched them with an expression of suffering as he noticed how passionate their embrace was.

They both turned towards him and his expression changed.—He smiled. He lifted his mood. And he beamed at them.

He acted as though he didn't have a bother in the world.

Jayne said to Ridley, "I just got a job working at Chet's company. ... Isn't that wonderful?"

Ridley instinctively shifted his weight to his rear leg.

"Congratulations," he said.

He caught himself falling backward and rocked his weight forward.

"That's great. I'm very happy for you."

Chet kissed Jayne on the cheek.

Ridley watched them—and inside he was now completely broken-hearted, but on the outside he played the part of a good sport.

To Be Her Friend
And how to do it

Ridley's Bedroom, Night

It was very late at night.

The world was fast asleep.

Ridley was lying awake, thinking about this girl.

And now to a "him beside himself" he spoke softly.

"To not be in love with her," he said.

"To just be her friend—"

That was Ridley's struggle. To not be in love with her. To resist the overpowering romantic feelings for her

He observed his breathing, observed his spine tensing and tightening. To release. To not be in love with her.

"To not want her," he said.

"Don't be a selfish dog. Don't be a jealous dog.

"To not kiss her. To not make advances on her. To not make passes. To not think about her. To not want her—There I feel better already.

"I wonder what she's doing tomorrow. I wonder does she think of me like—Does she think of me at all?

He lay there for a moment.

"Don't focus on your needs," he said. "Don't think about kissing her. Don't think about doing things to her. Instead, focus on doing things for her. Put the focus on her. That'll make it easier. Much easier. Put her first.

"Just get through one moment at a time. And worry about the next moment, next time.

"Learn how to lose," Ridley said to himself. "Love was everything they said it would be. Now it's sweet and sad and you have to learn to lose.

He thought about that for a moment.

"To not need anything from her. To not be needy with her. To not pull from her.

"Don't be needy. Don't need anything from her. ... Be her friend.

"Don't kiss her. Forget about kissing with her. ... Be her friend.

"Maybe, she could use a friend. Her life is stressful. ... Be her friend.

"Whooo. ... This is rough.

"To not want. You suffer because you want, so don't want.

"So this is what clear thinking feels like? It hurts. Son of a bitch—It hurts."

Ridley & Jayne & the Late Afternoon Sky

A Few Days Later

The Back Porch, Late Afternoon to Night

"How's the studying going?" asked Jayne. "It's animal behavior correct?"

"Last time it was," said Ridley. "I was thinking of becoming a zoologist for a while. I think that lasted a month. That was a rough month."

"You're off of animal studies?" she asked.

"In a way," he said. "The part I like is *man-watching*. So then I thought about anthropology. And then I thought about mankind's history."

"Ah huh," she said.

She smiled a kind smile at him.

"I understand," she said. "I love learning new subjects too."

"You do?"

"Yes. What do you want to do ultimately?"

"I don't know. There's so much."

"Yes, too much to get your head around," she said.

Mastering world history

"I'll show you what happened, so that you can picture it.

"I started thinking about people. Do I want to study people? I picked up this book."

He went into the house. He pulled a book from the shelf. He returned to the porch and sat down.

"It's called *'Mastering World History.'* It's a small book considering the subject."

He gave her the book.

"I like small books," she said, taking it from him.

"Then you might like this. It takes world history and gives it to you in a very simple way. ... See how, if you leaf through it, it gives you the fundamentals? ...

"It starts with *'Primitive Man.'* — Then *'Ancient History Begins in the Near East.'* — *'The Early Civilizations of Asia.'* — *'The Greeks.'* — *'The Rise and Fall of the Roman Empire.'* — *'The Middle Ages.'* — *'The Barbarian Invasions.'* — *'The Empires.'* ... The revolutionary wars. ... The world wars. ...

"It's a pretty good book." He looked at her. "As I went deeper and deeper into it, I found myself getting pulled in by what I was dealing with. ... What I found fascinating was where the stories started and where they went. And now where some of them were ending up in our time, Jayne."

"But then I started following some of the offshoots. I was following the stories through science, biology, psychology, social studies, anthropology, physiology. ... And then each of them had an offshoot. ... And each of them was so worth looking into it. It just keeps going and going."

"So that's where you're at now?"

"Yes." He turned back to her. "It's difficult don't you think?"

She laughed.

"It's a universe. ... It's like staring at a universe. ..." he said. "I like what I see in it."

"And what do you see?"

"Hope," he said.

He looked up at her. Looked into her eyes. And held her tenderly with his gaze.

"Hope is a big thing. ...

"If we can do this. If we can get through. ... Things will be better."

She looked at him. There was a longish pause.

She looked down at the book. There was a stillness and a quiet.

They sat there together.

"There's something else ... When you look into that ... When you really look ... What's interesting," he said, "is the structure, the frame of it, the fascination there, how it all works. How it all goes. ... Do you know what I mean?"

"That there's some kind of order there?"

"Well, ... what's fascinating ..." he said slowly ... "... is ... that ... it's ... all ... madness.

"It's absolute madness. The world is a madhouse. It's all insane. That's why it's interesting. You're looking at it. And you see all these levels of insanity and unreality. Levels you never thought could even be there."

She laughed.

"Yes, you look at the news headlines: In science, they're constantly finding things that don't make sense. You look at business—at politics—in every area there's constantly all this stuff that doesn't make sense. It's weird! Isn't it? And so you ask yourself, *'What's that all about?'* And then you start reading about it, and then you're hooked. It's got you. And it never ends. Oh, it's bloody exhausting.

"If life would make sense I'd have a lot less work. I could finish all my reading tonight, if it only made sense."

He was looking at her, ... and she was smiling. ... He felt that perhaps, ... maybe it would be all right, ... to keep talking to her ...

"It's like a flower and the petals keep opening," he said.

"You're at one level of magnification and there are all these patterns so you go in for a closer look. And what was stuff now becomes new patterns at the next level of magnification.

"It keeps opening. The further you go in, the more it opens. It's the darndest design. And the more you look at the design the more darned wild it gets."

"Are you a thinker?" asked Jayne.

"No, I'll show you my problem."

He rose and went to the edge of the porch.

She joined him.

They stood there, looking outward, far outward ... and upward.

"I look at the horizon," he said. "And I want to go to the next one. ... And when I get there, ... to go to the next horizon. ... My problem is I'm a boy scout."

She looked at him.

He looked at her. "And when I get to the next horizon, the next beautiful, gorgeous horizon, I want to come back, and show it to you, and ask you what you think?"

"Or any girl," she said.

"Yes, or any girl—as long as she is you."

"Now you're trying to beguile me."

"I'll stop."

She was looking at him.

He was returning the look.

"So am I an original thinker? Well, I think my problem is I'm an original boy scout. It's a different problem. My problem involves more travel."

"Lots of time away from the wife and kids," she said.

"Yes, lots of maps. ... Lots of asking yourself, 'Where the hell am I now?'"

She laughed.

"And when you're home what kind of husband would you make?"

"Same as I would a boyfriend," he said.

"Hmm. Would you be a good boyfriend?" she asked.

"I would be the best ever," said Ridley.

He smiled.

"You should be a boyfriend," she said. "You should be with someone special. I wish that for you Ridley. I hope you find her."

"Thank you Jayne," he said. "Thank you, that means a lot to me. ... One day ... One day she'll be there."

Fascination

Several Days Later

Jayne's Apartment, Day

Ridley and Jayne were finishing a dinner together.

"What's it like working with Chet?"

As Ridley asked this, he was wondering if he could bear to hear it.

"He's a major talent. He's a superstar," she said. "No wonder he got me a job. It was just normal horse-trading for him. ... Everyone worships him. He's a marketing wizard. ... He might even be a genius. I was really amazed."

"Yes, I hear he's very charismatic."

It hurt Ridley in a way.

He wished he could be the charismatic man in her life.

He was her friend. ... And he did enjoy that. He enjoyed listening to her. It was something he could do. It made him very, very happy to listen to her.

He looked at her. He didn't say anything.

She continued. "I've never seen anything like him," she said.

"He's a force of nature at a marketing agency. ... It's more than the work he does for the marketing clients—It's the way he markets himself. I've never seen anything like it. Everybody owes him a favor, and everybody comes to him for every tricky thing. It's like he controls the whole place already. He's command grade. And he's only 24 years old."

In her mind's eye she could see him relating to the CEO.

"Murf—that's Russell Murphy—he's the CEO. Chet keeps telling him, 'You're a daddy to me.' You know what he says back? 'You're the son I never had.' That's for real. He's really become the professional son. Chet is so good at getting ahead, it's uncanny."

She continued. "At work everybody is his family. ... His boss is his father. ... The partners are friends. ... The juniors are brothers and sisters. ... Do you know what I mean?"

"Hmm, that is brilliant," said Ridley.

Just then, Chet walked through the door.

"Sorry I'm late."

He joined Ridley and Jayne. He gave a nod to Ridley, and squeezed

Jayne's hand. He was a gentleman.

"Chet waits until the boss leaves," explained Jayne.

"The man always works late," Chet said. "I work a few minutes later than him. So that I'm the last one out. ... You have to play the game."

"How's it coming along?" she asked.

"He loves me," Chet said. "Everybody loves me."

He looked at Jayne. "Is that a new outfit? You look so pretty."

Tenderness

Later that Night

Ridley had gone home. Chet and Jayne were sitting alone on her couch. The lights were low.

They were looking into each other's eyes.

"I have to talk to you," said Chet, "about Ridley. ... Do you know what's on his mind? ... Ridley has been thinking of moving out."

"Why?"

"He wants to get an apartment of his own. He craves quiet. He studies a lot. And as much as I try to make our place a library atmosphere—there is still too much life."

"I'm sorry to hear that. I would really miss him."

"I walked in the other day. He was studying. I asked him why not at the library. They went to summer hours. ... In my house, it's a separate wing. It's almost like someone living in a completely separate house. It's a nice space. Very comfortable. But I think for him, it's too lively. You get so much street noise. And there's me. It's not like here. ...

"Your place is so quiet. ... It's a perfect place to read and study. This really suits someone like Ridley. Do you ever notice that?"

She gazed around her apartment. She was thinking.

"Housing," Chet said, "in this city is very, very modern. ... At our age, people move around all the time."

"Yes," she said, "that's true. My apartment is just somewhere I shower, change and sleep."

"That's right in a big city, you keep a lot in storage. Apartments are small. You move in and out of them. You can do it in a day. That's the way it is these days."

"I've been in five apartments in three years."

"I've lived in two places in three years," said Chet.

"Yes, the world is getting strange," she said. "Living in a big city is like camping.'"

"Camping that's exactly it. It's like a campsite. In the old days, you just picked up and moved. ... In a way it was nice. You didn't get locked down. You had freedom."

He looked at her. She was still thinking.

"Ridley," said Chet, "is thinking of moving. ... He's at that stage. ... Why don't we help him out?"

"Help him move? Gosh, I like having him around. He's fun."

"Right, I have an idea."

"Oh, I can see the wheels turning Chet."

"What?"

"You're about to suggest that I move in and Ridley moves here."

"You just want to have sex," she said.

"No, of course not. I'm not even thinking that way—maybe if we were going out for a few years the idea might drop into my head."

She stroked his cheek. Blew air into his ear. Then blew air across his lips. All the while she studied him.

"Is that a yes?" Chet asked.

"We're going to stay strong," she said.

"Brilliant Jayne. You're brilliant," he said, and meant it in every way.

"How long can you stay this strong?" he asked her.

"Longer than you," she said.

"Hell, I could go another month," he said.

"I can go a year," she said.

"We could be dead in a year—I mean, so much could happen, don't you think?"

"You're growing weaker by the minute, Chet my pet."

"No, I can do it."

"What's today's date?—A year from today we'll talk about maybe sleeping together. In the meantime we can talk about life and get to know each other."

"A year?" he asked.

"It sounds reasonable, I think," she said. "Are we clear?"

"So where are we at exactly?"

"Kissing and hugging for a year," she said.

"It would be like a new job," he said. "And then after a year, maybe you get a promotion?"

"Just so," she said. "I'm glad we're both strong. —It's just like running for president. You work your way through hell for a year and then, if you get the vote, you get to be president."

"There's an 'if' in there," said Chet.

"Yes, it's bloody fantastic, isn't it?" she asked.

He moaned. "Yes, strong. Isn't this a little bit strange Jayne?"

She said, "A year will go by quickly. We have so much to talk about. It'll fly by."

"Hmm."

She continued. ... "It's discipline," she said. "We wait until the moment is right."

"It's a sexy kind of strength. It's strength of will."

Chet loved that. "Why—that's fascinating. ... Strength of will."

Chet thought about that one.

"You know normally it's a very big deal for a woman to move in to a man's house," she said.

She looked at Chet and continued. "What if we do it for the summer?"

"How would that work?"

"Like a summer sublet. There's a lot of that that goes on around a university, every summer. ... I'll just move in for the summer. Then we look at where we are in two months. ... The move-in is a trial. It's testing with an exit strategy," she said and looked into his eyes. "We'll do a trial move-in and I'll be the judge. I'll come to a verdict at the end of the summer. Then we'll have a hearing. And that's when I'll do my sentencing. Now how do you like that? ... Do you think you'll be able to live with that? Do you think you'd be able to live with my ruling?"

"You know I'll like it," he said. "Of course, I'll like it."

"Jayne, you'll help me," he said. "You'll tell me how to do what's right whenever it's in question. You're a good influence. And I want you to influence me."

"Chet," she said. And smiled.

She said, "I know the schemes you're scheming, and I know the dreams you're dreaming. ... That was a nice thing to say. I expect great things of you."

She looked at him and said, "You have moments of brilliance. ... Like no one else. You've got it Chet. Whatever it is, you've got it."

"I know."

"I'll move into your house, if Ridley will be fine with it. I want him to be happy. His happiness is very important to me."

Chet's House, Night

Chet sighed. A long weary, drawn out sigh. A miserable, 'I'm in agony,' sigh.

He did this as he sat down to talk with Ridley.

He looked anguished as all hell. This would be difficult on him. He wanted Ridley to know that.

"Ridley, I have something to say about Jayne ... about me and Jayne ..."

He looked at Ridley with a conerned, friendly look.

Ridley looked back at him. He was already dead. What could happen? What could make it worse?

Chet said, "What we want to do may be very difficult on you ... and I have to tell you what's coming next ... Jayne and I care for each other ..."

"You want to move in together."

"You saw it coming?"

"I saw it coming. ... But this was fast. ..."

"Yes, ..." said Chet surprised. "Fast."

Beginnings & Futures

Chet and Jayne's Living Room, Day

Jayne was moving in.
    They put down some boxes.
    He put his arms around her.
    They hugged.

Ridley's Apartment, Day

Ridley stood in the doorway, sipping from a teacup. He was staring out at the landscape. He liked to stare at landscapes.

Days Later

A Hillside, Mid-Day

Chet and Jayne were on a hillside, having a picnic on a summit overlooking parklands and clusters of hillside estates.
    She was looking out at the landscape.
    Chet put his arm around her. They held each other tightly. A warm hug.
    It felt good, she thought. A hug that did not let go.

They were walking along a hill.
    "Sometimes I like to look at mansions," he said. "Eventually you have to buy one—it's the only place to raise kids. When we're talking about a mansion I think we could get a good one for a couple of million. In fact I saw one I'd like to show you."

Chet and Jayne walked around a bend in the hillside.
    "You have to look around. When you finally decide to buy one, you want to have an idea. It has to suit your personality."
    They stopped and he directed their attention to a striking mansion.
    "That's what I need to get. Something I could really be comfortable in. Where you live is very important."
    "That one is gorgeous," Jayne said.
    "That's probably a couple of million, but as long as I'm going to spend

that much on a mansion, I might as well spend a little more and get something I really like. You need a pool. And a vineyard. And acreage. I saw some Arabian horses that would knock your eyes out. You really have to have some room to raise horses."

He took a breath. "Yes, it's good to look around."

Flying in the big steel thing
Soon they were looking by helicopter.

The mansions they needed to see were so big and secluded.

"I need a lot of land. ... I need grounds. ... Because I like to play polo."

He turned to her. "Do you like to play polo, honey? ... You ever play polo, darling?"

"No I don't."

"I'm going to teach you. You're going to love it. I'm going to teach you how to play polo. You know, I came in second in the—What did I do with the trophy?"

He looked down at the ground.

"That's not large enough for a polo field," he said. "Do you like an Olympic-sized pool?"

He turned to her again. "Right now, you want to know something— I'm a businessman. Right now real estate is bad, very bad. We could get that same mansion for $2 million less."

The helicopter glided along more terrain.

The hills passed underneath.

It was a lovely day. Sunny. With blue skies. Just a perfect day.

Chet sat back. And relaxed.

He was enjoying the feel of flying.

He really liked this helicopter. It had good vertical thrust. ... He thought about it. He did an asset list of the helicopter's virtues.

It was a beautiful craft.

He turned to the pilot and called out to him, "Hey, if you wanted to buy a helicopter like this, how much would it cost?"

When they landed, off they went. He took her to play tennis. And she really enjoyed it. He was great fun.

Ridley & Jayne & the Breeze

The Balcony Outside Ridley's Apartment, Late Afternoon

Ridley and Jayne were sitting in yard chairs, staring outward, sipping tea.

They were talking about life, and relationships.

"Where do your relationships come apart?" he asked her.

"Well," she said, "I'm a bad girl. I'm a very bad girl. You haven't seen that side of me. You haven't seen how bad I can get. I can get downright mean. And they say 'like attracts like.' So I enjoy bad boys. That's where the fun starts. And the danger. That's always where these things come apart for me."

"What about the idea of opposites attract?"

"Yes, opposites attract ... then drive each other crazy."

"Or live happily ever after."

"I'm thinking about it. ... But ... bad girl meets nice boy. Thunderbolts ensue. I don't think it works that way for me."

"And there has to be thunderbolts."

"I think so."

"Yes, I agree Jayne. There has to be thunderbolts."

"Yes," she said.

She took a sip.

"I think ... I think ... I like guys that are hard to get. That might be it. I don't know," said Jayne, "I keep falling for the guys that are hard to get."

"Oh," he said.

"And when I get them. When the guy wants me, I ... well ... I ...," she said, "I react ... It gets odd." She left it at that.

"What do you like about bad boys?"

"I get turned on by masterful men."

"Are you masterful?"

"No."

"Then I think opposites attract."

They each sipped their tea.

"That's a nice tree," she said.

He was looking there too. "Yes that's a really nice tree," he said.

It was nice. They both were having a nice time. And now both were sipping their tea again.

The Street Leading to Chet and Jayne's House, Night

Ridley and Jayne turned to each other.

Jayne said, "Ridley, nothing can change the fact that you and I once had a good time together." And she smiled.

"Goodnight Jayne," he said with a tender smile.

"Goodnight Ridley."

They separated. And off they went.

The Haunting

The Gym, Day

In the morning, Ridley had told himself that he had to put himself in motion.

Ridley spent the day exercising. He worked himself to exhaustion. Worked himself to pieces. Worked himself through one exercise after another until he couldn't breath, couldn't stand.

He had attacked the gym. And attacked. And attacked until he couldn't attack anymore.

Finally he paused and looked around. *Was it all finally burned off?* he wondered.

"That was a good workout. ..." he said to himself. "I wonder what she's doing—*Err, stop it Ridley.*"

He had spent the day trying to burn off all of the waves of painful energy he was feeling. He had exercised like mad. It persisted, this thing.

Ridley's Apartment, Day

He couldn't control himself. He would be doing ordinary things around the house, and suddenly he found himself saying out loud:

"Jayne Holly Wyatt."

He lay down on the couch to read a book. And her face flashed before him. He put down the book and stared into space.

He made himself a cup of hot tea. He brought the cup to his lips and sipped.

"Jayne Holly Wyatt," he said.

It happened there too. ... Everything reminded him of her and everything made him think of her. Walking made him think of her. Sitting made him think of her. Not thinking of her made him think of her.

Thinking of anybody or anything in the world made him think of her.

"This has got to stop," he said. ... It didn't.

He took his cup of tea out to the balcony. He sipped it and stared out at the trees.

He marveled at the agony of it. At the complete and totally agony of it. It was really a many-sided agony. And filled with many levels of anguish.

He wondered about the pain. ... About how very much pain he felt and how there was just no way to stop it. It was a new side of life. It was *hell*. He was getting a chance to live through *hell*. He explored the experience. Hmm, he was getting a chance to experience *brutal pain*. So this was what *intense bone-crushing pain* was like. This was what it felt like to love a woman who did not love you.

Well, on the bright side, he thought, *it's better to be in love than not to be in love.* And that nice, bright thought *hurt.* Damn it all, did it hurt.

I'm very lucky, he thought, *when you take the broad view of it. It's a good kind of pain.*

He continued to stand there on the balcony looking out at the trees. He lifted his cup of tea through the pain. And took a sip, trying to enjoying what he could of this feeling—of this wonderful feeling that was so very much like falling off a cliff to your doom. He sipped the tea and stared out at the trees.

"Jayne Holly Wyatt," he said aloud to the trees.

A Friday Dinner

Chet and Jayne's House, Night

It was dinnertime. ... Jayne was on the phone.

She was calling a *secretary* from Chet's office—or what was more fashionably called a *junior associate* in the consulting professions. This beautiful young lady's name was Amanda.

"Hello," said Amanda at the other end of the line.

"Hi, it's Jayne. ... Sorry to bother you at home. You went over to the client with Chet today didn't you?"

"Yes."

"He seems to have ... disappeared again." Jayne tried not to sound needy. "Did he go out with Russell again?" she asked.

"He didn't call you?" said Amanda.

"No. ... He doesn't have to. I'm just wondering."

"Well, he's probably just working on developing the Russell thing. You know Russell is thinking of starting a new division and putting Chet in charge."

"Yes, I know."

"It's in the works."

"It's a good thing."

"Yes, so it eats up hours. What can you do? ... He'll be home soon."

"Yes right. What can you do? Okay, good night," said Jane and hung up the line.

To not be needy

That was what Jayne was going through in this moment.

To not be a jealous dog. To not be needy.

"When you have time on your hands you start thinking thoughts that you shouldn't be thinking," she said to herself as she sat down on the couch.

"Chet is a very busy boy. I'm needing to be with him but I shouldn't. We're in two separate time continuums. He's busy. Beyond busy. I'm open and making dinner.

"Okay ... slow down. Don't be needy. Pull yourself together young lady.

"Don't start thinking thoughts you shouldn't be thinking."

She sighed, "Oh, what the secretary must be thinking. Okay fix it. This'll be good for you."

Chet had told her, '*You're in your world. That's what people respect. They don't want to see that you're worried about anyone's reactions. You are. But you don't let on. You come on with an attitude.*'

This is like being possessed, she thought. *I wonder if you can get rid of this with a witch doctor? ... No, Jayne, you just have to talk yourself out of it. Don't let him get so far into your head. You're young, you're beautiful. Every guy wants to catch you. Don't let so much become about this.*

She was thinking about these things as she called Amanda again and said, "Chet just got home, never mind. ... You were right. Boys will be boys."

"Oh, good," came Amanda's voice.

"Thanks. Goodnight Amanda. See you next week."

"Goodnight Jayne."

Amanda's Apartment, Night

Amanda put down the phone. ... And turned to Chet.

They were having drinks in her apartment.

Chet came to her. "Ready for that dance lesson?" he asked. He put their wine glasses down.

They came together into a closed dance position and slowly started dancing to strains of soft music in her living room.

And the world disappeared around them.

It was a romantic interlude, a moment between Chet and a strong candidate for woman number 24 in his life.

Jayne's Living Room, Night

She had told Amanda 'he just got home' almost as a throwaway. She probably got the tone right, she thought.

Jayne was thinking about other things now. Although she had to ask herself: *Why did I tell the secretary that? Ah, what does it matter? What now my love? Did I just think my love? No, I didn't.*

Odd things were bubbling up. And coming out in her.

She wanted to redirect her attention. ... "Ridley, I'll ask Ridley to come over and we'll have dinner. ... He'll get my mind off ... he'll get mind off ... sex? Why would it be on sex? Stop it Jayne. Call Ridley."

Jayne called Ridley.

"Chet isn't making it to dinner. ... It seems a shame."

Ridley's Apartment, Night

"You're asking me if I want to have dinner with you?" he asked.

"Yes," came Jayne's voice.

Well, it turned out that Ridley would indeed like to have dinner with her.

Presently, Ridley made himself ready and rushed over to Jayne's place.

The House, Night

"You're not eating much," she said. "Don't you like it?"

"It's very good. ... I have trouble paying attention to food and paying attention to you at the same time. ... I'd rather pay attention to you."

She looked at him.

"We cover such great ground when we talk," he said.

"Yes," she said and smiled. "We do."

She took a bite.

"What should we cover next?" she wondered aloud.

"What do you know about posture?" he asked.

"Not much," she said. "Why? Is it an interesting subject."

"Maybe. ... I guess it depends on how you think about it?"

"Oh. ... Well, how do *you* think about it Ridley?"

"I don't know. ... Your posture is your attitude. ... It's how you say, 'I'm great. I'm wonderful.'"

She was intrigued.

"Posture is not just internal, it's also in relation to your surroundings.

"Posture is not just inner space, it's also outer space.

"It's how your body opens up to the world. How it opens to these walls, to this room, to this space ... to the people around you."

Ridley looked at her in a bashful way. "Maybe it's not for me to say but you're tense."

She looked at him. She became still and turned her attention inward. That was an interesting observation he made. "Yes," she said. "I am tense. ... So how do you tell that?"

"You're curled forward. Normally you're not."

She held still and listened.

"Think about the wonderful spring in your body. The spine is really a spring. Now it's designed to be an S-shaped spring but when people stress out, when they become tense they crush it down a bit into a C-shaped spring."

"What?" she asked.

"They tip it forward when it should go upward. Light and easy. Like floating upward. ... When your spine is relaxed and extended, when you have your full height, the spine is a stretched out S. Going up to the ceiling or to the sky.

"You have three big bony masses attached to your spine.

"Your body holds weight in but 3 ways: it can sit, hang or brace. The head sits, the ribs hang, the pelvis is braced.

"When your spine is in its proper shape. It's holding those 3 weights in that way.

"Starting from the bottom. Starting where you sit. Your hips. ... If you follow your spine up. ... It curves inward between your hips and ribs, then curves outward over your ribs, and curves inward again at your neck. It's an S and at the top is your head, sitting on the S.

"Now when people get tense they curl everything inward. To a C shape. You curl your neck so your head tips forward and comes down towards your chest. Your shoulders curl in, your rib cage sinks and shoulders come forward. Your hips and ribs curl toward each other taking out the curve in your lower back. ...

"It's like a cat, when he gets scared to death. Yikes! Suddenly his spine curls. ... With people, everybody does the same thing under stress."

He stood up and came to her. "Can I just show you some small things?"

"Yes, please," she said.

He sat next to her and showed her. ... She did what he did. ...

Your Hips

"Okay, roll your hip forward a little bit so that you're on your sitting bones more squarely. Now extend straight up into your ribs.

Your Ribs and Shoulder Blades

"Take your shoulders up, then back, and then bring them down. That rolling of your shoulder blades engages your lats, your back and side muscles, and opens your chest."

Your Head

"Tuck your chin in a little to make the top of your spine extend. Bring your head back so that your ears are above your shoulders. Imagine that the top of your head is a crown and it's being lifted up or that it's floating up. ..."

Your Look and Attitude

"And lastly, the final step in this is you look outward and you open your visual field. Spot the wall over there."

She did all these things as he was saying them and doing them himself.

"Now relax in that position and tell me—what do you think? Tell me your thoughts. What do you feel?" he asked.

Her posture was much better, much more open. Now she also took a beat to become more relaxed and light. To float herself upward a little bit.

She turned to Ridley.

"Thank you Ridley," she said. "This is interesting."

"Yes, balance is a wonderful thing," he said returning to his seat. "I have to keep reminding myself all the time. It makes life so much easier and so much more fun."

She looked at him as he crossed to his chair.

She hadn't noticed it before, but he seemed to be a body floating upward.

He gracefully seated himself. His movements were so light and easy, she thought.

She laughed. Not because it was funny, but because it was cute ... and new.

He smiled back, adoring her.

He said, "You'd be a great *Miss America*—but I'm drifting off the subject. ..." He caught himself and continued. "Want to try something?" he asked. "Go back to the way you were a minute ago and compare."

She went back to a tight curled spine. And then opened up again and relaxed.

She laughed.

He laughed.

"Where did you learn that?"

"I saw it in a little green book once."

"And you forget the title."

"Yes, I can't remember the title."

They both smiled.

"Ridley, you're sweet," she said.

"Thank you Jayne," he said.

She ate a little.

He shifted in his seat. And took a breath.

"Hey, Jayne, I'm attending a lecture next week. ... Would you maybe come with me? ... You might enjoy it. ... It'll give you something a little adventurous to do on a slow night."

"Hmm," she said and looked up. "What kind of lecture?"

The Lecture

A Small Classroom, Night

Ridley and Jayne were seated among a group of young people.

Presently, in came *an old man*, with a strange aura about him. This was the star lecturer. He might have been in his late eighties or early nineties.

At first he seemed to be a walking mummy. He seemed to barely be able to see, hear and walk. He shuffled into the room, and sat down to rest from his entrance.

He was a tiny man with tiny movements. But this was only what he seemed to be.

What Jayne soon discovered was that when he stepped from his seat to lecture at the podium he willed himself to become someone else. To enter a totally different state of being. ... At that point, he came abruptly to life and became a roaring emotional bull of a man. A man filled with a beaming passion for life and discovery.

Jayne was watching him with interest. *What a cute old man,* she thought. *And how strange.*

The lecture
Now he spoke. And when he spoke, he spoke with great color:

"Let me tell you a story—", he said. "This happened to me roughly sixty years ago—

"My professor asked me to drive him to a night class that he was teaching. He was legally blind at night and needed people to drive him. I said I would do it. And so I stopped by his house one evening to take him to this night class.

"He let me in. Then immediately started to ignore that I was there. With his back to me, he said, *'You're early. Have a look around.'* Then he sat down and started reading. He didn't say another word.

"He didn't seem to have any manners. There I was doing him a favor. But he didn't look ready and he wasn't making any attempt to get ready. He was going to wait until the last minute to hustle out. Then I would have to race to get him to class on time.

"I took a look around his living room. There were some cabinets with mementos and junk. He ignored me completely—as though I didn't exist.

"I walked through the rest of his house. It had some more old junk, some sculptures. Abstract ones. Who knew what they meant?

"I went out to his yard—more abstract sculptures! It all looked like stuff a child could have done.

"I went back to the living room and sat down. I was getting very angry. Who was he to treat me in that way?

"He said, *Are you finished looking?*' I said, '*Absolutely.*'—Just then he turned to me. And suddenly he had this tremendously broad, friendly smile. ... He said, '*You're a quick looker. Let me show you what you missed.*'

"I said, '*What do you mean?*'

"He said, '*Follow me. I'm going to show you what you looked at and didn't see.*'"

"We saw some really marvelous things.

"He was *hard*. And I don't like someone to behave *hard*, when he has a guest in his house. But he had a point. Sometimes you have to forgive the circumstances and enjoy the moment. ... I was always an observer, but I didn't always see what I was seeing."

Weekday Chet

The Driveway of Chet's House, Morning

Chet was going to his car.

He was opening the driver-side door, when he found himself saying: *"Jayne Holly Wyatt."*

He stopped. He looked around. There was no one on the street.

He paused. "Why am I saying that out loud to myself?"

Soon Chet was entering his office.

He was pulling the chair back and was about to sit when he said, *"Jayne Holly Wyatt."* He stopped in place.—"Why am I saying that out loud?" He shook his head.

Sunday Chet

Chet's House, Morning

Chet and Jayne were sitting on the couch.

"I want to travel with you," said Chet.

"My, oh my," she said. "Do you fancy me Chet Clifford?"

"It's more than fancy." He drew a breath and released it slowly. *"Jayne Holly Wyatt. ... I ... am ... I'm in love with you."*

"Well ... I didn't see that coming."

"Neither did I," said Chet.

"I can't believe I didn't see it."

"Maybe you looked at it and didn't see what you were seeing."

The Next Friday

The Street, Evening Twilight

Ridley was stepping out for an evening walk when he crossed paths with Jayne on the street.

She was returning home carrying a paperbag loaded with vegetables and groceries.

"How are you?" he asked. "Looks like you're cooking again tonight."

"Yes, I love to cook. ... Hey, I've really been thinking about what your teacher said."

"Have you?"

"He was right. On so many levels."

"Good I'm glad."

"Yes, Chet and I had a talk about it. It helped a lot."

"Huh? You and Chet. I'm not following."

She smiled demurely like a little girl.

She looked at Ridley and said in a kind of whisper, "Can you keep a secret?"

"Yes of course."

"Okay, don't tell Chet I told you this. You promise?"

"Yes, I won't tell Chet. What is it?"

"Well, when we started going together we struck a kind of romantic deal. It was my idea. I led him to believe we wouldn't have a sex life for a long time. Until it was really the right moment. Do you know what I mean? I can't believe I'm telling you this. ... I really don't know why I'm telling you this?"

"Jayne ... what are you telling me?"

She took a deep breath, and then blurted it out—"We've had a love life with no sex life. Do you know what I mean?

"Do ... you ... mean ... the sex hasn't been good?"

"No, silly. I mean there's been ... no sex."

Ridley fell back a step, onto his back leg.

"No?" he asked.

"No."

"Oh," he said, rocking back onto his forward leg to her.

"The truth is," she said, "I've been making him go slow. But I think it's time ... for us ... to have a sex life."

"What's the hurry?"

"Ridley!"

"No offense meant. I'm sorry I didn't mean to say that. It just came out. I don't know why. You're right. I'm happy for you Jayne."

"Thank you Ridley. ... I was waiting for the perfect moment. The thunderbolt moment that I'm always waiting for. ... Maybe waiting for that moment gets you nowhere.

"But I realized something important. ... Sometimes the moments that you want ... don't come in the ways you expect. ... Unprepared perfect can happen all the time. All around you. ... Isn't that a beautiful thought."

She hugged him.

"I hope it happens to you Ridley. I hope you find love."

"One day Jayne. One day. ... Goodnight," he said.

"Goodnight my friend Ridley," she said. She smiled and walked away.

He walked away, slowly. ... Very slowly. ... Not sure where he was now meant to go.

The Strange Moment

Ridley's Apartment, Early Evening

Ridley stepped into his apartment.

"I'm not a jealous dog," he said. "Never be a jealous dog."

"To not blow up. To not go mad. To not lose it. To not go crazy and embarrass myself ... in front of Jayne."

He sat down on the couch and took a very deep breath. He calmed himself.

Everything seemed to be racing. He was hearing a beating of nine thousand drums.

"Where are we? ... Where are we Ridley? ..."

He tried to control himself. To continue taking deep breaths. To calm himself.

"The stakes—he's upped the stakes. He ups the stakes, and then he ups the stakes again.

"This is war."

Ridley calmed himself and considered this for a moment.

"It's war ... War. ... War. ... War. ... Oh my God."

Ridley continued, "Holy shit, son of a bitch. This is street-style war. This is a street fight. I let him get a mile-long start over me.

"Ridley you son of a bitch this isn't about friendship anymore.

"This is war. It's time to woo her. It's time to see if I have a chance in hell of winning the battle. It's time to fight."

"Some people like to be chased," he said.

"Oh my God! That's it. ...

"Some people like to be chased.

"She's beautiful and sweet and a wonder—and she likes to be chased. Okay Ridley, let's start chasing. ... The first thing is to outrun Chet. ...

"I've been standing still while Chet has been advancing for miles."

He brought himself to his full height. And then standing tall, he walked out of the apartment.

He crossed to the door and opened it wide.

"Let's go get our heads kicked in by love," he said.

And he exited.

Act Three

Jayne Holly Wyatt
The Girl Made of Cool

Chet's House, Night

Ridley rang the bell to Chet's house.

The junior associate from Chet's office, Amanda, came to the door.

It threw Ridley. He'd never met her.

"You're in the right place," she said. "I work with Chet. I'm Amanda. Come in."

"Nice to meet you. I'm Ridley. Is Jayne around?"

Chet stepped into the living room.

"Hello Ridley. We're in a little meeting. You look unsettled. Are you all right?"

"I'm fine."

"You need Jayne? She's in the kitchen."

"Oh, thank you. ... If you'll excuse me then," he said to them.

And he went into the kitchen.

Chet and Amanda sat down on the couch and Chet whispered to her.

"That's the one I told you about. ... I think he's having sex with her."

"Him? Really? He seemed so sweet."

"Can you believe it? And whatever happened to hiding an affair? I bet you if I asked her, *Are you sleeping with him?*' She'd say, 'Yes.' She's that kind of person.—At least, have the decency to lie to me."

"She sounds like a bitch."

"I don't want to go that far. But I appreciate what you're saying. Why can't every woman be like you? Sweet. And simple."

He moved closer to her.

"We should go over this proposal."

Their work was laid out on the coffee table. He patted her knee.

"We'll be together soon. ... Don't worry. ... It won't be long. ...

"I can't lay it on Jayne yet," he said. "It's going to make her so sad. I hate to do it. It's going to hurt her. And it's not just about me. I have to watch out for her too. Listen, her lease is for another month. Now that's not the deciding factor but if she has to move, I have to consider her situation. She has bad credit. I didn't want to say anything but she has really bad credit. ... She owes a lot of money. Maybe I shouldn't say that. But that's part of it. There's a lot going on with her.

"Listen she knows a separation is happening. You see we're in separate rooms already. It's almost like she's just a roommate now."

"But you said she has a lease," said Amanda. "How does that work? She was your girlfriend but she had to sign a lease?"

"Oh, I can explain everything."

"Yes. ..."

"She wanted a lease. She's independent. She wanted to pay rent. ... Listen, I think that's a good quality about her. Don't you think? How can you fault her for that?"

"It's strange."

"Yes. Yes, it is strange. You're right. Yes. You're very right." He was trying to induce a trance in her, and get past the logic traps in this story.

"Thank you," she said. "You're so sweet. You always say such nice things."

"Well, you bring out the best in me. You have so many good qualities yourself. Do you know that? Do you notice that?"

She smiled.

The Kitchen, Early Evening

"Are you okay?" asked Jayne. "You look red."

"It's just an adrenaline rush."

"Oh, a nice Friday night adrenaline rush," she said.

"Yes, a nice Friday fight-or-flight response."

"You just get them out of nowhere?"

"Almost ... Jayne, do you remember how I said you were 'The Girl Made of Cool'?"

"Yes, I do. No one plays the love scenes like you."

"Sometimes I don't have the words to express myself. I didn't then. I want to do a better job tonight. Right now. This is *part two* of my 'Girl Made of Cool' speech. There's somewhere I wanted to go with the speech. I didn't have the words. Maybe I do now. Maybe I could just say a little if that would be all right?"

The Question and Answer Path to Enlightenment
"How does Chet lead to your enlightenment?

"Let's talk about *'The question and answer path to enlightenment.'* "

"The what?"

"Here it is, for you."

"Go."

"Question and answer. ...

"A question that you can't let go of, causes stresses. You keep thinking about the question. You get locked in on the question. The answer brings the release. 'Ah, I get it.' And then you don't have to think about the question anymore.

"The questions and the answers are the path to enlightenment. The question is conflict. It's tension. The answer is the release and it's enlightenment.

"So I have a question for you. ...

"The question is, 'How does Chet lead to your enlightenment?' How does he make you more of 'The Girl Made of Cool'? "

"Oh, I see," she said. "But Chet is ... fun. Dastardly, and naughty, and loads of fun—that's his reason for being."

"But what comes next?" asked Ridley. "You're going to have sex, but are you thinking about what comes next—what's out there? Are you thinking about Europe, and South America, and Africa, and Asia, and out to Australia?"

"I'm about to have sex and you want me to think of Australia?"

"Exactly. Yes, now you got it."

"Ridley!" She pinched his cheek. "You're adorable."

Cosmic being
"Let's just talk a minute about cosmic being. *'The Girl Made of Cool'* is a cosmic being.

"She's the Jedi version of you. She's your future. I can see it.

"I know I'm sounding like a little kid. ... But goddamn it it's true. ... Just please stay with me and listen. ...

"It's like an iceberg. The girl made of cool is this enormous cosmic being. We only see a little of her at any one time. But there's the whole iceberg under the surface. Right now, she's in Chet's house about to have sex with him and talking to me. But below that—"

He paused, to quickly resume, "—No, it's *body and soul.* That's what it's all about. She has body, and she's filled with soul. She has both.—You see there's body. Chet has body.—There's soul. I've got soul.—She has both.

Do you see how that works?"

"Wow, that's a hell of a cosmic being."

"That's what I was trying to tell you that night we had the fight—She's the girl made of cool. That's you."

She gave him an odd look.

"The thunderbolt sensation you're looking for is enlightenment. Let's call it that. It's the answer. The moment of, 'Ah, I get it.'—You got it? Are you following me?

She gave him another odd look.

"Let's go to the garden. ... Let me show you something," Ridley said. "Please."

He moved toward the door that lead to the garden.

She followed.

They stepped into the beautiful meditation garden that had always been a part of the old house.

Ridley and Jayne crossed the porch and stepped into the garden.

The Garden, Early Night

The garden was lit with an orange and yellow glow.

The fading twilight was still casting its dark bluish velvet glow across the sky.

Out in the distance were the stars, the moon, the hills. There was fertility all around her. It was the full bloom of summer.

"I'm saying too much." He took a deep breath. He released it smoothly. "I have a better way."

She looked at him.

"Are we ready?" She gazed into his eyes.

"Listen to this . . ." he said to her.

She entered a state of expectation. This was interesting. What would he say next?

He looked at her.

What next?

He did not speak. The world went quiet. Silence entered the corners. The world stopped moving on its axis. Time froze in place.

She felt quiet calm and she noticed her new state.

She looked out to the garden and then turned her gaze to him.

He was looking intently.

He smiled.

She smiled.

"*This* is it," he said. "This is what I've been trying to tell you."

"Well," said Jayne, "maybe a few words would help it. What is *this*?"

"*This* is us," he said.

He leaned back. That was how the conversation broke off.

There was a calm there. It was interesting to her.

Silence.

She spoke first, "What else?"

"You're waiting for thunderbolts—What if they happen all the time?"

"Yes, what if."

"Maybe, you've been getting thunderbolts all along," he said, "and you just didn't know. Maybe they're just garden thunderbolts, or porch thunderbolts, or small shivers of heat that you feel. ... Maybe you looked and didn't see what you were seeing.

He continued. "Maybe you get smooth bolts. Or maybe you get cool bolts. Maybe, maybe, maybe. ..."

She thought about it. And she said, "... Maybe ..."

"I figured it out. It's not a thunderbolt. It's this ..."

"And what is this?"

"... Stillness."

It brought out a laugh from her. "Indeed. I will think about that."

She went to the door. "You're being wonderfully mysterious. Keep it up Ridley. I like you when you develop an edge."

She looked at him as she backed into the house.

"Good night Ridley. I enjoyed our talk. Let's pick it up tomorrow." She softly turned and entered the house. The door fell closed lightly behind her.

Ridley stood there.

He breathed deeply.

He went to the door. It was locked. It had locked itself. "Damn."

He knocked.

Presently, Chet came to the door.

"How's it going Chet?" Ridley said.

"Well," said Chet. "How are you enjoying my garden?" He smiled.

"I forgot to tell Jayne something important."

Ridley walked into the house.

"Go ahead," said Chet, "but do me a favor wrap it up—what are you telling her the story of the rise and fall of the Roman empire? Tomorrow's another day, you know what I mean sunshine?"

Ridley walked off.

As Chet came back into the house, he and Amanda exchanged looks.

Chet nodded to her as if to say, 'Do you see what I mean about them?'

Amanda mouthed the word 'Wow.'

Connections

The Kitchen, Night

Ridley joined her in the kitchen.

Connections make the size of reality

"It's the pauses!" he said. "We're good on the pauses."

"Pauses and connections. We're good on connections."

"It's about connections. That's what that was all about. Making connections. Seeing many different directions and connecting them. So that you live in a bigger reality.

"Reality is only what you're aware of," said Ridley. "That's your reality. It's not even what you are potentially aware of. It's just what you are aware of. That's your reality. ... And the more connections you make, the bigger your reality. ... Most people live in a small reality, but you have the potential to live in a huge, bloody massive reality Jayne—That's why you're beautiful."

Ridley continued. "To reach it you need moments of enlightenment.

"So that's where my question comes from. *'How does Chet lead to your enlightenment?'* "

Ridley paused and then said: "Am I sounding like less of a lunatic yet?"

The Living Room, Night

Chet and Amanda were sitting silently, trying to overhear Ridley and Jayne.

"I can't hear a word. Can you?" she said.

"It's no use. I don't think they're talking. I think they're hugging."

"Do you think so? Right out in the open like that."

"Some people have no shame."

Now Chet gently touched Amanda. They got caught up in the moment. He moved toward her, and she moved her lips toward him.

The Kitchen, Night

"The size of reality," she said.

Jayne looked at Ridley. And then she continued.

"Getting a picture of reality," she said. "That's what we're talking about?"

"Yes," he said.

"Getting a larger sense of reality," she said.

"Yes," he said.

She suddenly had a bright thought:

"Come with me. I want to show you something," she said.

The Living Room

Jayne and Ridley emerged from the kitchen.

Chet was startled. He moved quickly to recover. He put a hand on the Amanda's forehead, to feel her temperature.

"You don't seem sick," he said.

"Maybe I just have a headache," she said.

"Gosh, I hope it passes. We're up against a deadline here."

Jayne observed this for a flashing moment and then withdrew her attention. She strode from the living room and Ridley followed.

The instant they made their exit, Chet raised his chin high and turned to the secretary.

"Do you see what I mean?"

She nodded. She was quite appalled at Jayne's scandalous behavior.

The Rock 'n Roll Session

Let me hear your body talk

Chet's Bedroom, Night

Jayne and Ridley entered the bedroom.

"Here we are. This is Chet's bedroom. This is Chet's bed. ..."

Ridley's eyes traveled to Chet's massive bed.

"We're two people in love. We're going to talk and kiss. Share our love for each other. If I'm wrong, then it's intercourse, physical commerce, carnal knowledge, coitus, sexual congress."

As she talked, she demonstrated some of the sensual motions they would get into.

"Getting it on, getting your snack on, doing it like animals."

She described and demonstrated the love-making with enormous delight.

"Thrust. Penetrate. Ram. Bend each other over; enjoy each other's curves; lick each other; have a baby oil party; have a hot time in the old town; get happy as a clam at high tide. "

She looked at him. "Everybody out there would love to spend tonight the same way. Will you answer one question for me?"

"I will answer any question you ever pose to me."

"Can you truthfully tell me that you don't want to spend tonight the same way?"

Ridley froze, rigid, solid, like a shock victim.

"A-ha! I'm right. I'm right. I know I'm not wrong. It's all perfectly natural. You study everything. You should know about these things. It's not dirty. Or obscene. It's a thing of beauty.

"Rock 'n roll—This is called a rock 'n roll session. Have you heard the expression? I've heard that is the original meaning of rock 'n roll. And who doesn't like at least a few rock 'n roll songs?

"You're jealous," she said. "I can see it in you, Ridley. I have x-ray vision.

"Here's what we're going to do, that's what's getting to you.

"You're jealous, because you can't get started with me—I mean with someone too."

She smiled.

"This is animal behavour. Fine young animal behavior." She was throwing him all the names for 'fucking.'

She could make a pro blush.—

He was on her eyes. Her gaze. Her beautiful eyes.

"Let's get physical. Let's get animal."

"It's body talk, baby. The sleep drain. The elements of horizontal style."

"You can sit in your room and worry about things. Or you can run, live fully, and get into the fundamental things that make life so worth living. There's nothing to be ashamed about here."

She looked at him. "That's what this is about."

"There isn't anything wrong here baby. This is horizontal blues music."

Ridley was seeing her. Seeing her in close-ups on her legs, on her neck, on her breasts.

"It's a good 'going over,'" she said. And she smiled in a very sexy way.

"Jayne ... you're ... being ... cruel ..." he said.

She stopped.

"What ... What do you mean? ..." she asked.

He suddenly looked very sad and alone.

"Why would this be ... Why's it cruel ... to you? ..."

"I ... don't want to say." Ridley let out a breath and looked down at the floor. Then back at her direction.

She didn't know what to say.

"It's okay," he said. "You didn't do anything wrong Jayne. It's me. Good-night."

He walked away.

He left.

He was gone now.

And she looked—at the empty place where he had stood.

The Living Room

In the living room, Chet continued putting moves on the secretary.

Ridley came into the living room, to find that Chet had his hand on the secretary's breast.

Chet immediately reacted. "Jesus," he said, "how do we get that stain off? Maybe if you put some seltzer on and dab it."

Over his shoulder to Ridley he said, "You think seltzer, right?"

Ridley acted as if everything was perfectly normal. He casually waved goodbye to them, as he walked toward the front door.

"Good night you two."

As Ridley opened the front door. Jayne appeared at the far end of the hall.

"Good night Ridley," she said.

"Good night Jayne," he said.

He walked out the door.

Jayne paused a moment to look at that door. Then Jayne continued down the hall and went into her room.

Chet turned to Amanda.

Chet gave Amanda a good long look.

She took in the look.

The Street, Night

Ridley was striding away—in inches.

He slowed down. Then went slower still.

He stopped.

He punched a shadow foe in the air.

"Ah, damn it," he said.

He turned and walked in a wide circle around Chet's house.

What to do?

To do something or just do nothing. He marveled at his fate.

He saw Jayne moving in her room through the lit shade.

He went to her window.

Her curtains were closed so he couldn't see into her room.

He climbed over some bushes to her windowsill. And drew a deep breath.

He saw Jayne's shadow moving.

He tapped on the window.

Her shadow stopped.

And then she appeared at the window.

"Jayne, I'm disturbed," he said. "May I say one more thing?"

"Of course, Ridley. ... But first, ... I, uhm, ... I'm sorry if I teased you. I was being naughty. I don't know. Maybe you disturb me too."

"That's okay Jayne." He leaned against the window. "Whatever you do is always okay with me."

He looked at the window. Then to her. "May I come in for a moment again?"

She nodded.

He climbed in through the window. She helped him in.

Jayne's Room, Night

Now they stood before each other.

She said, "Where do we go next? Are we going to do silence again. That was fun but it worked better in the garden."

He was silent for a moment.

"Well, this is a different kind of silence." He took a breath. "Jayne, here's what I think I see. ...

"What I'm starting to see in Chet Clifford is the gravitational pull of society. And orbiting bodies.

"Bear with me please. This is another one of those thoughts, and what I'm thinking is. ...

"He'll always be looking to get into better orbits. That's the kind of man he is.

"He's attracted toward the center. And that's where his talent is. He's very good at going deeper and deeper toward the center.

"Some of us don't move toward the center," said Ridley.

"I see," she said.

"Yes," said Ridley. "Some of us move away from the center. ... And some are in between."

He smiled at her.

"That's what I see in Chet," he said.

She was affected by what he said.

"I've been with him an awful lot," she said, "and I don't see the same person you do."

She looked disturbed.

"Well, I worry," he said. "Make sure the things you think are in his head are really in there."

He took hold of her hand.

And slowly, slowly ...

He kissed it.

It was a significant moment.

She was somewhat turned on by it.

She combed his hair back lovingly.

Then she quickly recovered.

"The food ... I need to check ... on the food."

She was actually quite flustered now. And had to break away.

The Living Room

Chet and Amanda watched Jayne pass them and head into the kitchen.

Now Ridley entered the living room. And he was a sight. His face was red and scratched from the bushes. His clothes were spotted with dirt from climbing through the windowsill.

"Hello," he said with great cheer. "It's good to see you again. Let me tell you why I've returned."

He considered how to explain it for a moment, then noticed their looks and decided to shorten his formal remarks.—They were looking at him as though his hair were on fire.

"No, you know what—I'll be back in one minute."

Ridley left to join Jayne in the kitchen.

"Do you see?" Chet whispered. "And he acts like this all the time."

"He's terrible."

"I hate to talk out of turn but that happens to be what he is. It's like letting a rhinoceros into the house. I'm not going to be judgmental but in one night he's come through the front door, the garden door and her bedroom window. I'm not going to say anything but I'm aware that this is happening."

"Where do you think he'll enter next?"

"I don't know."

Chet moved away from the secretary.

"Pardon me a moment please."

The Kitchen

Ridley joined Jayne.

He said softly to her, "I really care about you and I want you to have the best, ... and that's it," he said. "I fumpher. ... I do that. ...Tonight ... I fumphered and fumphered and fumphered. I hope some good came out of it."

She looked at him in a very odd way this time.

She seemed to be ... about to say something—

Just then Chet stepped into the kitchen.

"Hey, you two," said Chet. "Listen, we're finished working and Amanda's going home. Why don't you come say goodbye to her—Was I interrupting?"

"Oh no," said Ridley. "Not at all. Your timing is fine. We were just saying goodbye."

"Again," said Chet.

"Yes," said Ridley, "you want to get a goodbye just right."

The Living Room

Chet and Jayne said goodbye to Amanda who walked off.

Now Ridley came to them.

"Good night again Jayne, ... Chet." Ridley nodded respectfully to Chet as he walked away and through the doorway.

Chet smiled. "Hey, thanks for coming by Ridley. It's always nice to see you."

Jayne waved to Ridley. "Goodnight again Ridley."

Ridley left.

They closed the door.

"What were you talking about?" asked Chet matter of factly. As a throwaway line.

"Nothing. He had an eventful day."

"Oh, is that so? God bless him. He's such a sweet guy."

"Yes, he is," she said.

She embraced Chet.

And they stayed that way a while.

Chet & Jayne Night Sessions

The Living Room, Much Later

They were having a candlelit dinner.

The strains of soft music were playing in the background.

It was all quite nice. Just a wonderful moment between them and they both were enjoying just being with each other.

The Living Room, Later Still

Now it was getting quite late.

Jayne walked out of the living room.

Chet lingered to turn off the lights, to lock the deadbolt on the back door, and to close the blinds on the picture windows.

Once Jayne was gone, he spoke in an aside to his *'audience.'*

Tonight the audience was in a kind of hushed, muted state.

"Oh my god," he said, "she is going to have such a good time tonight. I'm going to make sex so wonderful for her.

"She's special. To me she's very, very special.

"I hope you're learning a little something. Watch how I make the night even more special for her. Watch the master at work.

"I'm going to take her to a breath-taking, out-of-control climax. I do it with them all. She'll be scratching and biting. She won't be able to get enough. How do I get her into that state?

"What's it any of your business?

"Nah, I'm only kidding around. You've stuck with me this long—and what—now I'm not going to tell you? Of course I'm going to teach it to you.

"Well, you might call what I'm going to do now more show than tell.

"Boy, we're going to have a good time tonight."

Chet's Bedroom, Night

Chet and Jayne were standing in the room with the massive, very comfortable cushioned bed.

"Let's go away together next month," he said.

"Where would you like to go?"

"East, or west, or south, ... or north. Any of those. Which would you like?"

"Hmm," she said. "Chet, that'll be fun. I can't wait."

"I can't wait either Jayne."

They kissed.

They walked together hand-in-hand to the bed.

They sat and kissed and lay down together.

At the end of a long sweet lingering kiss, Jayne said, "That was nice."

They looked into each other's eyes.

"Chet, do something for me ... before we make love."

"What, what is it sweetheart? What would you like?"

"Tell me about the other women."

"What? What part of it?"

"It's okay with me that you've been with other women. But before we do this, I need to know. Have you been seeing any other women while we've been together?"

"No, of course, not. But we've been friends Jayne. We haven't had sex until now."

"Have you been tempted? Have you wanted to sleep with other women?"

"No, of course, not Jayne."

"There are a lot of beautiful women out there. Not one. Not even one has tempted you? The whole time we've been together?"

"No one Jayne. Just you. There's only you." And he said it so incredibly sweetly that it made him adorable. He was filled with sincere and total love for her.

"Chet ..."

"Yes ... Jayne."

"It would be okay to admit it."

He paused. Took a breath. Looked her straight in the eyes.

"There's nothing to admit. Jayne, there's only you. ... *I ... love you Jayne.*" He was so sincere and handsome; he was dreamy. What a handsome, loving man.

"Chet ... sweetheart ... it's okay." She stroked his head and ran her fingers down his hair. It drove him crazy. "Sweetheart, it's okay to admit it. ... Please tell me."

"Jayne ..."

"Please sweetheart ... I want to hear. ... Men have normal urges. ... There's nothing to be ashamed of. ... Nothing ever to be ashamed of. ... Please sweatheart tell me."

He looked at her.

"Have you slept with anyone else?" she said.

He looked at her.

"Who was she, Chet" she said.

He looked at her.

"Oh, ... Jayne ..." he said. "It was just once, ... it didn't mean anything and it's over now."

Now she looked at him. And he realized nothing was moving. She didn't move a single muscle except to breath.

"Chet ..." she said. She was just looking at him now. Not moving.

"That was the wrong answer," she said.

"What?"

Now silence. She wasn't moving. She wasn't saying anything. She wasn't giving him anything he could react to.

What seemed to Chet like several hours later, she said ...

"Oh my God. You've been sleeping with another girl? While saying you love me?"

"You just said it would be okay if I admitted it."

She sat back and just nodded her head as she took it all in.

"You slept with somebody? Do you love her? You must. Why would you want to sleep with her if you didn't love her? I don't want to come between such a relationship."

"It's over between me and her."

"I wouldn't be so sure. Maybe you're in a transition phase. Give it another try. Don't drop her just like that. Forget me. Get me out of your life."

"I could never forget you. What you and I have is different—I love you."

"You slept with her and you didn't love her? Why would you want to sleep with somebody you didn't love? Where's the joy in that? Did you tell her that you didn't love her before you slept with her?"

"I don't remember my exact words.

"Who was she?"

"Let's calm down and talk this through."

"We are talking this through. Who is it?"

Jayne gave it some thought.

"Your secretary?"

"Let's leave Amanda out of this. Besides what I had with her is in the past—I mean with whoever it was."

"You're sleeping with more than one person?"

"No! Just Amanda—I mean just one person—will you quit twisting this around! You're putting words in my mouth."

"Why didn't I figure it out before? You spend long hours with her. The secretary, who was just here? ..."

She gave Chet a piercing stare—

"You didn't look like you were very affectionate, considering you slept with each other. Trying to hide something? Were you trying to fool me? Was that what it was Chet? Was that what you were trying to do Chet? Lie to me? Snow me? Very good Chet."

"Don't get worked up. It's over. This is now, that was last week. Listen she's a very attractive woman. Any guy would get involved with her. Did you see the body on her? I didn't know how strong our relationship was. I didn't know how in love with you I was. Now I know and her attraction has really dropped. From a ten she's dropped down to a three—three and a half, I swear. She doesn't compare to you—I really love you. She was a slip. I slipped with her. I didn't sleep with her."

"What's in it for her? She knows we're together so why does she do it? Let's figure this one out? Is she going to get a promotion? Am I going to walk into the office in a month and find out she's my new boss?"

"Probably not."

"You've lied to me. Used me. Why? Sex? All this just to get me in bed?"

"Do you have to hurt me? Why do you put it like that?"

"Why did you do it?"

He wouldn't tell her.

"Give me a reason."

"Maybe you need to cool down. If you go in your room for a while, I would understand. Just take a few minutes. Go in there. Or I can leave you here. Just breath easy for a few minutes. And then we'll talk."

"I'm not going anywhere until I have the reasoning behind this—What were you thinking?"

"We'll talk about this when you calm down. Go back to your room. You'll feel better, if you give yourself some breathing time. You'll see."

They were standing now.

"Why lie to me? Why such a big lie? Why a lie so deep? Why so thick? I want to know why?

"Who," he said, "am I really hurting? ... Myself. My own spirituality."

"What really happened?" she said. "What was really there? ... If you're going to be glib I'm really going to lose it on you."

"Okay, okay—just calm down."

"No—why. Tell it to me."

"You're not in a state to hear it."

She bolted forward.

Stopped herself.

She shouldn't kill him. Not until she got her confession and the truth out of him.

He said he was hers. He lied. Many men lie—but only Chet had raised it to the level of bastard. And stripping him to his bones would be her revenge and justice done under this moon and night sky. In this place—that Chet noticed was growing very, very hot. He was sweating now. And extremely bent out of his bastard shape.

He needed recovery time. He said, "Go in your room Jayne. ... Go ... in ... your room."

"Chet, don't make me hit you with my fist." Perhaps she needed a little recovery time herself. She let out a breath. There. Now an audible sigh. "Oooh, ..." She looked him in the eye. "I am *not* going to hit you. I'm the kind of lady, ... that ... I don't do that."

She walked out.

He stood there. Then he heard shattering sounds.

"Krrsh! ... Ka-krssh ... Krssh!"

It was a sequence broken up by subtle banging and thumping sounds. Then more shattering.

There was a definite melody. For those who appreciated the musicality of such moments.

The Kitchen

Chet found her standing there, very poised.

A set of broken dishes happened to be on the floor.

She was taking a plate, holding it out now, releasing it, letting it drop to the ground.

It shattered on the floor.

She took another plate, held it out, released it.

It shattered on the floor.

She picked up another plate.

He looked at her.

It went the way of other plates.

"I want to hear '*why*,'" she said. "I want to hear it from you. I enjoy listening to you ... darling. I want to hear your reasoning."

"What you know, you know," he said. "Why does anybody sleep with anybody? And so what, honey! She's just another one of the bunch. I can't turn my life around in a second. I just have to get used to the fact that we're in a serious relationship. It doesn't happen overnight. I have to break my old habits. But I'm trying all the time. I'm working at it."

She proceeded efficiently, she was releasing piece after piece of his precious collection of fine china.

They were making a kind of abstract art formation on the floor. All these little broken pieces. It was quite a lovely pattern, when seen from a certain vantage point.

How receptive to the beauty Chet was, ... well, that was very hard to tell.

He walked out.

The Living Room

As he walked through the living room, there was the sound of shattering chinaware in the background.

The Bedroom

Chet was back in the bedroom.

He heard shattering in the background.

Then silence, a pause.

Now new noises.

A little closer and louder.

It sounded as if she had moved into the living room.

And that big heavy things were suddenly being thrown.

He heard a loud crashing sound. Then there was banging and breaking involved.

The Living Room, Night

He came into the living room. She had taken some heavy objects and thrown them at some other heavy objects.

She had smashed some things. ... She had made a quick decision, when what was happening between herself and him had escalated to a point of life and death. She knew she had to act. ... It was better to smash "things" than to smash Chet in the face.

"Oh my God," he said—*She had smashed his television set!*

He walked over and looked. There was a stick speared through the television. His television was dead. She had killed his television. It had been a widescreen set. Such beautiful sound. So stylish. So modern. ... Now all that was over. ... He would have to get another television.

He had entered the living room, she was still pursuing. Not with any intention of having some tranquil moments on the couch.

She was suddenly on the other side of the Jayne Holly Wyatt spectrum. There was no physical sign of the sweet Jayne. ... She was now a very strong character. A tall, lean elegant lady fitted in steel and fire.

With smoldering eyes and commanding presence. Sexy as hell. But dangerous. Very dark and dangerous.

He was meeting a Jayne Holly Wyatt he had not even known existed.

She was sexy as hell. That's what she was to him. But she was out of control.

"Straighten up and fly right Jayne!" he said.

"I want to hear what you were thinking," she said.

"That was a wide screen television," he said, "with surround sound! All right I did something a little wrong, I'm not going to deny that, it was a little wrong but to make a production like this.

"I don't deserve this. I do so much for you. And what do I get for my good works? This—a broken television, is that my reward? What you did to that television set hurts me more than the television. How am I going to watch *'The Sunday Business Journal'* this weekend!

"I slept with her. Big deal. Sleeping with somebody. That's physical. Loving somebody. That's important. That's what this is about between us, but not breaking televisions! You know how I felt about that set Amanda!"

"I'm not Amanda! Amanda is your secretary!"

"Right! See what happens when you get me upset."

"I just want one thing Chet—to hear a clear answer as to why?"

He wouldn't answer.

"Tell me why."

"I'm a human being. I have my imperfections. Take me as I am, that's what love is."

He continued. "You want to hear what was going on in my head—okay. In most of the sexual experiences I had with her she was actually facing the other direction and I was thinking of you. It sounds crazy—I know—but from the back she looks a lot like you.

"Human beings are far more complicated than you imagine. I think what was happening is that I was trying to cope with my intense longing for you, by momentarily satisfying the animal part of me. I'm not proud of it but the animal part is there. And sometimes it just makes demands on me.

"I didn't want to force you to satisfy me. That would be very selfish. Listen, I don't want to marry my secretary. I don't even want to promote her. It's just that I'm a man. You and I aren't sleeping together. I had to satisfy my drive in some way. Have I made any sexual demands on you? No.

Why? Because of my secretary. If it wasn't for my secretary you would bear the brunt of my animal urges.

"Let's find a way to work this all out. Amanda is a very nice, sweet person. I don't want to hurt her feelings either. Maybe we'll invite her over and you'll talk to her. She's a very wonderful girl. Maybe the three of us could just sit down and get comfortable ..."

"You ass! "

"What? What now?"

"You bastard!"

She came towards him.

"I wasn't going to do this. But it's a woman's prerogative to change her mind."

"Go ahead smash me one," he said. He tapped his own cheek at the chin. "Go ahead smash me one," he said again.

Well, Jayne Holly Wyatt ... She wasn't reckless. She wasn't interested in smashing his face. She became very exact. She came forward and using hip motion to make a very graceful swing, she punched him in the solar plexus—She struck him hard in the gut.

She stopped in mid-strike. She was indeed very exact. She knocked the wind out of him but did not damage him.

He sank to the floor.

He panted a bit for breath, and then caught his air again.

He looked up at her.

And when he looked up, she said, "It's okay Chet. I'm finished. This feels like a fine moment to end it."

Now he had heard what she had said, and he took it in.

He absorbed it—and realized where they were now.

"Oh, I can see it now," he said. "This is not going to a good place. I'm going to break it off with you. You're the problem. You Jayne.

"This is a dead end," he continued. "I can see that right away. There's something wrong here."

He slowly rose to his feet.

"And you know what, you're the problem. You Jayne. You.

"I've tried," he said. "God knows. But I have to face the music. You know what the trouble with you is? You have an unbalanced value system. I take you to nice places to eat. I take you to meet interesting people. Those sorts of things don't seem to matter. The only thing that matters is that I slept with my secretary. And I said your name wrong once."

"This is unreal," she said.

"I'll tell you what's unreal," he said. "That now I have no television set. That's unreal.

"I've had problems with the relationship but I was in love so I overlooked things. Now I don't feel I can do anything more for you."

Jayne walked off.

And what happened next happened in a kind of whirlwind between them.

Jayne started packing clothes into a bag.

Mentally she had already left. She was just in the house packing, not even reacting. Nothing he said meant anything to her.

As he began watching this, Chet's adrenaline began to really pump.

"Did you fall in love with me?" he asked.

"It might be nice to tell you," she said. "But you're not in a state to hear it."

"And you're going to leave it there?" he said. "That is not right. This is what I get? After everything, this is what I get?"

"This is a breakup. This is how things go."

"This is a pattern with you. You've done this before."

"No, I haven't done this before."

"This is unreal. This is totally unreal. I'm a real person. Do you understand that? I'm real. Are you a real person?"

"No, I don't even exist. Forget me. Don't lose what you have with your other women."

"You're a head game. You're just a game player. You don't care whose heart you break. First you break Ridley's. Now mine—"

"Ridley's?" she asked.

"You just sleep with men," he said, "I mean you just have sex with men."

"We never had sex," she said.

"Oh, I get your game. You just don't have sex with men and then continue to not have sex with men."

"Under your scenario, I'd be a professional virgin."

"Are you?"

"I'm not a professional."

"That's only half an answer. What about the other part?"

"I don't think you'll ever find out the answer to that ... And it might be fun to leave it that way."

"Is that what this is to you, fun and games?"

"No. ... You're right. It's not fun, at all. It's an ending."

"Holy goddamn hell! I'm being played. I was such a good guy. I played it slow because you wanted it slow. What in the name of hell are you doing?"

She was finished.

She went to the front door with her bag.

She looked at him.

"Goodbye Chet," she said.

She walked out the door and closed it softly behind her.

He looked at it.

He walked toward it.

Walked away.

Turned completely away.

Then moved his whole body forward and with his arm made a kind of graceful swinging punch into the air.

"Argh!" he said.

He shot a lightning jab into the air.

"Grhh! Uhhh. Shwoooh ..." He whistled a long, soft descending whistle into the air.

It all went quite.

He straightened himself to his full height. Raised his head. Looked out at something.

Now he was alone with his *audience*.

Chet Finale

He looked around.

"Hey ... it looks like we've got a good group here tonight," he said. "You all can understand. I lay my case out in front of you. Do you see what's happened? Do you see what she's like? You never can tell what's buried inside of some people.

"Fellows—am I right? Women—can you understand her? She's a mystery wrapped in a question.

"I am so glad I broke it off with her—as soon as she started talking about leaving me. ... I saw where that was going right away.

"You see what she's like. She's manipulative. And you were feeling sorry for her. Admit it. You were. I was starting to feel a little peculiar about bluffing her too. On the surface she looks like such a nice person. Innocent. Loving. You never can tell what's buried inside of some people.

"She deserves what I did. Good for her.

"And don't worry about me, I'll get past this. I've made mistakes in the past. I'll make them again. The main thing is that I'm learning. You have to go through these things but I'll be fine.

"My secretary isn't that bad of a person. And she really cares a lot for me. And if not her then there's a new girl. She started working downstairs at my office. What a knockout.

"I've still got a lot of good things coming my way. I'm not down. Not by a long shot. I'll catch you later.

"Where there is hatred, I bring love.

"Where there is discord, I bring harmony.

"Where there is despair, I bring hope.

"Where there is sadness, I bring joy.

"Where there are shadows, I bring light.

"The approach I take really has to do with the future.

"I'll see you in the future," he said.

And he walked away ... into the darkness.

Outside of the House, Night

Jayne was standing and staring at the house.

She slowly walked away, into the surrounding darkness.

Heartstruck
The "Girl Made of Cool" Speech—Part Three

A Park, A Beautiful Day

Ridley and Jayne were sitting on a bench.

Looking at a field and a grove of trees.

She said, "That 'Girl Made of Cool' part two speech was a show-stopper."

"Well, that's nice of you to say," he said. He went quiet for a moment and then said, "Hey, do you want to know something? I figured out how I should have made the original 'Girl Made of Cool' speech."

"Let's hear it."

"I think I missed my moment."

"No, c'mon. You can't say you figured it out and then not share it with me."

"It's not like you're a reporter. It's about you."

"I like your speeches. I'd like to hear it."

"I should have told you that I had this feeling for you. ... It's not art. It's not clever. It's just the feeling that hit me."

He caught himself.

"Oh, never mind. It would come out silly at this point. Forget it. Sorry to disturb." He turned and looked out over the park. "... Do you want to get something to drink?"

"No, go ahead and tell me."

"Oh Jayne," he blushed. "Now I can't." He wiped his hand across his forehead. Looked at her. Then put his head in both hands. And drew a deep difficult breath.

"Ridley, go ahead and tell me. Please I'd like to hear your idea."

He slowly drew his head from his hands and turned his gaze toward her.

"Talking like this is so difficult," he said.

She looked into his eyes and her gaze was steady.

He looked into her eyes. Her beautiful eyes. And steadied his own gaze.

They connected. A moment of something passed between them. He began to speak.

He abruptly broke off, turned from her and leaned his whole body forward, away from her.

"I can't keep going here," he said.

Then he glanced over his shoulder in her direction, in a discreet, small movement. He said, "—Ah, all right. ... I'll go on. ... Somehow. ..."

She smiled. She got it. She laughed. He was a delight to her.

She looked at his back. She slapped him playfully on the shoulder blade. "Go on."

He laughed too. And then resumed. Quite sincerely. Very genuinely. And completely from his heart. He spoke.

"Sometimes when you just *state the obvious* to a girl—that can be the most significant statement you can make.

"Maybe a good speech would be just saying what it is—If what it is, is so big, maybe you don't have to add to it.

"Because ...

"When I think of you, I feel a strange sensation.

"This is a strong sensation.

"It's not at all in the place where I would expect. It's up here."

He put his hand high on his chest.

"It feels like my blood gets warm in this area, going out to my arms. Strange. Then I thought to myself, 'What place is that?' My lungs?

"I thought that's a strange place to feel for you. In the lungs. But, wait, the lungs aren't filled with blood. Then I realized that actually the lungs are around it. So I thought, 'What's in the middle?' Then I realized what place it was.—I don't know if you know your anatomy too well," he smiled a small pure smile, "so I don't know if you're following me on what that thing is. ..."

"Your heart," she said.

"Yes," he said, "that happens to be what they call it. I feel for you in my heart. ... And the arteries coming out. Into my arms up here. And also down into my diaphragm. ... Or I guess a better way to say it is it feels like my heart is suddenly bigger, so that it fills my chest and arms and head. ... I didn't remember ever feeling a sensation like that. So, I'm thinking to myself, *'What do you call that?'* And then I realized what people call it. Now I know what it is." He looked at her. "You know what it's called."

"Yes, I know," she said.

"You must get a lot of that sensation from men," he said.

"Yes," she said, "but usually it's in a different place."

"I see," he said.

"Yes," she said, "usually it's different."

"And I realized something about it," he said.

"What was that?"

"I'm in big trouble," he said. He turned and looked into the distance. "I'm in big goddamn trouble."

She went silent.

"There is beauty in desire," he said. "And this was a beauty that was trouble. Beauty and trouble in one. Beautiful trouble. ... There was something funny in that. ... Don't you think?

He continued. "What kind of basking is this for your body to do? Basking in blood streams. In a flushed feeling. I really believe beauty is truth, truth is beauty. So I started questioning. *'What kind of beauty is this?'*

"It's a flushed feeling, so you would think that would be good and feel pleasant. And it makes you feel great but at the same time it's crushing.

"It came to me—This new feeling—It was a *'flush crush?'*"

"Ridley," she said, "do you mean to tell me that you're realizing that instead of a speech about *'The Girl Made of Cool'* you should have given me a speech about—*'The Flush Crush'*?"

And right there, that stopped him.

"Foiled again," said Ridley. "I thought I had it."

"You're just going to have to face it," she said. "Ridley, *you have an imperfect speech,*" she continued. "You're faced with an imperfect speech."

Ridley was confronted with the cold hard truth of it. He drew a breath. He let it out. He looked at her.

He said, *"Jayne Holly Wyatt."* It was a very definite statement. He went quiet.

She looked at him.

"Ridley Richardson," she said. She was every bit as definite.

They both laughed. There was something funny in his plight. It hit them both at the same time. They laughed for a while and then stopped.

"You're probably wondering," she said, "what my feeling is for you."

"Yes, I have wondered."

"Maybe," she said, "one day I'll tell you."

They looked at each other, and then they looked out into the trees of the park.

They continued looking out at the trees.

No one happened by. They had the world to themselves for a few minutes.

After a moment she said, "They're very nice trees."

He said, "Yes, they're very nice ... They go well together. Do you notice that?"

They sat and stared at the trees.

The sun was low on the horizon in the background. It was setting.

And soon night would fall. It would be a warm night. Quite pleasantly seasonable. And very comfortable if you wanted to enjoy it.

The Gravitational Pull of Society

Several Days Later

The Metropolitan Museum, Afternoon

Jayne walked up to its huge front entrance.

She turned her head upward, and looked.

After a moment, she brought her gaze down to the doors.

Then she went up the steps and past the pillars of the large facade, into the lobby.

And slowly moved beyond.

An Exhibit Hall of the Metropolitan Museum, that Day

She was traveling very slowly now. ... Jayne was walking through the Metropolitan Museum of Art. Seeing it in a new way.

She paused.

For a long, long moment.

After a long slow while, her eyes started to move to the side. ... There was a young man a few paces away. ... Something about him looked very familiar. ... A familiarity that went back years and years. That had been with her since grade school. ... Since she was a little girl with big dreams about the future. Her future. ... He came to her and spoke.

"Hello," he said.

"Hi." She looked at him.

"You seem," he said, "to be really enjoying this."

She looked at him.

"Me too," he said. "... Have we met before?" he asked. ... And he was genuine about it. He really didn't know.

She smiled. "I know what you mean. I feel it too. It seems we've met before. Yes, it does. But no, we haven't."

"Hmm," he said.

They looked at the art.

"I'm David," he said.

"I'm Jayne," she said and smiled again.

"I like to look at the art. ... I'm very practical. But I'm learning to appreciate this."

"Yes, me too," she said. And she smiled.

"Well, I seem to be making you smile at every turn. We're off to a good start," he said.

"David," she said, "can I ask you something?"

He looked at her and she opened up.

"Do you work for a living?" she said.

"I do," he said, "... uhm, but my father is an attorney. ... There's quite a bit—well, there's a fund he set up. So if I want it, it's always there. But yes I work."

"David," she said, "if all artists had to stand on one side of the room, and all business people had to stand on the other side of the room. Where would you stand?"

He gave it thought. "Well, I would stand, in the, uhm ... I wonder," he said.

"In the middle," she said.

He looked up at her. "Yes, in the middle. That's right."

Yes, he was exactly what she thought he would turn out to be. She smiled. She laughed.

"David, I'm glad we finally met," she said.

"Finally," he said. He wasn't sure where this was going.

"Have a good life David. I have to go," she said.

"Ah," he said, "so we leave it there."

"Yes," she said.

"Have a good life Jayne," he said.

And this was how she said good bye to Mister Perfect Gravitational Pull of Society Man.

She was different now than she had been, and she was not going back.

The Park, Day

Jayne and Ridley—met in the park.

They looked into each other's eyes.

She put her fingers to his mouth. She didn't want him to say anything just then.

"Shush," she said, "please."

She looked at him.

"I want you to kiss me," she said.

And she continued to look at him.

"Would you like to kiss me?" she said.

He smiled a small smile.

She smiled.

"We are going to kiss aren't we?" she said.

"Yes," he said, "I would like very much to kiss you."

He stood in stillness.

"Can we, ..." he asked, "... kiss with ... our eyes closed?"

She stood, too, in stillness.

"And, ..." he said, "... can we do it slowly?"

They looked at each other for a moment.

She closed her eyes.

He brought his lips close to her lips. He closed his eyes.

Slowly, ever so slowly they kissed.

They kissed for years.

She pulled away slowly. Both of their eyes were still closed.

They happened to open their eyes at the same instant, and both slowly.

"I had," he said, "an ex-girlfriend who said I should stop pulling away first when we kissed. ... I think she was right."

"Yes, she was right."

"So that was our first kiss"—and they both happened to say it at the same time.

"Maybe," he said, "we'll do it again some time."

"Maybe," she said, and smiled.

"May I take your hand?" he asked.

She gave him her hand to hold.

He took it in his hand, very gently, tenderly, lovingly.

And they walked into the park like that.

New Year's Eve, Horizons, and Crossing the Years

Seasons changed. ... Before long it was new year's eve.

The snow was falling. Past the yellow lights of the lampposts. Touching down on the city's streets. Set against the dark cold of the night sky, the snow was bathed in the soft warm glow of city lights.

At the party ... Ridley and Jayne watched the show.

Then the stage was cleared, and the dance floor was opened. The band began to play. People stepped onto the floor.

Ridley and Jayne held hands as they walked on.

They danced and flowed. The songs drifted across the dance floor and the swirling couples.

Ridley looked at Jayne. And Jayne looked at Ridley.

There was something in the way they clung to each other after they had danced a while.

Soon they were home.

They kissed.

He peeked in the mirror while she stripped her gown.

Bare.

So in love with her, was he.

Whispering tenderly.

Into the night.

Thrill of the new was here.

Slipping into dreams.

So in love with him, was she.

Will it be? An affair to last? Summer love? Thrills of first snowfalls, seasons changing. Will he? Will she? Will they be in love? So in love next new year's eve?

The Fading Echoes of the Years

A few years later—there was this photo. Of Ridley & Jayne ... & beaming little children.

—The End—

Hell Has Blue Skies

The Business Age

I<small>T's VERY IMPORTANT</small> to have a sense of history.

From history, you can know the age, from the age you can know the form. From the form you can know the people.

From knowing everything, you can win. And when you win you can make money! ... Money, baby. We're talking lots and lots of money.

The era was the turn of the century. It was a time of traveling—From one business era to the next. From one presidency to the next. From one social age to the next.

Historically it was a hingepoint.

It was an era of great progress—of business progress and invention. Humanity was rising to the next level.

It was a "let's get rich" era, after the "world war" eras and the "cold war" eras.

Now, they say that: *Success at the top hides many sins all along the line.*

It hides many practices, like robbermanship and sonofabitchmanship. These were prevalent in the new "let's get rich" era.

Many businessmen were heady.

The fundamentals were still the fundamentals. A kiss was still a kiss. A sigh was still a sigh.

And a good racket that returned 35 percent (or more) annually was still a wonder to behold, a mother-of-all-rackets, a *"beauty."* ... The fundamental things applied as this time went by. ... And many pursued the modern sense of *"beauty"*—to a high standard of excellence—in this vanished age.

The time was actually the latest in a series of "let's get rich" eras. It came hot on the heels of two other similarly high-minded eras in between recent wars. This one was different in that it propelled itself higher, farther, faster.

People were blazing through companies. The returns were all that mattered. What were your returns to your company—and what were your returns to yourself? ... And if you knew what you were doing you would weigh the returns to yourself a little more heavily. Meaning 100 percent more heavily than your company. If you could make money by burning and destroying your company, why then the choice was clear. Your duty was clear. What was in question? Nothing.

How to Be an Expert

The Gentleman's Arts of Robbermanship, Scoundrelmanship, and Son-of-a-bitchmanship

Rob.
Lie.
Cheat.
Back-stab.

In the old days, robbermanship, scoundrelmanship, and son-of-a-bitchmanship were low-level lines of work.

Today, to practice villainmanship, and reach successmanship, you need a grooming school. Nowadays, it's the gentleman's art.

If you want to be evil, and you want to be a success at it, you have to do the same thing that a painter or a musician has to do—practice (stick-to-itmanship). And become better at what you do than anyone else.

In the old days, it was just horsemanship and pistol-whipmanship. You would rob people every several weeks and from these earnings you could lead a comfortable life. Nowadays—if you want to lead a comfortable life and not be apprehended—you had better have a good understanding of deal-making and how to profit from a corporation.

We're living in the modern commercial era of successmanship; a world of politics, of dirty deals, one after another. It's a very complicated and competitive marketplace. To be a ruthless villain in today's business climate you need superior training.

You must understand loopholes (clause-manship) and how to corrupt law enforcement officials (ownermanship); you must know how to supervise the processing of enormous amounts of paperwork (hide-the-baconmanship). You must know how to recruit good accomplices. That means you have to convert the honest to your way of thinking; you must be prepared to overcome moral objections, to get past the almighty "No!" that is constantly going to be hurled at you. Nowadays, everybody starts with a "No!" and it can be very daunting. You must cultivate your skill at lying and learn to perfect untruth to the level of art. There are so many things to learn. It's a wonder that anybody actually succeeds. Yet there are success stories, but we don't need to name names.

So where can you go to learn how to become rich and climb to the top in a scientific way?

Where can you learn quickly and neatly the things they don't dare teach you at the Harvard Business School?

Let's consider a *company* that is the perfect training ground for the up-and-coming businessman. Our organization is *The Blue Sky Company*.

We sell blue sky.

That is our only product. We do not have a monopoly on "blue sky" and therefore have grown very skilled at the "sell" part of our business.

Here are the principles of our profession:

How to be an expert. Don't spend too much goddamn time studying. Get your head out of the books.

That leads to the paralysis of analysis. Always be doing something. If it works, do more of it. If it doesn't, do something else.

How to be absolute. Let's say you put your hand on a hot stove. You don't just think it's hot. You get absolute very quickly.

Always speak with certainty.

The rules presented here are not opinions. They have been drawn from research.

How to select the right business promise. "The sky's the limit," is the right promise. "Blue skies from now on," is the right promise. "The harder you work, the luckier you get," is the right promise.

How to fight the battle. Learn the basics.

> "The race is not always to the swift,
> Nor the battle to the strong.
> But that's where to place your bet."
> — Damon Runyon

How to woo. The battle goes to the smoothest talker. Say all the right things and they will fall in love with you.

"The big lie is the key—tell it long enough and loud enough, and they will believe it: You're the only one in my life, you mean the world to me."
— Hans Von Gerring, famous Nazi general

How to approach your work.   Always go in with a really good attitude.

"It's not whether you win or lose, it's that you fight the good fight."
— Hiroshi Kamaguchi, famous Kamikaze pilot
(shortly before he died in battle,
which was shortly before his country lost the war)

Sweet lines.   Here are some things you should have in your hip pocket.
"I know what I like when I see it, and so often I see it in you."
Have sexy lines. Have family lines. Have all that ready.

How to say the right things.   People are stirred by traditional values. Good old fashioned American values. So you give them that line of horsesh**!
Also, use interjections like: "You're always smiling. We like that about you."
Additionally, the history of the rugged individualism that this country was built on shows us ... how to make it all about "me for me." Fill your head with thoughts like, "They all find me fascinating. They all love me. They all want what I have." And spend your life thinking like that.

How to handle injuries.   Do not bleed. If you are injured, you must not bleed.

How to counter aggression.   Sharks rarely attack without warning. Usually there is some exploratory aggressive action. The appropriate countermove is a sharp blow to the nose. The dictum [principle] is, "It's hard for your opponent to hit you, if your fist is in his face."

Do not indulge in the forbidden.   The wickedest of all sins are:
(1) whistleblowing
(2) honesty that loses you money
(3) being a prude for integrity, a.k.a., going over your boss's head.

How to say potent things.   Use a dictionary of winning words.

Always inject news into everything you say.

Always use the word 'new' itself. "We have a new way of doing things." "... for the new economy." "... in a new world." "... leading to new revenues."

Also here are the twenty-one words you should memorize and use at every opportunity: announcing, introducing, just arrived, important development, improvement, amazing, sensational, revolutionary, startling, miracle, magic, quick, easy, the truth about, hurry, and last chance.

You can further strengthen anything by throwing in words like darling, love, proud, friend and baby.

How to employ gamesmanship.   Say things like:

"Yes, but don't let's forget the big picture. What, after all, are we trying to do?"

Drip with cliches. Employ shopworn, hackneyed turns.

"Things are different now. They're not the same. It's a totally different situation. I mean it's new to everybody. They're moving forward from where they're at. You've got to understand where they're coming from and what they've been through. A lot of different situations. Nobody would have thought they ... or he would be where he's at ... after that beginning."

When they ask your opinion, say things like:

"That's how you win it. One play at a time."

"He's got a lot of heart and nobody can take that away from him."

"You never know. It all can change like that. You can't be too sure."

"They've got a lot of drive. They've got a lot of potential. But maybe this is not their year."

How to be political.   Gain admiration by offering new thinking.

"We have to end divisions. Religions, nationalities, states, cities. All of those are divisions. One day people are going to wise up. Borders are going to disappear. All the divisions are going to disappear. There won't be any separate cities, any separate states, any separate countries. The whole world will be just like one big country -- the United *State* of America."

How to talk like a leader.   "Shut up," you explain.

Once you have made that point perfectly clear, continue.

"Now, you can pick any color you want, as long as you pick red."

How to apply the first commandment of the expert, "Hell Hath Blue Skies."

Talk blue skies, promise blue skies and sell blue skies.

Now we have a sense of the art.

And a sense of the history.

First came the outlaws.

Then the confidence age, which brought the hustler, mechanic, burn artist, feather merchant and horse trader.

Now we are in the next wave.

Let's examine the present.

The tale of one young man progressing through our company represents an application of the principles described forthwith.

The path of a good guppy, of a typical guppy.

The path of a dreamer in the present tense. It's happening right now.

The dreamer awakens is the example.

We're looking at what's happening in the now. In business, known as "real time."

The Hero. The current hero—the hero of the fashion moment—Here we have an idealistic young guy who comes into the *company.* Although he has a college degree, he has to start at the bottom. In fact, he must start lower than that and then earn a position at the bottom. Unfortunately for him, the degree that he has is a Bachelor of Arts.

He's a nice guy; a go-getter; ambitious for the right reasons; anxious to prove himself a good company person. He's full of traditional American values. As a result, he's totally unprepared for the business world.

The Hero. In literature he is Odysseus, King David, Horatio Alger. The rags-to-riches man.

In folklore, he is the dreamer.

In business, he is "The Sucker." Also known as the also-ran, the neverwuz, the down-and-outer. The cold-dumper. The flopperoo, the bring-down-artist.

The fella-who's-here-for-his-shellacking. The guy-who-missed-his-cue. The guy-who's-about-to-go-thump.

The honest man.

The wipe-out-artist, a few other names. The guy-who's-about-to-go-snafu. The down-the-drain-man. The fizzle artist. The go-have-a-bad-go-at-it man. The rack-and-ruin man.

The all-American boy.

The cute, little ole' all-American boy. Let's get real. We're not selling opiates. And let's leave it at that.

The Company.   To the hero, at first, this company seems like a terrific place to be. They're in the business of training people in how to come on like *experts.*

That's how they make their money; they train high-level executives in subtle techniques for building up their reputations, and they teach winning mannerisms that enable these executives to come on cool and confident with the public, with venture capitalists, with potential lovers that they meet in bars, and all the rest of humanity. What could be better than that? A grooming school for experts.

The company believes everything has blue skies. Even hell hath blue skies.

The attitude is, "Nothing but blue skies from now on." The client is made to feel, "The field is filled with sun and sky."

There are nice landscape drawings on the walls.

Days are filled with walks down the garden path.

Such is the tone of the place.

The kid feels very lucky to have landed this choice job; he loves and trusts the people he's working with; he's as high as a blimp. Then he begins: *the learning process.*

First, he finds out that the training for becoming an expert is very similar to the training for becoming a confidence artist.

Next, he discovers that he's surrounded by liars and cheats; his associates are a bunch of arch-salesmen, up to no good.

Shocked by his newly acquired knowledge, he decides to work within the system to change it. In his heart, he feels he can counteract all of the evil he encounters. Unfortunately for himself, he's a do-gooder.

He sincerely believes that he can go in two opposite directions at once: Combat the corruption and at the same time make it big in the company. This is where the Bachelor of Arts type of thinking can lead a person.

Fortunately, he's working with some people who will lead him to the true path. They'll get his thinking on track and love doing it.

The Faculty.   In this "college" we have a group of first rate teachers who have been to hell and back and then to hell again, which is where we find them in the present.

First, we have the "Devil" in there. The boss is like the Devil; his embodiment. He's running the show. And he's always smiling.

I don't have to tell you that the devil—according to those in the know—has always been a smooth-talking guy who makes a lot of sense. In fact, many poets have written about how the devil is a pretty hip character. If you want to know more about the Devil, refer to Milton, Dante, Goethe. It's all in there. Unfortunately, it's beyond the scope of this story.

In here the Devil—or, uhm, I'm sorry—the *boss*, represents the common thinking of people today.

You can imagine what comes out of his mouth.

"Get ahead. Rise!"

He tells this kid things like, "You want to do good, heh? How are you going to do good if a bum comes up to you on the street and you don't have a nickel to give him for a cup of coffee? Which today is a buck and three quarter. Here, we'll teach you how to earn that nickel and more."

They say the Devil can quote scripture. Well, this guy cites passages from the Bible (and Forbes) to justify what he's doing. When he lies he starts with, "Ye shall know the truth. And the truth shall set you free. Ye shall turn the truth into cash."

It's a real battle for the kid to stay good because the Devil is a hell of a salesman—and this boss is a hell of a Devil.

Next we have the *senior associate*—a lower echelon of predator.

His expertise lies in using people. He doesn't call it using, he calls it cooperation.

He teaches the value of knowing your terrain. A good soldier needs a sixth sense about land mines. The senior associate represents one of the land mines. Maybe a couple of them. Stepping on the senior associate leads to dire consequences.

Now according to the Yin and the Yang, whenever there's a bad guy, there's a good guy. It's called the Good Guy/Bad Guy Syndrome. Hence, we have the Boss's *rival*. A different kind of leader.

———

The Learning Process. The hero—*of the fashion moment*—generally goes on what we might call the typical hero's journey. ...

He goes through *three steps of enlightenment.* There are only three steps.

Early Enlightenment. He starts off loving and trusting the people around him. He feels in his heart that they're totally well-intentioned.

The boss says things to him like, "You have a good attitude. You haven't complained about anything. That's a quality we like around here. You're always smiling. We like that about you."

The kid feels he's doing great.

Towards the latter part of the first stage he starts to become aware that he's surrounded by backstabbing liars and cheats. And that they're all getting ahead.

He's shocked but takes it in stride.

He decides this is as a test of his ingenuity; he'll straighten it out from within.

He soon sees that turning things around is difficult. With each attempt to improve his prospects, he digs himself a deeper hole.

Second Level Enlightenment. A very simple step. He realizes that he's not meant to straighten it all out. So moving at a snappy pace we progress to ...

The Epiphany. Eureka! He started off with a whole set of beautiful hopes and dreams, and now he reaches a final stage of enlightenment in which they're all dashed to the ground; and his eyes are opened at last. ...

———

Scene

The Eureka Moment

An Office, Day

This was the office of *Sam Bartlett*, the chief executive officer. Perhaps you've heard of him? He'd recently been featured in several business magazines. He was the CEO and president of an upscale business, a high-level shop of *image experts.*

Sam was sitting at his mahogany desk, in his wood-panelled office, when he looked upward and outward.

"Scooter!" said Sam.

Scooter—a young heroic junior associate, came in.

"The report," said Sam, "wasn't on my desk at 9 a.m."

"I'm sorry, sir," said Scooter, "but I didn't have enough time to finish it."

"You had one hour," said Sam. "You got in at 8 a.m. Why didn't you have the report on my desk by 9 a.m.?"

"It takes more than an hour."

"How long does it take?"

"Five hours."

"Five hours is too long. It should only take one hour."

"But it physically takes five hours."

"We only had one hour."

"I know that, sir. That's why I wasn't able to finish on time."

"That's not acceptable."

"Sir, how should I get it all done in one hour?"

"Work smarter."

"I'm sorry I'm not following you sir. Let's say the positions were reversed. If it was your responsibility to get it done in one hour, how would you do it?"

"It wasn't my responsibility. It was yours. I needed it done in one hour. You're telling me you'd like to spend five hours on it. I can't agree to that."

"But, sir, do you have a solution?"

"No, I want the solution to come from you. Give me my options and I'll pick one."

"Well, if I go at top speed, stay completely focused and don't allow any interruptions, that's about the fastest I can go."

"If you go at that pace, how long does it take?"

"Five hours."

"Listen to this. In sex anything worth doing is worth doing slow but in business it's the opposite. Now it is conceivable that this can be done in an hour, isn't it? It's not like I'm asking you to bite off your own teeth. This is imaginable."

"It is."

"Then let's do it that way."

"Do you have any suggestions for things that I'm not doing which I could be doing?"

"No, I don't care how you go about it. I'm only interested in achieving the result. I'm not interested in excuses why things can't be done the way I need them done. When I tell you I want something to happen, I want it to become reality. You're looking at me like you're confused. Does what I'm saying to you make sense?"

"Absolutely."

"If there's anything you don't understand, ask me and I'll clear it up for you."

"No, I understand what you're saying."

"Great. Now how long is this report going to take from now on?"

"Five hours."

Sam put an arm around Scooter's shoulder and patted him warmly. Scooter smiled.

Sam lead them to the couch and they both sat down.

"Scooter, this is getting so out of hand. I want you to understand what I'm doing. I'm trying to teach you so that by working with me, you become a better person. I consider every person who works for me not only an employee but also a student. I'm teaching you to look for answers. After all that is what we sell here—answers. Clients come to us with questions and we give them answers. This is an exercise in looking for an answer. The question is how do we resolve this? Do you have the answer?"

"No."

"Do you want me to give you one?"

"Please."

"The answer is—*You're fired.* Thank you for all your help and good-bye."

Sam was used to firing people and did it with great indifference. He immediately walked toward his desk to call personnel for a replacement. Scooter leapt at Sam, landed on the floor, and grabbed onto Sam's leg.

"Oh God, no please!"

"I'm sorry," said Sam. "This hurts me. I don't make a big show of emotion, but it doesn't mean I'm not suffering."

Sam pulled his leg free. Scooter remained on the floor from where he pleaded with Sam and tugged at his jacket sleeve.

"I have worked so hard," said Scooter. "Please reconsider."

"Please don't make this difficult for me. It's not easy to fire someone, especially when they're on their knees begging."

"You do feel that I'm intelligent, devoted, and a hard worker?"

"Of course. This has nothing to do with that."

"Then can you write me a letter of recommendation?"

"It's very difficult for me to write a recommendation for someone I've just fired."

"After all I've done for you I feel that you should at least help me in some small way."

"I understand where your feeling is coming from. But if you would please do this in an expedient manner I would appreciate it. I'll have payroll cut a final check for you and two weeks severance pay. That'll be ready in an hour or two. Now isn't that fair? Two weeks pay for no work."

"Very fair. "

Sam now relaxed and became casual.

"Now if you'll excuse me forever I'm going to call personnel and start looking for a replacement."

Act One

Early Enlightenment

The Next, New Hero—Cometh Boldly

It was a fine beautiful day in the big city. The skyscrapers looked so lovely set against the clear blue sky.

The Office Tower and Courtyard, Day

A crowd of office workers went happily on their way to work.
   What a lovely place to work, thought Jack Flynn.
   He broke away from the flowing crowd.
   Then Jack Flynn crossed the courtyard and entered the tower's lobby.

Sam's Office, Day

Jack and Sam's senior associate—*Ray Raymour*—stepped through the doorway.
   Sam was smiling warmly at Jack, as he moved to shake his hand.
   Ray made the introductions. "Sam Bartlett this is *Jack Flynn*. Jack this is Sam."
   "Good to meet you," said Sam. "Make yourself comfortable."
   Ray handed Sam a resume. Then Jack and Ray took a seat on the couch.
   Sam studied Jack's resume. "Forgive me. I haven't had a chance to do this."
   Sam read the resume while Jack, and Ray, waited on.
   Sam looked up at Jack.
   "I see by your resume that you've never worked for a company like ours. You have no experience in our industry whatsoever."
   Sam looked at Ray.
   Jack held still.
   "Do you know what we do here?" asked Sam.
   "I could always use more explanation."

"We are a school for experts. We show people how to come on like an expert. And you don't really have to be an expert to do that. You see experts all over the place. Have you ever asked yourself what do they really know? Of course not; because they come across like experts. You have to do what I'm doing now. I sound like an expert, don't I?"

"You do."

"Now please tell me why I should hire you and I want you to sound like an expert."

"I may not have the experience, ... but I, uhm, am ... a-uhm ..."

"Go on."

"I guess the only thing I have to offer you over other people is that I'm willing to run longer and faster than them. I make your life easier. I do a lot more. For the same money. I don't want a penny more."

"I see."

"I wouldn't worry about the resume. I have a lot of experience I didn't put on there. If you want, I can fix you one that you'll like. Besides in my case the person is even better than the resume. I make the job my life. I'm a very hard worker. I would get totally involved in *our* job. I don't need much sleep. I can start earlier than most people. And work later. I don't take breaks. I come in at 4. Stay till 11. Do you know how much I could learn in a day like that? There's no end. The more hours I work, the more I learn. I know I'm the man you're looking for. There is no one better."

Sam liked what he heard.

"Okay, that's the answer—"

"—It would be hard for anybody to match me—"

"—Let me stop you with a hot tip. Never keep talking after you make your point. People will think you're trying to understand what you just said."

Jack nodded.

"Let me tell you about how I operate. Then I want to learn more about you. My philosophy is simple—find the right people and keep them. When you have good people you can put work in their hands and forget about it."

Sam had a deep, true, soulful look in his eyes.

"This is a business that runs on people. If I had to walk away to-morrow and choose between taking all the bricks and mortar ... or taking the people. I would choose the people. People are the power in this business. Resources help us do the job—but what our clients experience is the people. On any given day, you can be bigger to your client than the entire organization. So for me, how I relate to my people determines whether I will succeed or not. And actually, this is where I pack a wallop. I'm very good with people. Let's take my last assistant, *Scooter*, who came to me with no experience. None. He didn't even know how to shine my boots. Some thought I was insane to hire him. I saw potential and developed it, to the point where he became an out-and-out star. Then he received an offer from the competition. I was floored. I said, 'Let me pay you more than them.' Money is never my main concern. But what's done is done. He had committed to them."

Sam was making up the facts as he went along.

"So I supported his decision. I told him any time you need a reference, come to me. Please. I said let's stay in touch—we're having lunch next week."

As Sam continued with his ridiculous self-aggrandizement, Jack listened with rapt attention—looking at Sam as if he had invented the light bulb.

Sam continued. "I'm easy to please. I'm just looking for someone I can train. I move you right up if you're not afraid of hard work."

The Hallway, Later

Sam and Jack stepped out of Sam's office. Sam's arm was on Jack's shoulder.

"Thank you for coming by. I'm going to make my decision in the next day or so."

Sam patted Jack on his back.

Jack walked off.

Ray and Sam watched Jack wait for the elevator in the distance.

"What do you think about him Sam?" asked Ray.

No response. Sam was thinking.

Ray said, "His brain plus four quarters would get him a dollar."

"Ray, if you knew your ass from a hole in the ground you'd talk a lot less."

"Right Sam. Very good point."

"You have to develop an eye for possibilities. If you haven't learned that from me then you haven't learned a goddamn thing."

"I agree completely, the Jack could work."

"How much was he told the job pays?"

"15,000 a year."

"Let's re-think that. There's no reason to throw a boatload of money at him. He's a good Jack. He'll take 14,000."

"What if he holds out for 15,000?"

"Tell him he'll get it in three months."

"What happens in three months?"

"Nothing. It's an expression like 'May your dreams come true.' He wants more money, you tell him, 'You'll get it in three months.' Then you don't have to give it to him."

The Offices, A Few Days Later

This was Jack's first day on the job.

Now Jack was a *systems thinker,* and he had gone into the office that first day determined to learn the systems of this place.

At the start of that morning, Ray and Jack were standing by Scooter's desk, which had not been touched since Scooter was fired. And it was a hell of a mess.

Jack was staring at the desk. It was littered with files and a wide range of papers.

"I think there's enough here to get you started," Ray said. "I need to get a memo out but then I'll be free to work with you."

"Okay. Great."

Ray returned to his own desk and absorbed himself in his work. Jack began sorting through the accumulated work. Then Jack looked around.

He noticed a large filing cabinet nearby.

Presently, Jack was carrying a large stack of files to the filing cabinet.

Now this filing cabinet was a massive thing. It was a large-double doored cabinet, and existed more in the sense of a large walk-in closet than a cabinet.

There seemed to be beams of *blue sky* in the cabinet.—He saw a light radiating from behind the doors. He felt himself being drawn in. What was this shining aura?

He opened the double doors. He stepped in. It was a lovely wash of light, and then he was flying through the sky.

He was standing poised. In a normal stance, but he was standing in the sky. Next to him were the slots, where you dropped the files into their appropriate positions.

He glanced up. He was entranced by this place.

There was something about standing in this filing cabinet that made him think of the great business impulses:

"Rise.

"Up, up and away.

"You can have what you desire.

"You can have it all.

"You can win.

"The sky's the limit."

Yes, he liked the feeling of blue sky opening on blue sky.

He felt it like a whisper in this place.

Though it's best not to get carried away, he thought. And he became practical. And industrious. He went back to his work.

Jack was a systems thinker.

He glanced through the files he had, and then the ones in the cabinet.

He looked at the binders and books in there.

There was something odd about this system and this place.

He began putting them into the sort.

Kate Greenway passed by outside the double doors. She paused and looked at him. Kate was a sweet, attractive young lady, who also worked in the associates area.

He looked up from within the *blue sky room* and smiled at her.

She smiled and continued to her desk where she went to work.

Jack couldn't take his eyes off her. He tried to return to the filing but his eyes traveled back to her.

Kate was sitting at her desk, sorting through paperwork.

She turned around and caught him staring at her.

He turned away.

She turned back to her own work.

Jack came out of the filing cabinet and approached her.

"Hi, you're *Kate Greenway?*"

"Right."

"I'm *Jack Flynn.*"

She smiled.

They shook hands.

"It's nice to meet you."

"Same here."

Then there was silence.

"I better get back to my filing."

He indicated the filing cabinet and then walked away. She stared after him.

Jack stood in the filing cabinet. He was dropping the files into their places.

But now something strange was happening—Kate was staring at him.

He did his level best to look graceful. He picked up his pace.

And now Kate was getting up and approaching him. She entered the small cabinet and paused beside him. Very close to him. He could smell her, and she had such a lovely scent. Then he looked into her eyes. Oh, so lovely.

She spoke to him in a whisper.

"You're doing great work."

"Thanks."

"But you're putting them in wrong."

"I'm putting them in alphabetical order."

"In the wrong cabinet. They belong there."

She showed him that there was a larger walk-in filing cabinet on the far side of the associates area. That was *The Lord Consulting Group* filing cabinet.

It had a reddish, purple, orange glow, with hints of yellow, radiating in streams from below the door. He opened it and gazed in. "Ah, I see."

"Yes," she said, "only the blue files go in the *blue sky room*. All the others go here."

"Oh," he said. "Thank you."

"You're very welcome," she said and left.

The original file colors were red, purple, orange and yellow. They now matched this room and it all made sense.

He stepped back and looked at the overall associates area. There was a red and purple wall with *The Lord Consulting Group* cabinet. And on the other side was the light, streaming, baby-blue wall with *The Blue Sky Company* cabinet.

In between there was a majestic picture window. Down below you could see clouds, and below the clouds, the streets of the city.

Jack considered the feelings in the filing cabinets, which were really on the level of rooms with distinct personalities.

The Lord Consulting Group room had a molding, thick feel—a solidity.

The Blue Sky room had a light and easy feel—as if you were floating free.

An interesting contrast, he thought.

Yes, he was a systems thinker, and found new systems exciting.

"Excuse me Ray," said Jack.

"You need me?"

"I'm confused about how these files are set up."

"I can clear it up for you. Our company is made up of two bodies—one large, the other small. The large one is *The Lord Consulting Group*. It's named after the person who started this business."

"Who is he?"

"She—*Lara Lord* is her name. A sharp woman. I'll show you the write-up they did of her in *'Fortune.'* She's absolutely brilliant. Anyway, the second entity is a small organization—*The Blue Sky Company.*"

"Why two different ..."

"First off, do you understand what we do here?"

"We're a school for experts."

"Right. We have all kinds of clients: manufacturing, public affairs and so on. Most people out there want to be experts and all the others want to hire experts. Now you can't make yourself an expert, you need us. We go to companies and find out what they need. Then we tell them, *'No—what you need is an expert.'* Then we sell you to them. Now we have two types of clients, very big clients and very small clients. The Lord Consulting Group is for the big jobs and The Blue Sky Company is for the small ones. I don't have to go on I'm sure, you see how that works?"

"Why not one company for everything?"

"Well that gets into other issues."

"It seems like the easiest thing would be for it all to go under one name."

"You really don't understand branding, do you?"

"Oh no, I get it. So all the accounts are divided into larger and smaller transactions."

"It's one facet of a process."

"You said Lara Lord started this company. Does she own it? "

"No, there is no one owner. This company is owned by a bigger company. Lara works for that bigger company."

"Who owns the company that owns our company?"

"Boy the questions just keep coming don't they? That's a pretty good one."

Ray left it at that. He went back to his desk and resumed his work.

Jack was just standing where they left off, wondering if their conversation was over.

Ray said, over his shoulder, "Have I cleared up a few things for you?"

"Thanks."

"Anytime. One for all and all for one. Right?"

Across from the Building's Motorcourt, Day

Sam and Jack were standing across from the motorcourt.

It was like a great businessman's garden.

Once you crossed the car bay, there was a great big open expanse. The outer area was fenced in by great trellises. Within there was a field and garden, and fountains.

Sam took a deep breath as if he was suddenly in the Swiss Alps. Jack also took in a calming breath.

Sam put his arm around Jack's shoulder.

"Always remain relaxed. If I'm successful in my training with you, you'll learn to operate without tension. You'll learn to release in the neck, the back, the shoulders. You don't need tension to get work done. Tension is the enemy. I work completely without any tension whatsoever."

Sam brought his feet together, kept his legs straight, bent over and grabbed his toes. He stayed in this position as he continued talking.

Jack followed Sam's lead.

"What's your morning been like?"

"Ray showed me my desk and I cleared away the files, so Ray explained how the company is broken down."

Sam got up.

"What did he say?"

"That the accounts are divided into two groups—large and small."

"Good."

"Why don't we just have all the accounts under one banner?"

"There is a company that owns our company and that company is run by a woman named Lara Lord. She's making a fortune by us. And her purse is running very deep nowadays. That's very good for us. The reason I'm telling you this is because I want you to keep something in mind. When the people at the top do very well, the ones down below can make out too."

Jack looked at Sam.

"Can I ask you another question?"

"Never be afraid to ask me anything."

"Our company is owned by a bigger company ..."

"Right."

"... And then that bigger company is owned by what?"

"A financial group."

"Who owns the financial group?"

"Who cares? Does it have any effect on your life whatsoever?"

"No."

"Don't you worry Jack. You will learn plenty from me. I'm going to tell you a few things over the next few days that will have you thinking like a true businessman. And then you won't be asking me these types of questions. You'll learn about efficiency which means getting the most done in the least amount of time. These questions take up unnecessary time. ... We should head back up."

They walked away.

"Remember—always stay loose."

The Offices, That Night

Jack was sitting at his desk. He had stayed to familiarize himself with the company's files.

He could hear voices drifting faintly out of Speed's. Speed was another manager in the company. He was Kate's boss and he was giving her a pep talk.

Jack rose from his chair and walked towards Speed's office. He would love to join them but he was afraid to interrupt. After some anxious deliberation, Jack decided against interrupting, and walked back to his desk. Then he changed his mind and turned back towards Speed's office.

While he was doing this, in the background he could hear Speed saying:

"We build *celebrity*. We super-charge a name. We build name equity. Equity is a process. Equity is performance based. There's no raw equity in a name. You need celebrity over time. Even the advertising geniuses are admitting they can't do what we do. We're innovators—over time, we've tried one of everything. We're pioneering the craft of building buzz. The techniques are something we're inventing here. And the business world is interested in investing in them."

Jack mustered up his courage and darted into the doorway.

"Hi," he said.

Speed's Office

Kate and Speed were huddled over some paperwork. Kate was sitting in an armchair. Speed was sitting on the floor. They didn't behave formally with one another.

"Hi Jack," said Kate.

"How are you?" asked Speed.

"I'm not bothered, I hope."

"I'm sorry. I'm not following you."

"I was just working at my desk and thought I'd say—but you're obvioubly viby—I mean visibly vizy—err, busy."

"I'm Denny 'Speed' Dalton. All my friends calls me Speed. I didn't catch your name."

Jack casually entered Speed's office with the air of a man who always knew what he was doing.

"Jack."

"I've got it now. Jack, huh. Nice. I like it. It hits you fast. That's good."

Speed was a man who exuded confidence. He did everything without hesitation. He'd been in the business for years, during which he'd seen and done everything.

Speed continued. "I'm going to have to talk and run here. I hate to do it. But I'm going to be off like a shot in less than no time. But quick as a wink, let me share what I was explaining to Kate."

As Speed delivered his monologue lickety-split, he also hurriedly gathered some work and headed for the door.

Speed continued again. "Here's our scene. ... We're in the business of lifestyle communications. Trends bubble up and then we bring them into the mainstream. I'll tell you, this is a hip, hot shop. And we're growing. And we have the latitude to create our own culture, our own new business initiatives. It's been sanctioned by the top. You're going to see how we connect the dots and get strategic—then, how it all comes to life on the streets."

Kate caught Jack's gaze and smiled warmly.

"Of course," Speed said, "it calls for extreme service. We're on all the time. We work hard all the time. There has to be a relentlessness to make sure it will all work. Maybe that's not the best way to put it. I'm still playing with the words. But it's because I'm trying to package what we do.

"We're a lifestyle company.

"The way an operation like this works is that everyone has to be busy and billable all the time. But we have to help each other.

"We have to get you to where you want to be in all the skills. And move you along the path to righteousness and success."

He laughed and then became serious again.

"I guess I shouldn't have a talk like this on the fly. But I'll throw you the pieces now. We'll connect them later. The concept is this: we provide the playing field, the tools—our people craft their own job descriptions.

"You start with entry-level apprentice—we gauge your character, you learn the craft. In leaps and bounds, you move onto the journeyman stage—with decreasing reliance on supervisors while increasing your supervisory skills—you start to aim yourself, until you become a teacher, a mentor yourself. Until you can counsel the client on anything.

"We create a creative environment. Our environment should engender nice people."

Speed moved into the doorway.

"We're defining a workplace that serves its people. And I don't want to skip over this part of it, it's very meaningful. I know I'm firing on all cylinders here but this stuff is important to say. We want to make sure caring and understanding are at least the norm. And we try to provide training and information modules. The training thing is hopefully going to be a real benefit. We're also going to offer Get-Out-Of-Jail-Free Cards, Spot Bonuses, and a Local Office Bonus Pool. But more about that later. I'm late for another meeting, so go I swifter than the wind.

"But don't you two rush out. Stay. My office is your office. Mi casa es su casa!"

And with that, Speed walked out the door. He continued yelling though. He was a marvelous madman. He was yelling Spanish to no one in particular as his voice faded away:

"Mi officina es su officina! Mi amigo es su amigo! Mi esposa es su esposa!"

Jack and Kate were sitting on opposite ends of the couch.

Their eyes met.

Jack started to rise from the couch.

Jack said, "Maybe I should beat a path back to my kingdom."

"No, stay," said Kate.

Jack sat back down, but a little closer to her on the couch.

Jack said, "Speed seems like the kind of guy that lines things up and lays them flat. He's so ..."

Jack made an expansive gesture with his arms.

Jack continued. "But not too much. He keeps it on the down-low. I think that's the way you have to be. You have to keep keeping it down."

Jack imitated some of Speed's delivery over the next few lines. And he was surprisingly good at capturing the guy's essence.

"He's got a bit of this ...

Jack imitated Speed's gestures.

"... And he's swinging a groove in this direction too ..."

Jack imitated his expressions.

"He's a fiddler calling a tune and you want to sing right along."

"Yes, he is," Kate said. "That's him exactly."

Jack put his hand on the back of the couch.

She glanced at the arm.

He brought his arm back and put it in his lap.

"What do you think of Sam?" asked Kate.

"Oh well, I've been to a lot of places and met a lot of people. I've been to a show at the convention center, I've been to a picnic, I've even been to a rodeo but I never met anybody like him. He shoots from the hip and he doesn't miss a trick. He fires you up and he sets you on the path."

"I hope you don't blush at compliments—words come out of your mouth in a very sincere way. You are out-and-out real. Way real."

"Wow, as far as saying things goes, that's like shooting me a breeze straight out of Coolsville. I mean holy act of Congress, thanks."

Jack continued. "Listen I know we only just met but when something seems right I'm not afraid to act on it right away. I've been thinking about what it would be like to go out for drinks with you some time. And it seems like it would be a lot of fun."

He took a deep breath.

She seemed bewildered. It was hard to read her reaction.

Jack said, "I shouldn't have said that. Oh good God, forgive me."

He backed to the other side of the couch.

"Boy did I pour it on and I don't blame you for reacting the way you did. I meant to say I think you're someone special and I really have strong feelings for you—"

He got on his feet and backed out of the office.

Jack said, "Holy shit—I mean, oh my God. I'm so sorry. I need to go kick myself some, put myself to bed with a shovel and then start off right with you tomorrow."

He exited the office but in the wrong direction—he had disappeared to the right.

A beat and then—he walked past he doorway heading left, pretending he meant to do that. He disappeared.

Kate said, "Wait. I didn't say anything."

Jack stepped into the doorway, looking at Kate's feet instead of her face.

Jack said, "Don't feel bad."

"How did you figure out that I'm attracted to you?"

His jaw dropped but he quickly recovered.

"Oh, I don't really want to say."

He smiled assuredly and put out his arm to lean against the doorway —like a 'Gentleman's Quarterly' cover boy. He was going to convince her there were methods to his madness.

But he was so concerned with being cool that he missed the wall and fell out of her visual frame.

Kate—reacted to a loud thud.

Jack leapt to his feet, pretending nothing had happened. He propped himself against the doorframe without any further difficulty.

Kate said, "Are you okay?"

"Oh sure, I've had worse falls than that."

Kate rose from the couch and walked over to Jack.

"You're clever, a Devil with the face of a Buddha ... pretending that you didn't know I was attracted to you. I wouldn't say no. But how can I say yes? We can't get involved. We're working in the same office. It could get complicated."

"I wouldn't talk you into anything that isn't right for you?"

"Okay. Friends then?"

He put out his hand for her to shake.

"Friends."

They shook.

The Office, Several Days Later

Ray and Jack were standing together.

Jack's appearance was changing. He was dressing better and his hair was more neatly groomed.

Sam came out of his office. "Ray. What ever happened to *Mr. Kalbert Kishkowitz?* I thought we had a meeting.

"Kalbert Kishkowitz? Not that I remember."

"Well," said Sam, "maybe you better set up an appointment. That man is sitting on a million-dollar piece of business."

"A million in fee?" said Ray.

"Maybe more."

Sam walked back to his office.

Ray plucked a card from his desk and walked over to Jack. "Jack, I need you to interface with this guy, Kalbert Kishkowitz. Set an appointment for him with Sam. But I don't want you to spend too much time on it. You need to be decisive and you need to be fast. We have a lot to do. I want to start getting you up to speed."

Jack dialed the number.

"Mr. Kishkowitz … is this Mr. Kalbert Kishkowitz?"

Kishkowitz said, "Do I have to shove a bat up someone's asshole to get some business done? Ray promised to call. When? Yesterday!"

Jack said, "I apologize for the delay sir."

"Yeah right. Let's have this fucking meeting next Wednesday?"

"I'm sorry sir but Sam's booked up on Wednesday and Thursday next week."

"You're shitting me. Ray said I could meet with him before the board of directors meeting."

"Pardon me sir. Can I put you on hold for a second?"

"Sure take your time. It's only costing me money."

"Thank you sir. It'll just take one second."

He put Kishkowitz on hold.

"Ray. He says that you were already setting up a meeting."

"Oh yeah, that Kalbert Kishkowitz. That's right. With a name like that, who can remember the man? ... Listen, that's really important. I even wrote that down so I wouldn't forget. Hmm, I don't know what I did with that piece of paper. Well, these things happen. Fortunately, we can fix it fast. This is a perfect example of what I've been talking about. Something comes up ... boom, you take responsibility. You make the decision and you complete the action. And you move on."

Jack picked up the phone and he overheard Kishkowitz make a remark to someone in his office. "Can you believe this? Some limp dick from business school putting me on hold. Last week it was, 'Do you want fries with that?' Now he's putting me on hold. I thought Sam was running a tight ship. This is unreal."

"Excuse me sir. I'm back."

"Hallelujah. Look, is his majesty available on the fifth? If it goes past the fifth my good friend Sam can canvass another client and kiss my ass."

"Let me check."

Jack put his hand on the receiver and turned to Ray. In the earpiece Kishkowitz could be heard carrying on in his office. "... Guys like this, you want to fuck their wives. ..."

"Ray," Jack said, "the only time he can meet is on the fifth."

"What's your recommendation?" Ray asked.

"Well, I would say the fifth. But Ray it seems like we have to set it in stone. On the fifth right?"

"Jack, what do you say you move on your one and only option. We're into a crisis here. You're going to piss Curlowitz off. Besides, we have more important things to get done today."

Jack spoke into the phone. "Okay sir. We can definitely do it on the fifth."

"Thank you. You're so kind."

"Come hell or high water, you will see Sam on the fifth. Thanks."

Jack hung up the phone.

Sam came out of his office. "I'm leaving now. You have the copies?"

Jack grabbed a stack of copies and handed them to Sam, who grabbed them without even noticing who was handing them to him. "Thanks Ray."

"No problem," said Ray.

Sam left. Jack walked back to his desk.

Ray picked up a hard copy of Sam's calendar.

Ray looked at it startled. "Awww! Argghhh! God damn!"

Ray brought the calendar over to Jack.

"Looks like you screwed up," Ray said.

"What do you mean?"

"You set the meeting with Kishkowitz while Sam's supposed to be on vacation."

"What?"

"He'll have to cut his vacation in half to get here for the meeting. You shouldn't have done this."

"Ray I asked you first."

"I thought you checked his calendar."

"How could I do that? You keep the calendar on your desk—and you write all these notes in it in your handwriting that I can't read."

"And that was too far for you to walk? You can't be lazy in this business."

The Office, the Next Morning

Jack and Kate were standing together, talking softly and discreetly about the Kishkowitz problem. Ray was listening nearby.

"I have to tell Sam," said Jack. "What's the best way to do that?"

Ray came into it then. "We've got to help him Kate. Sam is going to be a monster about this."

Kate said, "I don't see anything we can do but I'm sure Jack appreciates your concern."

"If only I could have prevented this," said Ray.

Kate doesn't realize this is Ray's fault.

At that moment Sam appeared. He was in a great mood, smiling from ear to ear. "Hello all." He waved to them and darted into his office.

Ray said, "I'll go in there and explain it. Let me handle it."

"He should get it from me," said Jack.

"No, I was a part of it. I'll smooth things out. I've worked for him a long time. I know how to talk to him."

Sam's Office

Ray was sitting across from Sam and said, "I want to talk to you about this new kid. He's turning into a problem."

"Ray, let's get one thing straight—there is no such thing as a problem; just an issue. Occasionally a concern or a debate. Never a problem."

"I'll strike it from my vocabulary."

"No feel free to use it—when you describe the competition. If they suffer from anything that cripples their business and we are immune to it—that's a problem. When it affects us it becomes an issue."

"I always learn so much from you."

"Of course. Now what did you want to discuss?"

"It's about this new Jack. Now don't get me wrong. I like him. He's a good guy. But do you know that I have to help him with everything. And I'm a busy guy. I don't have time to do his work. But I'm stuck because he keeps making mistakes. Did he tell you what he did yesterday? Listen to this one. We're scheduling a meeting and I specifically told him, 'Make sure you plan around Sam's vacation. Check the calendar,' I said. My last words. I leave the office. I've got a number of clients to meet. I come back within the hour. Sam, he has scheduled a meeting and an important meeting I might add with you on Wednesday while you're supposed to be on vacation after me specifically saying, 'Make sure you plan around Sam's schedule.' So we're stuck. I don't know what we're going to do Sam. We're stuck."

"We're stuck?"

"We're in a situation where you're on vacation and we need for you to meet with Kishkowitz … the million in fee. Wednesday the fifth. Right in the middle."

"Bring the Jack in. Call the Jack in here."

"I don't think that's necessary Sam. I think under the circmstances I could rearrange my schedule a little bit."

"Send the Jack in here."

"I think I sent him out. He shouldn't be all that long Sam."

"Go get him."

"Sam I thought we could just straighten this right out and arrange something whereby we could have you have the meeting. I would change my schedule around and accommodate yours. Just sort it out right now."

"Send the Jack in. Ray. Send the fucking Jack in!"

Jack's Desk

Ray walked over to Jack.

"Sam wants to see you. Be careful. He's in a terrible mood. Who knows what's gotten into him."

Sam's Office

Sam was sitting calmly at his desk as Jack walked in.

"I'm very sorry about this," Jack said.

"Please close the door."

"I'd love to explain what happened."

"Have a seat."

"Thank you. Sam please let me tell you how this happened so you can judge the wisdom of what I did."

"I'm going to give you two weeks severance pay." Sam looked Jack directly in the eye and waited for a response. He got nothing. Jack didn't reveal what he was thinking. "I'll have a check cut and you should be free to apply 'your wisdom' in a new capacity within an hour."

"Sam, I know my mistake hurts you and if you have to fire me then I understand."

Sam couldn't believe this.

Jack continued. "It's your decision?"

Sam looked at him, ... and then said, "I'll give you an extra week of severance pay."

Jack said, "And we'll stay friends, I hope."

Sam looked at him.

The Hallway, At the Same Time

Kate went barreling into Speed's office.

She closed the door.

An instant later Speed came dashing out of his office, heading towards Sam's.

Sam's Office

Sam and Jack were interrupted by a knock at the door.

Sam said, in a sweet, mild voice, "Who is it?"

From outside the door a voice said, "It's Speed. Can I talk with you?"

Speed entered the office before Sam could respond.

"Speed, let's talk later. I'm in the thick of things with Jack."

"He's taking the blame for my screw-up. I told him to book you with Kishkowitz on the fifth."

Sam froze. He took it in. And his attitude instantly changed to very friendly.

"You don't say. Well don't sweat it Speed. We all make mistakes. It's not a tragedy."

He turned to Jack. "We don't need to discuss this issue any further. Let's get back to work, what do you say?"

Apparently, the matter was dismissed. Jack and Speed turned to leave.

"Speed since this is now your issue, I presume you'll be meeting with

Kishkowitz instead of me."

"Of course Sam."

The Hallway

Jack said to Speed, "Thank you so much."

Speed said, "A little advice—whenever there comes a time for telling an unpleasant truth, figure out how to say it, imagine yourself saying it, and then, unless you're absolutely sure it's going to shoot you into a better position, don't say it. The truth is lethal, even in small doses."

The Office, Late that Night

Jack and Kate were the only two people in the office. Kate was at her desk assembling kits. There were stacks of paper everywhere. Jack walked over to help her.

"I hope this whatchyamacallit you've got to *do*,

"Is a thingamudoo that can be done by *two.*" he said.

Kate looked at him, "I'm okay. But I love you for asking."

"I'd truly love to STAY.

"If you had something that had to be DONE,

"And it could only be done by ONE,

"Then there'd be nothing more to SAY.

"But when you've got something like this to DO,

"I'd be so happy to be doing it with YOU."

He grabbed a sheet.

She said, "Then that's what we'll do.

"We'll go at it as two." And she smiled.

They began working in unison.

"How do you feel about what happened today?" she asked.

"I think thoroughness was the lesson. I need to be thorough, through thick and thin, for better or for worse, in good times and in bad, until death do me part. I let him down and I had another think coming."

"You made a mistake; learning is making mistakes."

"He gets worked up, but it's out of worry for the company. When you get to the top, you go at it alone. And there's a lot at the top that can eat away at a body."

"Let me help you out here," she said. "When people get to the top, a lot of times they go off on a power trip. I think that's what's happening here. I think you two are playing a game and neither one of you sees it. Think about this: How can people do bad things to other people and not feel guilty later? Nobody ever thinks of himself as a villain; evil people never think of themselves as evil people; so how can someone justify victimizing other people?"

She stopped and waited for him to take it in and then continued. "He has to find flaws in the victim."

This insight into human behavior came as something very helpful to Jack. "The victim has to deserve being a victim."

"Right. If you murder an old woman for her money and you get caught, and the police ask you, 'Why did you murder that woman?' If you're really evil, you don't say, 'Because I wanted her money.' You say, 'Because she was old and dying anyway. Because she hated me. Because she beat her dog.'"

"It's not why I deserved it, but why did it mean so much to him?"

Jack sprang away and marched across the room. His blood was running hot and his breath was coming quickly.

"Exactly why are the accounts divided into *The Lord Consulting Group* and *The Blue Sky Company*?"

"Money," said Kate, "tends to pile up in mountains. Any time you see someone taking money across a valley. You have to wonder from what mountain to what mountain is he taking it. You're not going to find *Lara Lord* at the top of the *Blue-Sky-Company mountain*.

"No? Who's mountain is it? ...That only leaves Sam."

She looked at him. "Now you've got a fix on it."

"Let me get this straight. Sam is stealing money from the company? Is he crazy?"

"Of course he's crazy. Everybody in the business world is crazy. You haven't noticed that yet?"

"Wait a second, you mean to tell me the business world is full of crazy people?"

"Yes."

"I hadn't thought of it that way. Are you crazy?"

"Yes."

"You don't look crazy."

"Thank you."

"And he's crazy."

"Yes."

"Am I crazy?"

"No. You're not. But you better get crazy if you want to fly the friendly skies. If they find out you're not crazy, they blow you out of the sky and turn you to dust."

Jack was pulsing with anger.

Kate was being infected by his energy.

"What happened to Sam's last assistant?" he asked.

"He fired him."

"Why?—No, don't tell me. I'll invent the reason."

"Any one would fit."

"Was he crazy?"

"Of course not, if he was crazy, he wouldn't have gotten fired. ... If you can't get crazy, then act a little crazy. Just so that they're convinced you're crazy. Going with the flow, that's the name of the game."

He pulled away from her.

Now he was moving about the room very swiftly. He moved into a stream of gliding rotations. The way a whirlwind does.

Kate looked at him.

And he was changing before her eyes.

He aged years. He grew from a slight, mild-mannered Jack to a tall, sinewy, muscle-bound adult hulk.

He pounced onto the floor, like a businessman seizing opportunity.

He took one arm, and in sweeping line, arched a fist above his head and brought it into a streaking pound onto the floor. ... He looked like the legendary Norse God of Thunder—Thor, oh mighty Thor—pounding his hammer into the ground and creating lightning all around.

He was suddenly electric and crackling with energy. That was how he looked—to Kate's beguiled eyes.

Now he rose, slowly, smoothly, sleekly, with tremendous grace. He reached his arms out into the air. He took up great space. And he turned to Kate—As he came out of his maelstrom what he said to her was:

"No, I can't do crazy, Kate.

"Crazy is not my way.

"The world has gone mad today.

"And good is black today,

"And bad is white today,

"And day is dark today,

"And night is light today,

"Crazy is not my way,

"But at long last, I've arrived at where I should be.

"Thank you. Now straight is the gate and narrow is my way."

He took a few graceful, gliding steps toward Sam's office, threw his arm into the air, arched it in a direction outward, and in a newfound voice of fire exclaimed—

"I am standing on the warpath now, baby! And I'm going to blow through him, because I'm shooting to the top and nobody's going to stop me!

Jack's blood was boiling. He couldn't remain still.

He prowled about, but there was nowhere to go. He turned around to face Kate. And now with his blood running hot, and this gorgeous woman standing within arm's reach, he lost every thought of Sam—

And *he kissed Kate.*

He kissed her mightily.

He kissed her with great tenderness.

He kissed her for a long time.

She enjoyed it.

They pulled apart and neither knew what to expect next.

Then they exploded into a tempest of kisses and caresses.

Kate said, "We can't go off the deep end here."

She pulled away from his embrace.

"We can't do this? We shouldn't."

She caressed his cheek.

She said, "Thank you. Let's just do the work and not think of how we feel until we calm down."

They separated. She went back to assembling the kits. He joined her.

Jack said, "Okay. I'm not thinking about it. How about you?"

She said, "Neither am hot—I mean it's hot in here isn't it?"

"It's a steambath."

"Neither of us wants to get in over our heads. Don't you think? I mean is it just me because I don't want to put words in your mouth."

"You don't want to say what I'm not thinking."

"Let's talk about something else."

"Throw me a subject," he said.

"Business," she said.

"Management," he said.

"Who's on top—err, I mean what's going on at the top," she said.

He picked it up. "Too much of a focus on short-term profit at the expense of long term growth."

She jumped into it. "That's it. We'll talk trends—the problems with business today."

"It's all the consolidations," he said.

"All the mergers," she said.

Whoa—they halted talking there.

Now there was nothing but silence. They continued assembling the kits.

Act Two

Middle Enlightenment

Sam's Office, the Next Day

Sam and Ray entered.

Sam said, "You've been doing fantastic work lately."

"Thank you Sam."

"First rate. Absolutely first rate. No question of that."

Sam's tone suddenly turned somber.

"We've been approached to pitch a major deal for General Developers—GD."

"We're going to work with GD! Wow! ... Isn't that good news?"

"Marvelous news. I look forward to the challenge. ... We're going to make a proposal for a complete reorganization, a total overhaul for them. We'll be presenting that in ten days. And you're going to be my number one at the presentation. You'll give them the works.—That's in ten days."

Ray became alarmed—Ray became *very* alarmed.

"With everything we have going, that's tight," Ray said.

Sam fired back immediately, "I don't appreciate that kind of language Ray. Don't fuck with me today Ray! I'm not in the mood for this! What do you think this is? *'Fuck with Sam Day'*?"

Ray swallowed hard.

"I'm sorry Sam. I lost my mind for a moment. I don't know what happened there. I can't explain it."

"How many hours do you sleep a night?"

"About seven."

"There's your problem. You're oversleeping. They've done studies on this. Don't be a victim of sleep."

Sam continued. "That's why you're so sluggish. This business requires speed. That's part of the training here. I've noticed your work has been slowing down over the past few weeks. That's why I keep coffee in that kitchen. We shouldn't be having these kinds of problems. I didn't address it, and I may be the one at fault there, but now it's time to face the issue head-on. It's going to be a strain on all of us. But we've got a good team in place and we'll show them what we can do when we fire off our guns."

"I learn so much from you Sam."

"That's the spirit. Now here's another issue. My first vacation day was supposed to be tomorrow."

"Oh, I'm really sorry. I know you were looking forward to this vacation."

"Thank you. But the only sensible thing to do under the circumstances is to go ahead and take my vacation."

"What?"

"This is a big job. It's important that I pace myself."

The Offices, Later

Sam and Ray were going over the new business pitch.

Jack entered with two cups of coffee and served them to Sam and Ray.

"Did you remember to put sugar in mine?"

"Yes I did. Would you like to look at the dessert tray?"

Sam scowled.

"Look at me. Do I look like I eat dessert in the afternoon? What the fuck is the matter with you?"

Jack asked, "Sam, do you think I'd be able to work on this project?"

Sam looked at Jack. "Don't be ridiculous." He moved on to serious busines. "Do you know where the dry cleaners is?"

He handeds Jack a dry cleaning ticket.

Jack said, "The one that's two blocks up?"

Sam said, "You go out the front lobby, then travel two blocks."

Jack was attentive—and pretended he need these valuable walking instructions.

Ray interjected, "Sam, involving Jack could be an option."

"We can't take him away from his duties."

Jack said, "My accounts are on schedule. As for the special projects—I could work those out. Like maybe pick up your dry cleaning during my lunch break."

"Then that's what I'm going to have you do. Have a seat," Sam said.

Presently

Jack was sitting in one of Sam's armchairs. He was listening attentively to Sam, who was moving about.

Sam was talking directly to Ray.

"They've provided us with a dossier."

Sam rose from his chair and approached Ray with the *dossier* about the prospective client. He took a position beside Ray and began leafing through it.

Jack happened to be on the other side. He got up and crossed to a position behind Ray and Sam, so that he might peer over their shoulders.

Sam handed Ray a card.

"This is the contact person. During my absence, she can direct you."

Ray dropped the dossier into Jack's hands. And then very carefully grouped the card with a *golden notebook* (that he carried about the office).

The sleek, modern *golden notebook* was an interesting attribute and companion object in Ray's act.

Ray's notebook was in a jacket of true gold. Inside was a folio of Ray Raymour's thoughts, such as they were.

Ray carried this golden notebook about proudly.

He was just an old-fashioned genius. He did the hard work of thinking. Then put the thoughts in his notebook.

That's how it worked with him. ... He saw himself as brilliant. And he was sure he was. ... In every way. ... That's what he knew. And it felt good to know it. ... He was also constantly letting others feel it—nearby others such as Jack Flynn and Kate Greenway. *Oh lovely Kate,* he thought to himself from time to time. One day they would get to know each other better, he thought.

The Offices, the Next Day

Sam's office was empty and the lights were out.

Nearby Ray's voice was bouncing off the walls.

"Ohhh! Arghhh! Ahhhhh! This is going to be a lot of work. You have no idea how much."

The Associate Desks

Ray and Jack were each sitting at their desks.

Ray said to Jack, "I really appreciate your support."

"I'm ready to start."

"All right Jack."

Jack leapt eagerly out of his seat.

Ray lifted a stack of files from his desk and handed it to Jack.

Then Ray brought over several stacks of files and dropped them all on Jack's desk.

"Excuse me Ray. Aren't these your accounts?"

"Of course."

"I thought I was going to be helping you with the pitch."

"You are. But you can't build a house without a floorplan. ... You need a floor plan. ... And I've got to tell you it's going to be tough. But I'll do fine I'm sure. In the meantime, you can help me best by tackling lower priority issues."

The phone rang.

Ray grabbed his *golden notebook* and a pencil. He didn't answer the phone, even though Ray was closer to the phone.

Jack stepped closer to the desk and glanced at the phone.

"That's your line Ray."

"Could you do take a message?"

Ray didn't wait for a response. He walked away and disappeared into Sam's office. Jack picked up the phone.

"Hello ..."

Sam's Office

Ray seated himself in Sam's chair. He opened the dossier and began composing his pitch in his *golden notebook*.

Jack appeared in the doorway and asked, "Can I help you in any way?"

"I wish you could but this is a little too complicated for you. Having said that, I would go on to say that I really appreciate the support you're giving me—"

The phone rang in the background.

"—by handling some of the trivialities while I—shouldn't you be getting that?"

Jack walked off to answer the phone.

Later

Ray was reviewing notes that he'd written into his *golden notebook*.

He was also, at the same time, standing in the middle of Sam's office casually dancing to some soft music coming off of Sam's sound system.

Kate appeared in the doorway.

"Break it down for us Ray."

"Hello Kate. Come on in. Take a break."

Kate stepped into the office.

"That's a lovely dress."

"Aw yeah, sweet ruby Ray, tossing the compliments my way. "

"I'll be right back," Ray said.

The Associates Area

Ray walked over to Jack.

"Do me a favor Jack—no interruptions." Ray winked at Jack. "You know how it is."

Sam's Office

Ray stepped into Sam's office and closed the door. He gave Kate his most winning smile.

Presently

Out in the associate's area, Jack heard strains of laughter coming through the closed door.

Later Still

Jack was on the phone with a client.

"No, I'm sorry Ray is not available ... I'm not sure when he will be ... is it anything I can help with ... all right, hold on please. I'll see if I can locate him."

Jack approached Sam's office, hesitantly. He knocked on the closed door. He heard Ray and Kate laughing inside but got no immediate response to his knock, so he opened the door—to find Ray sitting beside Kate—so close that he was practically in her lap.

"Sorry to interrupt Ray but I've got a client on the phone who needs to speak with you."

"Come in here for a second."

Jack stepped into the office.

Ray continued. "Are you familiar with a mysterious, hard-to-develop technique called 'taking a message?'" Now Ray said, charmingly but acidly, "Perhaps if you could ever so kindly help me here, you could do that for me."

Ray stood up and stepped into the hall.

The Hallway

Jack joined Ray in the hall. Ray pointed to Jack's desk, to suggest that Jack should go sit down, but he did it as if he was communicating with a dog, whom he wanted to fetch a stick.

Jack went toward his desk, but not quickly enough to suit Ray—who *shoved* him with some solid force from behind.

Jack spun around and *punched Ray in the jaw*. With surprising street aptitude. He hit him in exactly the perfect spot to knock him senseless, and Ray fell to the floor.

Kate stepped out of Sam's office and saw Ray trying to lift himself off the floor. He was woozy and couldn't quite do it.

"What happened?"

She turned to Jack and found him leaning over his desk, wrapping up the phone call.

She turned back to Ray.

"It's okay. I'm fine."

But in truth he was not. He was approaching Jack—but he couldn't quite lift himself off the floor. So he was crawling over.

He mustered up his strength and managed to rise into a half crouch. He then curled his hands into fists.

"Let's go tough guy."

Jack didn't move.

"Come on. Let's take it outside."

Jack not only didn't move. He didn't even seem disturbed.

Ray said, "That's what I thought." He turned to Kate as he rose to his feet. "He came up behind me and sucker punched me."

"If you consider your ass your front then I came up behind you." Jack turned to Kate. "It was in self-defense. ... Ray got carried away and did something emotional. He's not having a good day."

"Be a wise guy. We'll see how far it gets you," Ray said.

Ray stumbled away and down the hall.

Jack and Kate were alone.

Jack said, "I lost myself. I don't know what came over me. I didn't hit him that hard. Who knew he passes out so easily."

The Office, End of the Day

Jack was watching Ray, who was leaving for the evening, and who was entirely ignoring Jack.

"Goodnight Ray." He said this pleasantly.
Ray didn't respond, he just left.

Sam's Office, Early Evening

He found the dossier and opened Ray's *golden notebook.*
   "How can this be our business proposition? It's weak Ray."
   Jack looked to the ceiling.
   "It should hit them harder ... we're general business consultants that deliver communications firepower for brands. And for the people who need to become brands."

The Associates Area, Night

Jack dashed to his desk with the dossier. He was going to create his own draft of the presentation, starting from scratch.
   "We use and push mainstream marketing science to work on your most valuable asset, which is your name and how your name is perceived. We build brand equity and brand personality."

   Jack worked in a *green folder,* a simple, earthen object, and filled it with his fertile imagination.
   He was a dreamer, and in this he kept the stuff of his dreams.
   He was a systems thinker and in it he developed the mechanics of his systems.
   He had an inventive mind that built business models and in this he kept his understanding of business designs.
   He felt that every brand and every business should have a supremely clear and specific focus. And in this folder was where he worked out his ideas.
   He opened it and began to imagine the presentation.
   He would give it a sharp focus—and dramatic people.
   Speed's vision.
   Sam's sagacity.
   Kate's loveliness.
   Ray's deliberate deftness.
   And how the qualities lent force to the company focus.

Much, Much Later in the Evening

Jack was growing exhausted, but he was still aggressively working on the presentation.

"We develop positioning and creative themes out of that positioning focus that bring brands and people to life. We select the most powerful messages built on that focus. The ones with broad appeal. We build a message package. A creative umbrella with a central focus that unifies all messages and program elements to make the sum more valuable than the parts."

The Offices, A Few Days Later

Sam had returned and was sorting through his mail.

Jack was working at his desk. He looked down at his hands, where he was now holding his *green folder* that contained his alternate version of the presentation.

Jack took a deep breath and then started walking towards Sam's office. Ray glanced up from his desk and watched Jack enter Sam's office.

Jack closed Sam's door.

Ray wondered what was going on.

Inside Sam's Office, A Few Minutes Later

Jack said to Sam, "I know this pitch is very ... it's our most critical project. And we want to present, ... uhm, to put our best foot forward ... Ray is of course in charge—"

"And doing one hell of a job. I understand we're almost finished with a preliminary."

"... As I understand it, our intention, was to have me contribute under Ray's direction."

"If he feels you're too busy or the work is beyond your abilities then you can't take that personally."

"But I've been free to do the work and I feel I'm capable of it."

"What do you want me to do, spank him?"

"No, Sam. What I'm saying is I came up with my own pitch."

Jack withdrew the presentation from his *green folder* and handed it to Sam.

"That's absurd. We don't have time for you to make a second pitch."

"I already did it."

"You can't do that."

"Why?"

He got no reply to his question.—Sam was now carefully examining the presentation.

"Have Ray bring in what he's got, so I can review it, then let's call a quick meeting."

Sam's Office, Day

Sam was comparing the two presentations as Jack and Ray looked on.

"I'm getting very angry here. Let's talk about why. And I'm going to try not to kill somebody today."

He held up Ray's presentation.

"Ray, this is your presentation. It's okay. Now Jack, this is your presentation. It's better."

Sam took Jack's presentation and tore it in half.

"It's never going to see the light of day. Let this be the lesson: Ray is a senior associate. You are a junior associate. Never under any circumstances go outside the chain of command. Every time you fly over your boss's head, I will blow you out of the sky and turn you to dust. So sayeth the Lord. Understood?"

"Perfectly," said Jack.

Ray looked at Jack and then turned to Sam with a lot of love in his heart and said, "Thank you Sam."

"You're welcome Ray," said Sam.

Sam turned to Jack.

"It may have been done with *good motives*"—said Sam and made 'good motives' sound as rigid as if he was actually saying 'bad motives'—"but it was not done with *military behavior.*"

Sam continued to look hard at Jack. "I cannot command a rabble, no order no discipline. I must rebuild the battalion. Show them methods of efficiency. ... Stay in line soldier. This is an outfit, not a ball club or a fucking playground. This is a place for adults."

His look remained locked on Jack. "When I was a child," said Sam, "I played the games of children. When I became an adult I put off childish games."

The Offices, A Long While Later

Sam was rushing down the hall. Jack was at his desk.

"Sam, can I talk with you for a second?"

Sam didn't slow down. Apparently, the answer was *no.*

Later, Sam was rushing in the reverse direction.

Jack said, "Sam, would you be free for a few seconds?"

"Do I look available?"

Sam's Office, Day

Jack was finally meeting with Sam.

"I didn't want to upstage Ray. I just wanted to do some good work. I'd like to learn from you how I can do that. You're a businessman; a successful, experienced, and smart businessman. And with all my heart, that's what I want to become."

Sam looked at Jack.

He said, "You could feed me more and more and then some, but let's cut to the chase Jack. You want to get ahead of the pack. And your brain is spinning, trying to come up with the game plan. I can read you. You could give me every kind of lie but I could still read you. And I've got a way to get you what you want. So let's do that. I mean we could share every variety of put-on right now but instead let's talk the truth. The truth shall set you free. When I say that, it's not just me talking, that's the Lord speaking through me. The truth shall set you free. What does that mean? Okay, let's get into it.

"You've got a head full of ideas.

"But ideas are not valuable commodities. Every fucking fool has ideas. Experience—that's precious. That's what you want and I'm going to give it to you. I'm going to let you work on some of *The Blue Sky Company* accounts."

Jack was thrown. "Uhm, ... Sam, ... isn't uhm, ... *The Blue Sky Company* reserved for—"

"Say it—you've figured it out, haven't you. *The Blue Sky Company* is an embezzlement outfit."

"You would characterize it in that way?"

"A turkey is a turkey. Blue Sky is a fraud. A deceit. It's also Valhalla. You know what that is?"

"No."

"Have you learned nothing from me? Yes is always the answer. You say 'yes' and then you look it up. Clients don't pay you to not know things. I hear 'no' come out of your mouth one more time, I'm going to rip your fucking jaw off.

"Back to my point ... in this life, you fight and fight and in the end, you want to know there's somewhere you can go ... your own company, where you can relax and be yourself. There's nothing sadder than someone coming to the end of their life and they don't own a company.

"I had a good friend, he died that way, without owning a company, poor fellow. Nothing. Not a limited liability company, not a subchapter-s corporation, not even a sole proprietorship. He was nothing. I'll be honest with you, he didn't even need to retain his lawyer at the end, let alone his publicist. That's the way most people end up.

"Now, I know stealing is a terrible thing. I'd be the last guy to tell you stealing is good. But it is a widely used, highly accepted method of building a life.

"Behind every great fortune is a great crime. Stealing is a part of business. It's expected. And respected.

"You want to know the ways of the world. That's what you're going to learn here. You think life is a bed of roses. Life is a business. And if embezzling is part of it, that's part of it. Breaking the law—that's not part of it. If you're good, you do everything within the law. I'm not talking about stupid, low-level embezzlement. They'll catch you and they'll lock you up. We didn't get where we are by teaching that. I'm talking about real, artistic embezzlement."

Jack said, "I feel like Moses in front of the burning bush."

"Absolutely," Sam said. "And now let's take a look at The Blue Sky Company. When you examine it along these lines, you find that it's brilliantly constructed."

"I'm listening."

"The art of arts is to turn a 100 percent profit. That's what I'm achieving here. The Blue Sky Company has no costs, no overhead. Just profit. And it's all legal. Do you understand the secret principle involved here?"

"What is the principle?"

"If you rob from a store you become a crook, if you steal the whole store you become the owner."

"And then no one can touch you."

"That's how to embezzle. To steal from the accounts is stupid. I'm not doing that. I'm stealing the accounts themselves."

"Sam, that is so simple and yet it's sheer genius."

"That's right. Now that you know the secret, I'm betting that you'll want in on the action. Or would you prefer to be a loser all your life?"

"Oh, I don't want to be a loser all my life. Just a third of my life."

He gives Sam an amiable smile that he did not really mean at all. Jack was going to lie to Sam. He had no intention of participating in this embezzlement scam. But if he were to tell Sam the truth at this point he would be fired immediately. Therefore, he was going to pretend that he would join Sam's plot until he could come up with a way to get out of this predicament without getting fired.

Jack continued. "I'm just surprised that you're opening up like this to me. This is a hell of an opportunity. Thank you for your trust. And thank you for the truth. The truth shall set you free. Ye shall know the truth. And ye shall turn the truth into cash."

Sam turned to Jack and said, "There's such a shortage of people with a natural feeling for this business. The schools just aren't turning out qualified people to fill the spaces that are out there.—What kind of degree did you get?"

"A Bachelor of Arts. In philanthropy," said Jack.

"Those fucking colleges!" Sam said. "That's the business I should have gone into. They have the best legal excuse for robbing people blind, because 'They're teaching them.'

"They have to make their money. But if the colleges weren't such dens of burn artists, feather merchants, lip gloss dealers and banana oil salesmen it would make my job a lot easier.

"Now you see what you have to go through to get good accomplices? You have to convert the honest to the true way.

"You have to be prepared to overcome moral objections, to get past the almighty 'No!' that is constantly going to be hurled at you—everybody starts with a no.

"Don't ever let something important die at the hands of no. No means maybe. No can be a lot of fun if you're willing to work with it."

Speed's Office, Night

It was now evening, a few days later.

Jack and Speed were meeting together. Everybody else was gone for the evening.

Speed noticed that Jack's appearance was—picture perfect. He was becoming polished.

"How does the head office feel about Sam?" said Jack.

"The head office is Lara Lord. And Lara is very fond of him."

"She is?"

"Sam makes sure of that."

"I want to let her know Sam has been implementing a customized profit participation plan."

"You want to get him fired?"

"Exactly. Let me you show you this."

Jack raised a set of documents.

"I got hold of Sam's employment agreement."

Speed reached for the documents.

"Look at the language that defines company business. It applies to the Blue Sky accounts. He's in breach of contract. What he's doing is flagrantly out of bounds and he knows it."

"If we talk to Lara it may hurt Sam, but will it help us? It'll look like a vendetta—it will come across wrong for what we want."

"What he's doing is wrong. He deserves to be outed."

"That's not enough of a reason to do this. We're not prosecutors, we're businessmen."

"Okay. The problem is ... you want to move up in the company but you want to do it because you're for something, not because you're against someone."

"Right. If we're doing this to benefit ourselves then we have to get the results we want. She shouldn't end up handing the job to a bigger nightmare."

"Then we don't tell Lara, we tell her business affairs person—in confidence. Then he'll look like the good lawyer for nailing Sam. And Lara will be upset because she had to discover the scam. By the time it filters up to her through two or three execs it'll be a major fiasco. What do you think—yes, no, maybe?"

Speed sighed.

"Is that a yes?" asked Jack.

"We're getting within walking distance of a yes," said Speed.

The Motorcourt, The Next Day

Jack walked over to a bank of payphones.

Back then, people dropped in coins into public phones to make calls. That was how you did things when you were outside an office.

He looked at the bank of payphones. He lifted a receiver. He looked at the phone. He touched the coin return and the silver buttons on the pay phone.

Then he went into his pocket and pulled out a *cell phone*. He dialed the number and as the phone rang, he looked at the bank of payphones. What a wonder yesterday was. That's how they did things in *the last business age*. That's how they made a secret call in *Sam Bartlett's day*. It was another world. ... Hmm, they were moving into the new business age now and a new century.

A voice came over the line.

Jack said, "Hello. My name is Jack Flynn. ... I work with Sam Bartlett ..."

On the other side of the motorcourt, Sam rushed out of the lobby toward the car lane, where a car was ready and waiting for him. Sam was heading toward the passenger side of the car when he suddenly stopped—

On a side angle—he noticed *Jack on the phone.*—

Immediately, lightning crackled across the heavens and a storm erupted in Sam's mind.

In the distance, Jack noticed Sam. He waved a hello with a charming smile. Jack made some comments into the phone and then hung up.

Presently, Jack was standing beside Sam.

"I was just talking to my girlfriend," said Jack. "We've been fighting so I thought it would be best to make the call outside of the office."

"Couldn't the call have waited until after hours?" said Sam.

"Well," said Jack, "you know how it is when you have a fight with your girlfriend."

"I don't want you conducting any personal business during office hours."

"You're absolutely right. It won't happen again. Is there anything I can do while you're out?"

"I've got two shirts and a pair of slacks that need a pick-up."

Jack smiled warmly as Sam handed him a dry cleaning ticket.

The Office, Night

Jack and Kate were working at their desks.

Everyone else was gone for the day.

"Would it bother you if I put on some music?" said Jack.

"Not at all."

Jack went to Sam's office, turned on a slow big-band song, and returned.

He put out his hand to Kate, she took it, and they began a slow dance.

"Can I pose a tender question?" she said.

"Please do."

"You and Speed have been meeting a lot lately. Are you working on something together?"

"Speed and I have been putting a few words into Lara Lord's ear."

"What are you telling her?"

"A story that's been told many times before, of a big kahuna—who is in charge of a pile of money—being led down the garden path by a charmer who speaks with a forked tongue. We didn't want to crowd his act, but we wanted to move her along in her fool's paradise—to show her the scene at the end of the road—where the fool and her money are parted."

"What's she doing about it?"

"Nothing yet. She's coming into town to drop in on him. The subject will probably come up."

"How'd she take the news? Is she angry?"

"Of course."

"Good. I wouldn't want a thing like this to backfire on you. It worries me. You're breaking an organizing principle here. You're behaving sanely. And sanity is lethal in the business world, even in small doses."

"Sanity does have its day, here and there. She's going to catch him with his hand in the cash box. It's going to be an … awkward … one could almost say uncomfortable meeting but it should work out for the best. I'd say Sam is a man very likely soon to take his leave without notice."

By this point, they had stopped dancing and were standing close together. Too close. They were getting hot for each other.

The background music went into a fast swing number.

Then she leapt onto him, wrapping her arms around his head and her legs around his waist. From there, they progressed into a whirlwind of kissing, caressing, and moaning.

They began to take off clothes.

Speed's Office, Night

It was now raining outside the window.

In the soft glow of city lights, they made love on the couch.

They were both finding it sinful, but very lovingly romantic—

Suddenly, Kate froze.

"Wait, did you hear something?"

Jack listened.

"I heard a sound," she said.

"Not to worry. I'll check."

Jack cracked the door open and had a look.

He saw two security guards in the hallway. ... They picked up his slacks and inspected them; then stepped a little closer to Speed's office, where they picked up Kate's blouse. They both turned in the direction of Speed's doorway and began to move.

Jack whispered, "You can fire a person in an office. You can sign a person's death sentence in an office. But just try to make love to a person in an office, and all hell breaks lose."

The Associates Area, Night

Jack stepped out of Speed's office. But he did it casually, ignoring the guards. It was a perfectly ordinary evening in the office. Except that he was naked.

The guards turned, startled.

Jack casually noticed them.

"Oh hello. I'm Jack."

He extended his hand for them to shake. They didn't respond at first.

Then slowly one guard stepped forward and shooks Jack's hand. But he didn't look happy to meet him.

"I'm Shake." He pointed to his partner. "This is Bake. ... What are you doing?"

"Oh nothing much."

Jack looked at Bake who was a very large, somber man. Bake looked even less happy to meet him than Shake.

But Jack showed no fear. He smiled charmingly at him.

Bake said, "Do you work here?"

"Absolutely. This is my office."

"Is it?" said Bake.

"Certainly," said Jack. And he was very convincingly definite about it.

"You'll pardon my appearance, I was catching a nap."

"Sir, you are naked."

"Of course. But it is getting nippy here."

He took back his slacks and put them on.

"My clothes'll take away the chill. How about you guys? What are you up to?"

They just stared as he put on his slacks.

Then he took Kate's *blouse* from them and put it on. It looked very odd on him—this silk shirt, with its feminine pastel color—but it was passable, and he just smiled as them oh so amiably—As though it was a perfectly ordinary evening.

"Is it a slow night?" Jack asked.

He patted Bake on the shoulder playfully. And Bake looked at Jack's hand grimly.

Bake said, "If you ever strip down naked again, I'm going to take your head and put it into a wall."

"I understand," Jack said. "Would you two care for some coffee before you head on your way? I'll brew you a fresh pot. No?"

"I'm wise to you," said the guard.

"Now my dear Mr. Shake—"

"—I'm Bake. He's Shake."

"Forgive me." Jack smiled at him. "Mr. Bake, sleep is a very important thing.

"I have to work through the night. We have a very important presentation in the morning. I need to get some sleep. Now we're chatting here very enjoyably but I have obligations.

"I'm sure if you research the subject, you'll understand why I will now leave you gentlemen.

"When you listen to clinicians talking about the effect of sleep on the brain, about disorders of sleep and alertness, then you will conclude that the mechanisms of sleep and arousal are linked. You cannot work well until you have slept well.

"Sleep is not 'time out' from life. It is an active state essential for mental and physical restoration.

"I'm going to share a secret about the great short-sleepers of history. Do you know why they got away with not sleeping a lot? Because they napped a lot.

"Well, if you'll excuse me, I have to get back to sleep. I have to start work in about an hour and then work through the rest of the night. We have a very important presentation in the morning. Let's look forward to talking again soon."

He went back into Speed's office and closed the door—leaving the Guards to face blank space.

Speed's Office, Night

Jack pasted his ear to the door and listened. Kate joined him.

"I lie occasionally. I don't believe in being a compulsive truth-teller."

They waited for a few long beats and then Jack opened the door.

He saw the guards disappearing in the distance.

The Offices, The Next Morning

A bouquet of flowers was sitting in a vase on Kate's desk.

Jack was sitting at his desk. Smiling. He had bought the flowers for Kate and was awaiting her arrival.

Kate arrived. ... She saw the flowers. ... She turned to Jack with a smile. Then she leaned in and smelled them.

Sam came out of his office and stopped by Jack's desk.

"What are you working on?"

"The expense reports," said Jack.

"I see," said Sam. He turned to Kate. "Kate?"

"Yes, Sam."

"Do you have a few minutes to spare?"

"Sure Sam."

"I'm trying to pick out a present for a lady friend. You know how bad I am at those things."

Sam's Office, Day

Kate and Sam entered, and Sam closed the door.

Sam motioned towards the couch. "Make yourself comfortable."

She sat down and he took a position beside her on the couch.

"I have to tell you something that has registered with me over the past few weeks—that you're doing a terrific job. First rate. Absolutely first rate. No question of that."

"Thank you."

"You're welcome. Now, I'm a teacher. I consider everyone who works for me a student of mine. And I'd like to teach you the lesson of how things grow. Would you like me to do that?"

"By all means, yes."

"We start, as always, with the truth. The truth shall set you free. Now when I say that, that's not just me talking. That's the wisdom of kings and queens passing through me onto you. The wisdom of moguls.

"You want to know what the truth is? The truth is what is. And what should be, is a terrible, terrible lie.

"You've been in the business world for a few years. And where are you in the scheme of things? What is your net worth? Is it more than zero, yet? You don't have to answer that. I'm sure you're still less than zero, from a financial perspective. That, to me, is very sad.

"Do you want to move ahead? You need to want to move ahead. You don't have the option of letting grass grow under your feet. That's not how it works when people are involved. When you stand still, others move ahead. When you stand still, the ground erodes from under you and you descend into the abyss. If you're not protecting yourself, then you're opening yourself up to an attack. I'm speaking in truths. I know no other way to speak to a mind that has to be turned. The truth is music—mighty, fine music—and it's calling out to you.

"How do people become millionaires? You're a brilliant, beautiful, magnificent woman. You know the answer. If a guy is earning a dollar and you want to earn a million dollars. Do you work a million times harder than him? No. You find a million guys like him and feed off each of them to the tune of a dollar.

"The world is a feeding game. We live in a mutual feeding society. I go to sleep each and every night wishing it were different, but it never will be. Man lives by eating flesh and screwing flesh.

"I've watched you closely. I know what's behind the curtain.

"You're as smart as you can be. The act you put out to the world is as wonderful as wonderful can be.

"But, I know the secret of you. Do you want me to put the secret into words? You want more and more and then some.

"Time to come out, from behind the act. Time for you to grow."

Kate's expression was inscrutable.

Act Three

Final Enlightenment

The Conference Room, Morning

Speed, Jack, and Kate were prepping the conference room for the meeting with Lara Lord. Preparations for a visit by Lara were always meticulous. She was the center of the universe at this company and more latitude could be allowed for a visit from the President of the United States than could be permitted for her.

The Hallway

Jack exited the conference room and found Lara Lord standing before him.

She was a charismatic, attractive woman who had command presence.

She was traveling with the two security guards, Jack had encountered previously.

"Hello Lara. It's a pleasure to meet you. I'm Jack."

"How are you? Where's Sam?"

"You got here in very good time. We're still just setting up."

"Fantastic. Is Sam here?"

"Not just yet. He should be here any minute. Can I lead you to our conference room? So you can have some coffee and pastries while you wait."

Lara threw a hand into the air. That was apparently a "yes."

Jack turned and lead them away.

"How was your flight?"

"Why?"

"I was just wondering if it went well."

"We got here didn't we?"

The Conference Room

Speed was reviewing some documents and Kate was setting up the table.

Jack arrived with Lara and her entourage.

"Well, hello Lara."

"Speed."

Speed pulled out a chair for her at the head of the table.

"We're all so sorry to drag you out here. I realize this is an enormous imposition." He turned to Jack. "Do we have an estimated time of arrival on Sam?"

"I'll go keep an eye out for him."

The Hallway

Jack was waiting by his desk.

Sam arrived with Ray.

Sam's Office

Sam and Ray were standing together, when Jack stepped into the doorway.

"Excuse me Sam."

"Yes."

"I'm sorry to have to tell you this ... but Lara is here."

"Oh good," said Sam cheerfully.

Kid was surprised by Sam's manner. "She's here to discuss The Blue Sky Company."

Sam, still cheerfully, said, "Really? "

Ray started laughing. Sam joined in.

The Conference Room

Lara, Speed, Kate, and the two security guards watched as Jack, Sam, and Ray entered.

"Lara, my dear, how are you today?"

Lara nodded to the guards and they took up positions on either side of Sam.

"Sit down Sam."

He complied.

Lara said, "We all know you are taking me for a ride. You are therefore fired."

"I am?"

"I am only here for an explanation."

"True I was running a small concern of my own in these offices."

"Why you pretentious son-of-a-bitch. Who do you think you're talking to?"

"You're right. I was stealing."

Lara did not react adversely to this.

"It's inexcusable," said Sam. "It hasn't been sitting well with me at all. I made a big mistake. But now I'm going to atone for it. For the sake of our friendship I'm going to put all that money back into the company."

"Whoopee," said Lara.

Sam and Ray each looked at her.

"You have no idea how I regret it," said Sam. "I took advantage of you, a very dear person to me. You're my mentor. I want to make it up to you.

Lara didn't do anything.

"Consider this," said Sam, "it may be very good news for you that I'm going to put all this money into the company. I took out that money over the course of years. We can put it all back slowly so that at the end of this year when you have to meet with your boss you can add an extra chunk to the profit margin. Maybe you add 10 percent. Bring it into that meeting and he's going to say, 'Very good Lara.' If he asks where it came from say, 'The Devil sent it from hell with a note that said *To an old friend.*'" He'll laugh and laugh. I know him. He has a good sense of humor. He'll get up from his chair and hug you. What do you say to the offer?"

Lara said, "I'm thinking about it."

Jack stood up.

"Let's talk about sanity for a minute. I urge you to not let a thief run your company."

"He's right," said Sam. "He's a vicious, horrible Jack but there's truth in what he's saying. I'm part thief but I'm learning to tone down that part of me. I can't promise to give up stealing completely, but I won't steal anything from you."

Jack turned to Lara. Jack was a systems thinker and now he just said what he knew to be true. He said it as plainly, and as simply as he could. "You need to stand for something," Jack said. "What do you want your business to be about? Sam can keep the company going and keep it profitable. But do you want it to be all about the money?"

Lara remained poised. She looked as if she was listening with an open mind.

The room went quiet.

She started laughing. She thought Jack made a dumb speech.

Sam courteously got her attention again.

Sam said, "I'm a requisition artist. I'm not saying no. He's going to call me a thief, all right. I like to operate by moonlight. I'm a flim-flam man. I'm a grifter. I'm also a good businessman. A clean-up artist. A make-a-haul, do-the-trick, and fill-the-bill artist. It's all one. That's what you want working for you—someone who brings home the green velvet—right?"

Lara smiled. She liked what she was hearing from Sam.

Sam continued. "Isn't this kid something else? He's the one who leaked the story of my embezzlement to your attorney."

"Oh, is he the one?"

"He has a certain style. He likes to fly outside the chain of command. And he likes to talk sanity. Let's talk sanity. Without the chain of command, where are we? Anarchy. You and I could not exist. I promised him a raise in three months. I'm not going to give it to him. He's going to fly over my head to you. If he does are you going to give him the raise?"

The room went silent again.

"No," said Lara.

"Of course not. What would you do?"

She turned to Jack.

"Fire him," she said.

"It's time to fire him," said Sam.

Jack started pulsing with anger. He was going mad with fury, but only internally. On the outside, he stayed stock still. If looks could generate heat, his eyes would have scorched Sam and Lara.

"Lara, what if I expose what I'm seeing here today?"

"There hasn't been any law broken here."

"There's a breach of contract."

"We'll renegotiate Sam's contract and make it retroactive. That'll make it a problem that never existed.

"We're making our numbers, it's legal, what else is there? Go talk to your congressman, ask him to write a bill, I'll be the first to support it. In the meantime, this is all legal."

"You can't fire me," said Jack.

"I can't fire you for racial reasons, I can't fire you for reasons of sexual discrimination. But I'm firing you for no reason. There's no law against that. You see how the system works."

Jack was really burning up now. He fought to not lose control as he slowly walked out of the conference room and gently closed the door.

Lara turned to Sam and smiled. All was forgiven. They both stood up and hugged like best friends.

"You're a character," said Lara to Sam.

Jack's Desk

Jack was emptying his desk of his personal possessions while a security guard monitored him.

Speed stepped out of the conference room. And Speed wasn't at all flustered. He shook Jack's hand.

"Well," Speed said, "I guess this is goodbye. You've got to hand it to Sam. He pulled a winning move."

"Speed I don't think this is funny."

"Oh cheer up Jack. You'll find another job in no time."

"I'm sure we both will."

"Oh, I already have."

"What?"

"I got an offer from the competition. I was going to stick around here if we could make the restructuring happen but now I might as well move on."

"Do you suppose you have a position there for me?"

"Of course. I'll try to find something there for you."

"Thank you. How can I get in touch with you over there?"

"Oh, that's okay. I'll get a hold of you."

Speed walked away.

"I just realized something," said Jack.

"What's that?" asked Speed.

"You don't care about anybody. You just put on an act."

Speed laughed.

"Everybody puts on an act. An act is the way to live. Good luck my friend."

"Help me out with one thing—is everybody in the business world crazy?"

"Absolutely. I thought you knew that already. Take care, Jack. I'm sure I'll be seeing you around. You've got too much might and main to meet your end on this field of combat. ...

"And when these unlucky deeds I relate,

"I shall speak of you as you are; nothing extenuate,

"Nor set down aught in malice, then must I speak

"Of one that loved not wisely but too well.

"Good day, sir. Enjoy the weather. It's beautiful outside. Blue skies, nothing but blue skies."

Speed left.

Now the others stepped out of the conference room.

"Let's have dinner together tonight," Lara said to Sam.

Lara glanced over at Jack. Jack met her gaze and there was something sad in his expression.

Lara turned back to Sam.

Sam stepped between them.

Sam said, "You have a lot more to learn than anyone can teach you. Don't get me wrong. I personally like you. But you're not right for the business world. You're a troublemaker. You have a bad attitude. You don't know what cooperation means. You're a loser Jack. You're a fucking loser. You need to recognize that you don't fit into this business. Or any business. You would drive it into the ground. You would put people into bankruptcy the way you think.

"Wise up before it's too late. One day, you're going to get married, you're going to end up the same way—fired. You're going to get fired from your marriage. You're going to start a family, you'll destroy the Jacks. You won't be a good parent.

"And I'll give you something else to think about—you're not liked. In this whole place you don't have one friend. I'm telling you this for your own good. Get a clear vision of who you are and where you are on the ladder. You're on the bottom. I think you're getting the picture.

"You have to recognize when you're not wanted and we don't want you because of the aforementioned. And I would leave before people actually start to get angry."

He has the two big security guards behind him.

Lara cut in. "Let's have Shake and Bake here facilitate his departure, that way you and Ray can walk us out."

Lara directed the guards to stay with Jack.

Everyone else left except Kate, who took a position by her desk.

Jack was doing his best to not be overcome by the humiliation of it all. He gathered his personal possessions as the security guards stood ominously at his side.

He looked past a security guard at Kate, who was standing a dozen feet away. Their eyes met. He had to say goodbye to her.

He walked toward her but was followed immediately by the larger
security guard, Bake. Jack stopped and with a vulnerable plaintive whisper
asked—

"I only want to say goodbye to her. Do you think you could just stay on
this side of the room for a minute?"

"No."

Jack sighed. How much more humiliating did this have to get?

He walked over to Kate and the guard trailed closely behind him. Jack
pulled Kate into a goodbye hug as the guard hovered beside them. Jack
kept her in the hug as he whispered in her ear.

The guard must have felt left out because he separated them.

Jack said, politely to the guard, "Come on. Do we really have to do it
this way?"

"Eat shit."

Jack stared at him, blankly. How do you respond to "Eat shit"?

He turned to Kate. "What are you going to do now?" he asked.

"Oh, I'm staying here for a little while," she said.

"Really? What about your problems with Sam?"

"Don't ask me why but Sam's actually going to promote me."

Jack was speechless.

He turned toward Sam's office.

He got an image in his head:

Sam's Office, Day

*He saw Sam and Kate sitting side by side on the leather couch. Jack felt himself
suddenly a presence in that room he saw in his mind. And both of them facing
him.*

*Sam said, "The truth shall set you free. The truth is what is. And what
should be is a terrible, terrible lie."*

Jack turned back to Kate. Now he understood.

She was not who he had imagined her to be. He had clothed her in the
colors of his longing but now he saw her—differently.

He became overwhelmed with a sense of loss. He didn't know what to
say, all that came out was:

"That's fantastic."

He looked up at the ceiling and then back down at Kate.

Jack continued. "Congratulations."

Jack stepped back. Apparently he was going to leave.

"Well God, good luck," said Kate.

"You too," said Jack.

"I don't know what to say."

Kate's expression was inscrutable.

Jack said, "You've made a big mistake. But I'm not going to be judgmental. You must have had your reasons. I hope you can live with them. I think it's a shame what you've turned yourself into. I'm not going to call you a bitch. But I have to be honest with you. I'm a little disappointed. You've lost your soul. I hope you can live without it."

Kate was still inscrutable. Maybe she was starting to regret what she did. Maybe not. She didn't say another word.

Jack turned to the guards.

The guards wondered what was happening now.

Jack scanned around the room.

He dashed to his desk and grabbed a piece of paper. He looked at it very intently and then:

"This is it. The evidence I need," said Jack.

He turned to Shake and Bake.

"This paper proves what I've been alleging. It's all illegal. And gentleman you are complicit in the act. I am, therefore, placing you under a citizen's arrest."

The guards were bewildered.

They approached Jack. Cautiously. Like they were ready to beat him to the ground but they wondered if there was any truth to what he was saying.

Jack did not move.

Jack said calmly, "This paper proves that a crime has been committed in my presence. And a private citizen—when he witnesses a felony—has the right to arrest wrongdoers.

"But have no fear, you will be turned over to a policeman without unnecessary delay.

"Now, you have the right to say nothing.

"Once in police custody, you will have the right to retain and instruct counsel without delay.

"Ultimately you will be brought before a judge and the question of bail determined.

"If you do not have a lawyer, I recommend you consult the local telephone book for a lawyer referral service number, or a complete list of lawyers in the yellow pages under 'Attorneys.'

"All right. I need you gentleman to step back."

The guards stopped and looked at each other. Did he really expect them to obey?

Jack continued. "Gentleman I do not have the time nor the inclination for this. I need you to step to that side of the room."

"How dumb do you think we are?"

"I don't think you're dumb gentleman. Now you need to move to that side of the room until the police arrive.

"Fuck you."

Bake raised his fist.

Jack said, "Put down the fist! A citizen's arrest is a constitutionally protected right under the ninth amendment as its impact includes the individual's natural right to self-preservation and the defense of the others. If you prevent me from completing my arrest, then I'll arrest you for violating my ninth amendment rights and then you'll really be in deep shit."

The guards slowly stepped back. Hesitantly.

"You gonna tell us this is a for-real bust?" asked Bake.

Jack turned toward the hallway.

Jack said, "Stay where you are gentleman. "

The guards were now in a position from which they could not see the hallway. So they stepped towards Jack to get a peep in that direction. Jack turned back to them.

Jack said, "I need you to not move. Don't make me tell you four times."

The guards froze.

Jack darted down the hallway and disappeared.

The guards looked at each other for a spell. What should they do?

They cautiously inched forward until they could get a view of the hallway.

The hallway was completely empty. Jack was gone.

Motorcourt, Day

Sam, Lara, and Ray were converged by the curb, beside Lara's limousine.

Sam was bidding farewell to Lara. His back was turned and he didn't see Jack approaching. Jack ran over to Sam and tapped him on the shoulder. Sam turned around.

Jack clenched his fist—he was about to punch Sam.

He had a clear shot at Sam's jaw but he hesitated.

Time stood still for a beat and then Jack decided against punching Sam. He unclenched his fist.

Sam turned back to Lara and ignored Jack, as if he was completely inconsequential.

Jack kicked Sam in the behind. This sent Sam flying into Lara and they both tumbled onto the pavement. Sam and Lara look into each other's eyes. And it was a romantic moment. It was love.

Jack, with enormous dignity, tucked in his shirt, combed his hair back with one hand and then patted one hand against the other, as if shaking off loose dirt. He slowly turned around. He was going to walk away with some dignity.

Ray leapt into Jack's path. Now Ray was going to be the hero. He lifted a finger into the air and pointed it menacingly at Jack's face.

"You and me," said Ray.

He bellowed these three words as if he was the voice of God. He was all confidence and bravado.

But the theatrics didn't stop there. He left his finger hanging in the air for a long moment. Then he slowly clenched the hand into a fist.

Ray continued. "You were lucky last time but this time I'm going to teach you the meaning of the word pain."

"You mean pain-in-the-ass," said Jack.

Ray got into a boxer's stance and approached Jack.

Jack stood still and calmly waited for Ray to step forward. The moment Ray got within reach, Jack punched him in the jaw and Ray instantly crashed to the floor. Unconscious.

Then the guards arrived.

The guards approached Jack ominously. They were going to toss him a beating.

"Gentlemen," said Jack, "you don't want to do this. You'll feel guilty later. And I don't want you to suffer."

But these guards didn't seem worried. They just wanted to beat him all the more because they didn't like speeches.

They started the beating. Lara and Sam, moved back a few paces for clearance room.

The guards beat him casually, as if they were baking a cake. They sprinkled a little kick here and a little punch there.

They were pretty methodical but one of the bodyguards hit the other by mistake.

Shake said, "Oh shit, I'm sorry Bake."

Bake said, "That's all right. Let's get back to work."

They were talking to each other throughout.

"What time have you got?" asked Bake.

Shake showed Bake the time.

"Okay," said Bake, "after this we each take our breaks. Son of a bitch."

Bake kicked him in the balls twice and then dropped his knee on Jack's crotch. Jack's head popped up and got clocked by Shake.

Shake said, "So remember I was telling you I went out with this girl. Holy shit, she got me so upset. Every time I think of her, everything I look at, I just see her."

Boom! They hit Jack.

"You just gotta get over her," said Bake.

"I'm going to get over her," Shake said. "Fuck her."

Shake lifted Jack's head by the hair and gave him three sharp, quick jabs to the face.

"That bitch," said Shake. "She didn't know what she had with me. I'm sensitive, you know that."

"You're a good man. Honest, bro."

Then they stopped.

"All right. This looks good enough."

Then these two "artists" of beating stepped back in sync.

Jack rose from the ground very slowly. He turned to the guards and smiled warmly.

Jack was happy. He didn't have the emotions that a person would typically have in this situation. He was not depressed. He was relieved. He was thinking, *I've graduated.*

He didn't play up any of his pain. He acted more like he was punch drunk.

Jack said, to the guards, "Thank you gentlemen. I'm so glad you were here. I was really getting out of line. Who knows how far I would have gone? Incidentally I couldn't help noticing you guys do a very good job. I had no idea. When we first started into the beating I thought you guys didn't know what you were doing. But then I started to see the results. Gentlemen, I may need your services someday. Do either of you have a business card?"

The guards were stone-faced.

Lara and Sam were looking at Jack.

Jack now addressed them. His tone was not hostile in any way. He smiled and said ...

"I am become enlightenment; a seer of wheels within wheels."

To them, he didn't make any sense.

Jack continued. "It was a pleasure meeting all of you. I had a rip-snorting good time.

"Ya'll are good people. I feel warmer toward ya'll than I do toward my own kinfolk. I came to you with nothing and ya'll been paying me enough to buy two meals a day. I tell you what, I just got a whoopin but I ain't hungry. I feel pretty good."

Over his shoulder to the guards, he said:

"And by the by, I can't thank you enough for everything you've done for me here today. Ya'll done taught me to be a man. You whooped the tar out of me, but real proper."

He turned back to Lara and Sam.

"And ya'll taught me the meaning of good manners and courtesy. Ya'll made me feel real good by accepting me into your offices. I'm sorry it all has to end here. I just hope that the next guy you find can fill your heart the way you have filled mine with joy everlasting. Now if you'll excuse me, I really need to go to a hospital. Oh now, let's not try to talk me out of it. I should get going before I lose consciousness."

Now Jack walked away.

It was not steady going. He was dizzy. But he did his best to look co-ordinated and dignified.

Lara and Sam watched him.

Jack stumbled, regained his balance, and then kept going.

Lara and Sam continued watching.

Jack turned around and blew his enemies a big goodbye kiss.

Jack said:

"I'm off to do my thing.

"Going to swing it.

"Swing it, swing it, swing."

With that said, Jack walked off.

Lara started laughing.

Sam smiled.

Lara put an arm around Sam.

"What was that line about?" asked Lara. "That didn't make any sense at all. What is he going to swing?"

"It breaks my heart," said Sam. "I think he's lost touch with reality."

"How could you hire that psychotic?"

"He started off as such a nice kid. I don't know what happened to him. It's impossible to find good associates."

"There's the truth. Well, I should get going."

She moved toward her limousine.

Lara said, "We were talking about something before that no-account varmit showed up."

"Whatever it was, we can talk about it later."

They took the next few steps to the limo, walking hand-in-hand. It was turning into a love story.

Lara said, "Let's try to live it up tonight and not let that flaming queer louse up a perfectly beautiful day."

Sam kissed Lara on the cheek, very tenderly and lovingly.

Lara brought her lips to his. And they kiss.

Lara climbed into the limo. Sam closed the door and the limo drove away.

Sam joined Ray, who had regained consciousness. He helped him to his feet, then the two men along with the security guards walked back into the building.

The motorcourt was now very quiet. Very peaceful.

And it was indeed a perfectly beautiful day. The motorcourt was bathing in the golden glow of a loving sun. The trees and plants that ringed the court area, were basking in the rich colors of a spring bloom, and a soothing breeze was playing upon the leaves.

Some pedestrians passed through.

The Front of the Office Tower, Day

Jack was walking away from the office building.
 Across the great tree-lined garden area.
 Into the park ... and the rambles.

The Park, Day

He strode through the rambles and came out of the other side.
 He crossed a bow bridge over a narrows in the lake.
 He joined the long scenic walking path stretching across to the horizon.
 He was heading off to recover, but he suddenly was very happy.
 He was feeling better.
 Cheery.
 As he crossed the place he leaped forward. He followed his momentum into a turn and kept going across.
 He was traveling in a direction that took him to a terraced lawn, leading upward to a stone pavilion.
 He paused on the terraced hill to enjoy the view.
 He felt it now—You had to force things to be simple.
 The world made things into:
 Chaos.
 Disorder.
 It forced you to lose focus.
 You had to force life to be simple.

He came to a spot on the terraced green hill, open and level.
 He angled into a dynamic posture.
 He stood in *a ready position*. One leg behind the other.
 His weight was angled forward. His center of gravity held low.
 He stood poised on the balls of his feet.

He jumped.
 He landed.
 He jumped. He went high.
 He landed.
 He jumped higher. And higher.
 He jumped higher still.
 He jumped into a ten-foot rise. He landed, poised.

He jumped much higher.

He landed in a ready crouch. *The international ready position.*

He jumped higher.

He jumped higher than the small buildings lying along the backdrop of the city.

He landed poised and ready.

He jumped and he went higher.

He jumped higher than the office tower.

He looked straight out. He was not looking down.

His arms were out in a dance frame. Wings spread before him.

He came down into a landing. Crouched. Poised. Ready to jump again.

He jumped and went much higher.

He jumped. This time he was aiming his momentum into the clouds.

His jump rose and rose.

His jump took him far above the city.

As he shot into the clouds he was looking straight outward.

Like a dancer in full flight he was "spotting" the horizon line.

Now coming through the clouds he rolled himself into a great big ball—and kept flying upward.

In that cannonball shape he continued hurtling upward, at great velocity.

He was shooting upward.

His whole frame went into a flip. Then he opened. Spread wide. And came gliding down.

Coming down through the clouds he could see the city spread below him.

He was getting it all. He was seeing the wide view.

He looked down at it all.

'That's life.'

He descended.

And landed.

He landed, poised. Crouched. In a dynamic posture. His weight on the balls of his feet. His arms out. Balanced. In the international ready position.

He held still. Looking straight out he spotted the horizon.

He looked along the horizon line that stretched behind the office tower.

He came out of this thing now. He exhaled. Relaxed. Released.

He came out of it in a slow, moving graceful shape of motion. And he came to his full height.

He stood now with his full weight on his right leg. His left leg held out before him poised. And his arms floating outward from him in a gun-slinger position.—The international ready position.

He smiled. And relaxed. Released more. He was free.

Now he was spotting the horizon and he noticed a figure moving from the direction of the office tower toward him.

She was coming out of the rambles.

She was walking toward him.

It was a woman. Walking straight and sure toward him.

It was Kate. And she was looking quite lovely.

She was hip motion. And long legs. And a lovely frame moving toward him.

Her motion was gracefully level. There was no rise and fall she was moving in a line toward him. Her hips were powering the motion. Her hips swayed. Left. Right. Left. Right.

She was moving toward him.

She had crossed the bow bridge.

And set on the path toward him.

It was a long distance. Almost like crossing a dessert.

Jack held still. His eyes were spotting outward. Seeing her. Taking her in. Watching her walk toward him.

It took a long while. It was a distance. But in time she crossed it.

Now she came to him. She entered his space. And paused very close to him.

They looked at each other.

They stood there a long while.

"I'm sorry," she said. Life was tearing at her. ... So very, very much was tearing at her.

"I am so, so sorry," she said. "Sometimes, I get mean. I get very mean. I hate being mean."

"Kate," he said.

"Jack, I'm sorry. ... I'm ... so ... sorry."

He looked at her.

"Please forgive me," she said. "I did something very wrong, and now I want with all my heart to make it right. ... I'm not who I thought I was. ... Now I'm me. The real me. ... And I'm so very ... very sorry."

He took her hands into his, ... and brought her toward him.

They kissed.

They hugged.

She took a good look at him now. "Are you okay?" she asked.

"I have good news," he said.

"Good news?"

"Yes, they've just turned me into *the comeback kid.*" He laughed.

She smiled.

"I'll go somewhere else," he said, "with what I've learned, and I'll start over. I'll do better next time."

"Don't let them own you," she said.

"What do you mean?"

"Don't let their problems own you."

"Oh."

"You're not finished here yet," she said.

"What do you mean?" he asked.

"Don't rush to *next time*. You're still in *this time,*" she said. "Before you go on to be the comeback kid—Have you really lost here? It's not who wins the battles, it's who wins the war."

"Wow," he said. And looked at her amazed. "You have real courage."

"I do," she said. "You're going to be a success Jack. I know you will be. I believe in you. I trust you. ... I think you have a war to finish."

He looked at her.

"Actually, we have a war to finish together," she said.

"Together," he said.

When they came together they felt it.

Sometimes two people together are more powerful than the two on their own.

It was two coming together in a bond of very simple force.

These two were now to dream together.

She was feeling what he had felt. They had to force things to be simple.

'Together'—was a nice word.

They saw things together. Things that they did not see separately and on their own. Yes, sometimes two people together are a lot more powerful than two people on their own.

"Now," she said, "let's get the recovery part of our day done, and then I think we should have some good strong drink. ... Do you like single-malt Scotch whiskey? ... We have a lot to talk about, you and I, ... Mr. Jack Flynn."

"I believe we do, ... Ms. Kate Greenway," he said.

They smiled, and began to walk away from an eventful day, to brace for a more eventful tomorrow.

———

A Skyscraper, Days Later

High atop one of the city's most graceful and spectacular skyscrapers, Jack Flynn had arrived—for a meeting.

He entered the offices of a CEO, a rather world-famous one, by the name of Lee Manning.

"Hello, I'm Jack Flynn."

"Lee Manning."

They shook hands. And Manning noticed Jack's grip. There was something there. He looked at Jack's face. Yes, there was presence there.

"Sit," Manning said.

They sat in two armchairs, beside the CEO's office couches. It was quite an office. Lee Manning was a multi-billionaire. The office was simple and graceful, but had loads of accommodations for conducting business in a comfortable setting.

"This is about Lara Lord?" asked Manning.

"About Sam Bartlett," Jack said. And paused.

Manning smiled. This young fellow was smart. He was waiting to get a reaction from Manning that he could read before even beginning.

"Sam Bartlett?" Manning asked.

Jack nodded slightly.

Manning said, "I know the name." Manning looked away. Out at the wide view of the city. "Let me see. Sam Bartlett. I've read about him. ... I remember meeting him. ... Lara acquired his company for us a while back."

Manning turned back to Jack. "It's an image firm. ... A school for experts, I think is what the media called it."

Jack nodded.

Manning said, "Are you from there?"

"I worked there until recently."

"What happened?"

"I was fired."

"I see."

Jack paused for a beat. It was a balanced pause. Not too long, not too short. He was giving Manning enough connection to get a flow moving and at the same time giving him the sense they were equals. They were separated by about 40 years of business experience and several billion dollars in personal worth, but Jack felt they were equals, and Manning was beginning to sense that.

Jack gave Manning a good strong gaze. Now without blinking, without moving except to breathe, he continued. "To me, the most beautiful thing in business is *the fundamentals*. I have a story to tell you about the fundamentals within your business. ... Now I know I'm jumping past seven layers of chiefs and vice presidents—of important divisions—to tell it to you. Normally that's not done, but I think you'd like to hear this story. ... Can I tell you my story?"

"Yes," said Manning. He looked at Jack who had now settled into a graceful pause once more. "What did you say your name was, again?"

"Jack Flynn."

"Jack—I'd like to hear your story very much."

The Skyscraper's Courtyard

Kate was waiting down in the building's tree-lined courtyard.

She saw Jack Flynn emerging from the lobby.

He stopped. And raised a graceful fist into the air for—victory!

... And then he smiled. ...

She jumped into the air.

Then ran toward him.

And jumped on him.

They kissed.

And then Jack Flynn and Kate Greenway walked into the city, hand in hand.

— The End —

The Lovely Lady
at
The Love Museum

A COLLEAGUE OF MINE IN ANTHROPOLIGY—REED FLEMING—
was pretending to be a real-estate crook. So that he could get close to, and study the rip-off deals of, a real-estate billionaire in New York City.

"What?" you ask. Believe me my friend I was shocked too. ... And my God the things I heard about poor Reed next! Shocking! Just outrageously shocking. Surprising even. ... Do you remember him? He was such a good man. Funny, bright, so promising—who would have thought he would end up this way.

Oh you don't remember him. ... What's that? ... Oh no, I couldn't tell you about what I heard. It wouldn't be right to talk about it. ... Well, maybe I'll tell you a little bit.

————

An Anthropoligist in New York

R EED FLEMING WAS AN ANTHROPOLOGIST—that is a long word for a people specialist. He was studying a game. It went by names such as the "territorial imperative." The game was, put simply, the game of *"one-upmanship."*

Now, *"oneupmanship"*—is the art of placing a person *"one-down."*

"One-down" is the psychological state of mind that exists in an individual who is not "one-up" on another person.

One of the most powerful prizes of "upmanship" is territory.

Many feel that Mr. Sigmund Freud got it all wrong when he said life is all about "sex." It is actually all about "territory." People are driven by the need to seek and acquire "territory." And territory is not just land. It is everything that you can imagine acquiring. It is a great many things. And thus we will label the prize, "things." We are talking about the pursuit of things. A favorite "thing" is "money." Money equals territory.

In nature, territory leads to sex.

If you have a lot of territory, you will tend to have a lot of sex. If you have very little territory you will tend to have very little sex. Among a species of deer in Africa, the female will only have sex with a male that possesses a *stomping ground.* The male that does not possess "turf" will not get a female.

Reed did not have territory, which placed him in a one-down position within society. Consequently he had very little sex, which also placed him one-down.

For Reed, this was quite all right for a very long time. You see, he was an anthropologist who spent ten years in remote wildernesses, studying primitive peoples. He was in the "Stone Age," removed from the modern world. This was jolly good for a very long time.

But in time, he ran out of money for his field studies.

He returned, with his skills, to his quaint little home town of New York City. In this country town with a Main Street population [in its central area] of merely 7,920,000, he found a rich gameland, a territorial zoo.

He found a master oneupman who was acquiring lots of territory.

... And a very sexy woman ...

But it all began with trouble, an upmanship problem—or rather, he found himself a leading example of onedownmanship.

Now, *the moves* in the oneupmanship game are called *"ploys."* A ploy is a move or gambit which gives one an advantage in a relationship.

To be an anthropologist in New York City—was to be without effective ploys.

Reed couldn't find a job, a one-down experience. He couldn't earn money, a one-down problem.

When he told a New York businessman that he was an anthropologist, the reply was, "What is this a joke, I mean, what are you fucking kidding me!"

The last thing a New York businessman wanted to hire was an anthropological genius.

When he talked to New York businessmen about the bushmen of the Kalahari or the First Nations people of the Pacific Northwest, they asked him to, "Speak American!"

Reed's every ploy landed him one-down. This filled him with anxiety, a one-down emotion. Knowing that he was one-down filled him with terror. Knowing he was in terror, filled him with horror. He proceeded, spiraling downward, along the spectrum of one-down emotions to madness.

Amazingly, Reed discovered what very few know, that the extreme state of madness is actually a one-up state. He who does not give a damn anymore, is one-up.

Frankly, he had become a Rhett Butler figure.

And the world was his Scarlett O'Hara.

Insanity

At this point, Reed got a vision. He would build a beautiful luxury apartment skyscraper, and plop it down on the most expensive street corner in the United States.

Surely a "one-up" territorial idea, consisting of putting a "one-up" building on a "one-up" corner.

Then, he would go to a "one-up" territorial king and fire him up about the idea, a "one-up" maneuver.

The way one became a one-up territorial king among the many one-up men of New York City was via a one-up practice called "stealing." The greatest real-estate crook in all of New York City was *Lloyd Belasco.*

Belasco was a rotten son-of-a-bitch, who was one hell of a good salesman (and very charming). Thus, reasoned Reed ... Belasco was a jolly good target for a one-up ploy.

Tracy

In Belasco's world there was an interesting woman, *Tracy Redfield.* She was tired of being one-down. She was born poor, a one-down condition. She became a police woman, a powerful position, but she who serves and protects is one-down.

Also, to be in the police racket in New York was to be a bribee, and she who takes bribes and pay-offs is in a one-down position.

The one-down life was not the life for her, and she threw it aside.

Now she was a real-estate wheeler dealer, a one-up job, but she was in the employ of a monster, Lloyd Belasco—and she who serves a monster, is temporarily stuck in a one-down position.

She had a secret passion for anthropology; consequently, she was a beautiful, kick-ass people watcher.

She was beholding her boss Lloyd Belasco. And she liked not what she saw.

Belasco was drunk with one-upness.

Belasco presided over an empire. The Belasco name was splattered over skyscrapers, casinos, helicopters, restaurants, planes.

His people were working in a pressure cooker.

He yelled and tossed fits.

Cheated on his wife. Cursed his managers.

He was a foul-mouthed, bullying billionaire. He hated ordinary people. He was drawn to celebrities.

He was always bragging. Always talking like a winner. Always in the right. Any mistakes he made were just because he trusted the wrong kind of people!

Lloyd's way of talking to his people was, "This is the best place in the world to work and I'm the best guy in the world to work for.

"I'm America's most successful businessman. I've made a lot of money. I've done things nobody thought could be done. And I've got big plans.

"You'll never have another job like this. There will never be another guy like me. So don't ever leave."

Lloyd's reaction when his wife shook hands with one of their fans was, "Forget them. Why do you let these people touch you? Don't pay attention to them. Forget them." … "Forgetting" the average person was a cornerstone of Lloyd's philosophy.

His act was the standard one in business. His speeches were standard. It was, "Work hard and you'll be a success." … *Just like Belasco.*

It was the *'come in early, stay late'* song.

Belasco's repeating chorus was, "The harder I work, the luckier I get."

He didn't mention the mobsters, dirty businessman and crooked politicians. They were simply "rough-and-tumble guys who are real sweethearts once you get to know them."

Tracy watched Belasco … and suffered privately.

As long as she was stuck in one-down service to this Phillistine, she couldn't have the one-up life she sought; the life with the one-up shelter, a two-story house; and the one-up home-life, that of a mother and wife.

The Deal

Reed went to Belasco with a pitch.

He got an upmanship session with the billionaire—in business known as the "sales meeting."

Aware that Belasco was a master oneupman, Reed started with a one-up attack.

"Across the country, people talk about the 'Brittany' location. Your office is across the street. You look at the shop window of 'Brittany's' every day. But do you really see it?"

Belasco said, "Get the hell out of my office!"

Reed said, "Shut up you prick and listen to me."

Thus, the battle of upmanship was joined. Belasco had asked, "Why should I do business with you?" And Reed had implied, "Because we can make money together."

He who plans how to make money is one-up. And he who follows the plan, Belasco, is one-down.

Reed took Belasco over to the office's picture window, which overlooked Central Park in the distance, and in the foreground Fifth Avenue, with it's ritzy shops, with the world-famous, proverbial "Brittany" location, and other prize real-estate properties.

"Look at the Museum of Anthropology down there."

"It bores me."

"No, it's marvelous. It just has a boring name. It's the '*Love Museum.*'"

"The Love Museum, huh?" Belasco could see the marketing opportunities opening up.

"The building next to it is Brittany's. If you can get the air rights, you can build a skyscraper across both."

He looked at Lloyd.

Reed continued. "The guy in charge of Brittany's loves the museum. You can tell him you want to build something beautiful above both so that they will be protected from guys who want to tear them down.

"At the top of the museum is a roof sculpture garden. You could spread that across both buildings and build 30 floors above.

"And then sell apartments.

"You re-do the museum. Call it the Love Museum. The building becomes the Belasco at the Love Museum. What do you think?" Reed asked.

Reed stopped there. He looked at Belasco.

Belasco's response was, *"Hold the phone a minute!"*

Belasco stepped out and brought in a lawyer, Harry "Holy" Bailey.

Belasco now treated this like a Pentagon secret. He started whispering in his own office. He said to Holy Bailey, "Do you think we can do it?"

The lawyer asked Reed, "How do we get the Anthropology Museum?"

"The company that owns the land and holds the lease is in financial trouble. They brought in a new CEO to hold a firesale. Just buy the lease."

Belasco asked, "What do you want out of this?"

Reed said, "I want the Love Museum."

Belasco and the lawyer turned to each other.

Reed understood what they were in Stone Age terms. Belasco and Holy Bailey were swine, and they had now entered the state where they devoured raw meat—ribs, legs, thighs—they gnawed like wild boars. They couldn't eat it all fast enough. Other Stone Age people could go hungry in the background, it mattered not to men who were pigs. Reed had seen these men many times before.

Reed repeated himself, "I want the Love Museum. Am I going to get it?"

Preparing a "Stab in the Back" Ploy

After the meeting, Belasco told Bailey, "While we make the deal, find out how to demolish the museum. I want it gone.

"And hire Dr. Love here. I want his mouth shut and I want him under contract. This guy is a total shmuck! But I like him. Let's see if we can work with him."

Soon, the lawyer put a contract in front of Reed.

Reed said, "No need for a contract. We shook hands."

The lawyer said, "We need to put the agreement on paper."

Reed said, "I'm offended. I stand by my word. Why wouldn't you?"

Reed knew his world history. And history favored the honorable. ... He who acted with total honor was always one-up in the long view of history. Perhaps he was not seen as that immediately. But the long arc of oneupmanship bent toward the honorable.

Reed was employing the best of historical and anthropological principles in his deal making. Lloyd was employing ... well, ... alternative principles.

Also, Reed noticed that he had no bargaining position whatsoever and the contract was a stinker. It was not a good time to sign a severely binding contract, it was not a good time to get "legal" with them. He would bide his time, and get very, extremely legal with them should the need arise. And, he would do it at an honorable time.

Lloyd and Holy Bailey thought he was eccentric. ... They reasoned in a very traditional way. ... If need be, they might have to damage him later. Or destroy him entirely.

Tracy Gets Angry

Lloyd Belasco was practiced in doing people wrong.

The way he got land and emptied existing buildings to make way for his skyscrapers, was to behave like a mobster.

Everything was done with brutishness.

The problem under everything in his empire was that everybody was on a treadmill.

You see, his empire was built on debt. Every property had to service enormous debt payments.

For Tracy Redfield, this was where all the difficulty lay. This was her job, making sure people made their debt payments.

She was what she was as a police woman, very sexy, very attractive, very charming muscle. She was vice presidential brawn.

She was employed by Belasco for her kicks and punches.

She was furiously riding the debt payments.

Then, she saw an opportunist come along—one *Reed Fleming*.

This was the last thing she needed in her life.

Belasco needed to scale down. Not add risks to his load, and borrow more money. For what? To build a beautiful luxury skyscraper that was probably going to lose money.

And what killed her about the whole deal was that she loved the Anthropology Museum. It was not stated overtly, but she could bet there was a tacit agreement to destroy the museum. Museums didn't make enough money for Lloyd, the museum amounted to a cash drain.

A damn shame, she would miss it.

The 'Belasco at the Love Museum' Goes Under Construction

As the Museum shuttered for "re-construction," Tracy was standing across the street. It was good-bye to something beautiful.

She saw Reed Fleming in the distance, and walked over to him.

"I'm Tracy Redfield."

"How do you do, Tracy? It's a pleasure to meet you."

"Mr. Fleming, I work for Lloyd."

"Is that so?"

"We'll be seeing quite a lot of each other as this skyscraper goes up."

"I look forward to it."

"I do as well. I'd love to punch that smile right off of your face. I think you're a rotten son of a bitch for what you've done here, but I won't hold it against you. On a bright note, we're about to make a lot of money together."

"What?"

She walked away.

The "Knife into the Back" Ploy

Months later, Reed was in a conference room sitting among a throng of Belasco's turks, when Belasco casually killed him softly.

Belasco was making a speech, "... To maximize the revenues from footage, we're dropping in a shopping atrium where the Anthropology Museum used to be. Once we re-open the building for business, the emphasis is going to be on renting atrium space—"

Reed was shocked.

He went out of his mind with rage. He tried to control himself. Fighting to restrain himself, he stood up. "Lloyd what was that middle part again?"

"The Anthropology Museum is off. We're building an atrium instead."

"NO, LLOYD, THE DEAL IS GOING TO STAND."

"It's gone, Reed. Get a grip. New circumstances. It's a cash problem. The building is going to have to re-pay the cost of construction. It cost a lot more than the original deal. Now we need money. We need a shopping center. The museum is dead."

Reed stood there. All eyes were upon him.

Belasco resumed his speech.

Reed cut him off again, "Hey Lloyd, do you know what the museum was? I loved it like a living being. You've raped it for some quick money. But I don't hold it against you. the museum had it coming.

"Nature's law is be rough-and-tumble. It should have been a fight museum, instead of a love museum.

"Violence sells tickets. If it's love, then you have to make it sex. You partner with *'Hustler'* or *'Penthouse,'* and then you'll have a business. It was bad planning on their part."

Belasco said, "I love this guy. You're like a jester. You make me smile."

Reed was growing angrier. He lashed out. "It should have been the *'Be a Prick'* Museum!" Reed climbed onto the conference table. "The *'Fuck You'* Museum!!" He stood above Belasco as he continued. "The *'I'm-a-Fucking-Shithead'* Museum!!!"

Belasco said, "I love this guy. He has the right attitude. I want to see a little bit of this from everybody. As we sell square footage for a beautiful new atrium."

Reed's Ploy, the Way of the Cash Guzzler

In Belasco's office after the confrontation, Reed explained, "Lloyd I can help you with other deals."

Reed had learned a lot about the game of upmanship. Sometimes, you pulled a few one-down maneuvers, in order to get a huge one-up win.

Now Reed used the *"I'm your friend"* ploy with Lloyd. He played that into the *"I'm your consultant"* ploy. He puts thoughts into Lloyd's head.

"You're in a position to make some big moves Lloyd, but you don't see them. You know what's holding you back? You went to the Barton School of Finance. Those guys don't like risk, they're pussies."

Lloyd liked that. "You don't know the half of it."

"But you're a prick Lloyd. Pricks fuck finance pussies. Pricks shoot high-yield bonds. Debt is a potent juice."

Lloyd liked the sound of it, "I like your scientific theories. Who would have ever though I'd start to like science?"

Reed pressed on, "Look at it from an evolutionary perspective. You are the next step in the financial animal. You buy trophy properties. You only buy things that other people want. You're smart. That's been the reason for your success. Everything you buy goes up in value.

"Now you're known, now you can do what lesser men cannot. Borrow what your buildings are going to be worth.

"Come on strong. Don't borrow less, borrow more. Make money by bluffing. Borrow what your hotel will be worth. Borrow what your casino will be worth. Borrow it all now. Use the money, to make more money, while you pay off the loans. And repeat the cycle."

Days Go By

Belasco liked the pitch more and more.

Reed rolled in one-up reasoning, into this pitch.

"The brand name. Belasco is a one-up name. You slap that on everything in gold letters. That's your one-up mark. The minute you slap it on, the trophies go up in value.

"You are about building things. Raise the value of your name.

"Your name is your fortune. When you buy these trophies, you put your name on them, raise the value, and then cash in.

"It's okay if some of them lose money. It's okay if a lot of them lose money. You own the name. Belasco is the fortune. And the Belasco name you always take with you, even if God forbid, by some fluke, one or two, or twenty of these buildings go into bankruptcy.

"You walk out with the billion-dollar name, Belasco."

The Deal Addict

Tracy watched as Reed turned Belasco into a deal addict.

She warned Belasco that he was headed for trouble.

Belasco told her to, "Shut up and eat a ham sandwich." Anthropologically speaking, he was telling her to become carnivorous, to learn to live, to get one-up on a piece of meat.

Belasco's bankers and investment brokers tripped over themselves to help make him a deal addict. His addiction put them in position for a one-up game of their own.

Debt became Belasco's one-up drug, and the loans routinely grew larger than the price of the purchases, leaving an excess for his organizational needs, thereby repeatedly putting him one-up.

Once he discovered he could take overdoses on his cash fixes, and only end up one-up, he lost all remaining fear of the fastlane.

The major New York banks syndicated his loans to Japanese, German, French, Canadian and British banks, all of which were willing to pay stupendous fees to the American banks to buy pieces of his one-up mortgages.

Foreign banks that had been one-down, in particular, were willing to put forth what were effectively entry fees to break into the one-up American real estate market, and few loans sold better on the Japanese market than a piece of a Belasco deal.

The combination of the immediate one-ups from the syndication fees and the certainty of being able to dramatically notch down bank exposure overnight by dumping the bulk of the financing on eager foreign banks mad Belasco's bankers quite willing to take on gigantic Belasco loans.

Everybody was getting one-up.

Reed was biding his time in the one-down position of servitude, until he at last felt the time was ripe for him to head one-up via the time-tested "hostile takeover" ploy.

The Hostile Takeover

Reed revealed to Tracy that he had been setting Belasco up for a fall.

He wanted to get one-up on Belasco. All the pieces were in place. Would she help him?

She revealed that she'd been concocting plots to get one-up on Belasco as well. And she had been looking for an opening.

They proceeded as a team.

They held a breakfast meeting with Lloyd's bankers.

On the table, they placed a bowl of corn flakes. Next to it, an empty bowl.

The brimming bowl represented the extent of Belasco's cash hoard. They showed the bankers the rate at which Belasco was running out of money. Each flake represented a day of debt payments. One by one, the days moved to the empty "payment" bowl. Soon they were all gone.

Reed assured the bankers that Belasco did not have any more corn flakes, anywhere. Once his current flakes were gone, he would begin to miss bond payments.

He turned to a set of dominoes beside the bowl. "We know what happens then." He knocked over the first domino, and the rest toppled.

Then Reed brought in a very famous financial reporter.

Reed explained, "He's going to break the story. It'll be a hell of an exclusive for him. A career maker. But he is willing to hold the story if we can add more to the end. So the question gentlemen is, do we want to read about *'How Belasco Went Bankrupt'*? Or do we want to work together and read about *'How Belasco's Bankers Took his Business Away and Saved It'*?"

The hapless bankers didn't need to answer. They had just learned they were one-down. They only had one way to get one-up. But one banker did have a question for Reed, "What are we going to give you out of this?"

Reed said, "The Love Museum."

The Must Scene

The bankers came to Belasco's office. Belasco had been told they were there to toss around ideas for future deals.

Belasco felt he was still one-up on these men.

He explained that he would like to borrow some more money, to handle a liquidity issue. Everything was fine. He had some great trophy properties. But he could use some more money to bridge a gap until some capital events happened.

They told Belasco to sit the hell down and shut up.

Now Tracy and Reed entered the room.

Entrance
Reed said, "Will Wyndham."

Everyone went still.

Reed looked at one of the bankers. At a distinguished old fellow, who looked back at Reed with a steely gaze.

Reed said to him, "Hello, I'm pleased to meet you. I'm Reed Fleming."

He went over and shook Will Wyndham's hand.

Wyndham extended his hand firmly and said, "Pleased to meet you as well Mr. Fleming."

Now Reed stepped back and took all of the bankers into his gaze—sweeping across the line of men and women.

"I'm pleased to meet all the rest of you as well. Now I know we're all in a hurry, so I'll be brief."

Reed looked at Will Wyndham, nodded, and proceeded.

"I'm pleased that all of the rest of you could be here to join us. Some of you I've met, and the rest I look forward to meeting after we've finished here."

"And now I know we're all in a hurry." He looked at Wyndham. "May I begin right away. I'll be brief."

Wyndham motioned for him to take it away.

Improvisation

Reed went a-improvising. Like a jazz band, he started bringing in different instruments, different lines, different layers.

This was a one-up game.

And Lloyd would have a hard time reacting, if he didn't know what was coming next.

So Reed started moving, swiftly. And laying on the music.

He was an anthropologist who specialized in territorial behavior. Now he showed them what a scientist could do. He strutted his street-science stuff.

You see a people scientist could be a street artist, and he was about to demonstrate how.

When people would meet Reed, they would often say, "You're an anthropologist? What's an anthropologist?"

"A people expert," he would say.

"Oh," they would say. ... "So what does that mean you do?"

He was about to demonstrate the work of an anthropologist, in full flight.

Reed said, "Lloyd you're no longer in charge. I know it's bad news and I feel bad breaking it to you. But we have new circumstances here.

"The banks have decided to take your properties away from you."

Lloyd was very smart. He was stunned, at first, but recovered his bearings immediately. He recognized that he was in a one-down position, and looked for an opening to get one-up.

Reed, while he was one-up, struck lightning fast with some "surprise" ploys.

"We're going to put Tracy in charge."

This was news to everyone. This was even a surprise to Tracy. The bankers had no idea what he was talking about. And Lloyd was pissed.

"She's the brains behind the operation. It's time we came clean. The world should know. While you've been coming up with ways to spend money, she's been inventing ways to make money. Now she's going to be in charge."

Reed turned to the bankers, and continued to lie through his teeth, a one-up maneuver.

"Belasco is actually a little stupid in the head. Tracy has been covering for him but that's all over know."

Belasco said, "What the hell are you talking about?" Thus, inadvertently putting himself in a one-down position just when he most needed to get one-up.

Reed continued with a series of surprise ploys—a one-up strategy.

He told the bankers, "You'll get great press. He's going to miss a debt payment, that's where all the trouble is going to start.

"He's going to miss a balloon payment on one of his Atlantic City casinos.

"She can help with that situation. The Casino Control Commission will pull the licensing away from the Belasco organization."

Lloyd cut in, "What the hell are you taking about?!"

Reed's line of bullshit was actually succeeding in getting Lloyd confused.

Reed fired a one-up shot, "Shut up Lloyd." Reed didn't stop for a beat, "Atlantic City will pull the licensing. That's a given. She can save it. You know why? She's a police woman.

"That's where you're going to get the great press. The mayor's a law-and-order man. You're putting a police woman in charge."

Lloyd said, "Reed, Tracy can't run this organization. It's preposterous."

Reed said, "Shut up Lloyd. One of the underlying parcels of land on one of his casinos is owned by a mobster. You didn't know that, there's no way for you to know that, that's why I'm letting you in on it. It's going to be another reason that the Control Commssion is going to revoke his licensing."

Lloyd cut in, "He's lying! Don't let him pull this shit!"

Reed continued, "He'll be driven out of Atlantic City. He'll have to sell his three casinos at a loss. But you don't let that happen. Instead you give control of the Belasco organization to a police woman. You do it today. Tomorrow the headlines read, 'Police woman becomes millionaire.' Can't you see the nice happy headlines? 'Police woman becomes queen of real estate.'

"Then she uncovers the mobster connection herself, problem solved, everyone cheers."

Lloyd said, "Reed, you're feeding them an asinine line of shit."

The lead banker, Will Wyndham, said, "Shut up Lloyd. Continue Mr. Fleming."

Reed ran with the one-up position and fired another surprise ploy, "Of course, you'll have to force Belasco to sign a non-compete clause with the Belasco brand. And force him to sign it this morning, while you have him in your grip.

"It's simple. He signs a little paper promising he'll never use the Belasco name on a building again. Otherwise, he could set up across the street from your Belasco buildings and steal your business."

Reed turned to Lloyd, "I'm sorry Lloyd but you're going to have to sign away your name."

Belasco smoldered. He saw this for what it was. *To give your name away*—It was the ultimate one-down transaction.

Wyndham asked Reed, "What do you do here?"

"Oh, I'm an anthropologist."

"In a real-estate company?"

"Yes?"

The bankers were puzzled. An anthropologist in the business world? What on Earth could be the purpose of such a thing?

Wyndham saw the benefits.

Wyndham was against him, thought Lloyd. This judge was a rotten son of a bitch.

He decided that Will Wyndham was a horrible person.

He decided that Will Wyndham was a worthless piece of work—who liked pretty women.

Will Wyndham was full of it.

So Lloyd turned to the jury to help him against the judge. These others might be business people. He could talk some sense into them and save the situation.

He felt confident. Hell, he felt supremely confident. He was Lloyd Belasco. The name had a frightfully immense power with these people.

"I'm part of what's right with America," said Belasco.

"Under our system our country has developed into the greatest country on Earth. Is it perfect? No. But it works.

"It's our business energy. Our freedom to grow and develop in surprising ways. I'm building a megabrand. I'm laying a solid foundation for a big-tent enterprise.

"Belasco means *luxury*. And under my direction it's becoming the biggest name in luxury. That's where we're going.

"Now are you ready to change horses? To bet the entire business on a novice? On a newcomer with nothing to her? She may get you headlines. But what are you really getting with her?

"You don't know. And you won't know until it's too late. If you put her in charge it'll be a disaster. I guarantee you it will be a big mistake—a total and complete disaster.

"She doesn't have the right stuff to run this business. There's no way she can do it."

He repeated, *"There's no way she can do it.*—And that is the truth of the matter."

Then having made his closing argument, he left the case to the jury. In a moment of high drama, he returned to his seat, and composed himself like a great king. Then he sat poised, and stared outward. Seeming to envelop great lands in his management vision.

Tracy rose to speak.

"Gentlemen, ladies. ... Thank you Lloyd.

"Now nobody here is a fool. So let's get down to business."

She turned to Will Wyndham. "You once put out an ad in the business journal asking to hire leaders that were *'trumpeter swans.'*—Leaders who could understand business and could understand creativity—trumpeter swans you called them."

"Yes," said Will Wyndham. "I did."

"I'm here and I have my trumpet ready," she said.

She turned to the others.

"You have a choice for who ought to run the Belasco holdings—Lloyd or Tracy?

"The problem here is that Lloyd is only interested in art, and we're only interested in money."

"Now here is something that scientists know and that is very important for you to know.—

"Belasco owns a lot of brands. He has towers called Belasco. He has hotels called Belasco. He has jetliners called Belasco. He has clothing called Belasco.

"He has a lot of things called Belasco. He brought together a lot of brands to make one Belasco mega-brand. He converged about 12 brands.—

"From a scientific standpoint, that's wrong."

"Brands are species of animals.

"Species of animals do not converge they diverge. For example, a cat never merged with a dog to create a catdog. I'll tell you, in fact, the only place species ever converge is in make-believe. A fish with a woman becomes a mermaid. A bull with a man becomes a centaur.

"But that doesn't happen in real life. Business people like Lloyd think it does, but it doesn't.

"Now Belasco is making everything into a Belasco brand.

"I know how to unwind that, so that you'll make more money. His brands will be worth more separated than together. I know how to make that happen.

"The lion is a species much like a brand. It diverged from an ancestor called panthera. That ancestor also diverged into the tiger, the cougar, and the leopard. One brand diverged into four great brands.

"That's what we can do with Belasco."

"If the Belasco brand is an animal. What kind of animal is it?

"The primary function of a marketing organization is to position the brand.

"Names are important. People believe that the name a company uses has real meaning.

"If you want to sell everything under one brand name, ... then the name itself can't mean anything.

"Common sense is not marketing sense.

"If your objective is to lose money, you'd be well on your way with Lloyd Belasco. He knows how to lose a ton of money. He has the perfect way.

"You know what a Belasco stands for? ... It's a luxury, affordable, cheap, expensive, small, large, building, or home, or tower, or hotel or casino that is also an airplane and a line of shirts, pants and ties. A Belasco is fashionable clothing for young and old, business and casual. Belasco is also resorts. It's golf courses. And where does it end? I don't know. Do you?

"And that ladies and gentlemen is how you lose money while earning billions every year—by taking 12 good brand names and turning them all into one no-name brand.

"It's not a one-up strategy. It's 12 one-down moves in a row until you're down and out. That's where we are today.

"It's like going into a boxing match. Losing 12 rounds in a row and saying I'm going to come roaring back. It's all part of the plan.—Some plan.

"And that's why you really may want to put a lovely young lady who you never heard of before today in charge of a multi-billion dollar business.

"The choice is yours. I know you'll make the right decision.

"What you face today is a oneupmanship problem—the answer is to go one-up. Let's step it all up a level. Shall we?"

"If you combined the top 5 cities in the U.S., they'd be worth less. If you put New York together with Los Angeles, together with Chicago, together with Philadelphia, together with San Francisco—the new city wouldn't be worth anywhere near as much as the five cities separated.

"If you combined a lion with a tiger with a cougar with a leopard with a jaguar, the new combined animal would be worth less than the separate animals.

"Lloyd has taken 12 brands and combined them into one. ... His holdings would be worth a lot more if you separated the holdings, if you divided it into 12 names, and cleaned up the mess. He's offering to make the mess messier. I'm offering to make the mess clean."

"That's the reason to put me in charge. I know you'll make the right decision.

"This is oneupmanship. The answer is to go one-up."

She left it there. Walked away. And returned to her armchair. Where she one-upped Lloyd in graceful sitting.

They all looked at her. No one spoke.

Most of the people in the room were thinking through a math problem. Did they want one big brand that was losing money—but was backed by big solid name like "Lloyd Belasco"? Or did they want to risk everything on a future with a lovely lady who might very well be able to give them 12 brands that each made money? Oh, plus one "Love Museum."

The Love Museum

The Re-Opening Day
Reed walked into the place amid a throng of new patrons. In the foyer, he broke away from the crowd, and headed toward a small circle of people who worked there and were gathered to listen to—*Tracy.*

She was standing in a leadership stance and she was directing them confidently, with clear, lucid instructions.

She was running the show here and she was doing it with supreme ability.

She was stunning, thought Reed.

She's a lady. ... Whoa, she's a lady. She's got style. She's got grace. She's got all you'd ever want. Whoa, she's a lady. What a lovely lady.

Presently Reed and the lovely lady were walking through the Love Museum.

People were enjoying the new opening of this place. Word had gotten around the city. Tracy had *branded* the place—the way it should have been branded from the start.

Now it was a hot spot.

A lot of big names were coming to the museum now and many, many people streamed in to enjoy the place.

Tracy had made a change to the scheme of the place—She opened a new wing of the museum devoted to the game of *oneupmanship* and the acquisition of territory.

Reed and Tracy passed under an arch, and walked into the wing hand-in-hand, and took it all in together.

The young man and the lovely lady at the love museum were in love. That you could see.

And that was where their love story went.

— The End —

www.ingramcontent.com/pod-product-compliance
Lightning Source LLC
Chambersburg PA
CBHW052034020726

47501CB00004B/1400